THE SYSTEM

GEMMA MALLEY

HODDER &
STOUGHTON

First published in Great Britain in 2013 by Hodder & Stoughton
An Hachette UK company

1

A CIP catalogue record for this title is available from the British Library.

Trade Paperback ISBN 978 1 444 72288 8
eBook ISBN 978 1 444 72289 5

Typeset in Sabon by Palimpsest Book Production Ltd, Falkirk, Stirlingshire

Printed and bound by Clays Ltd, St Ives plc

Hodder & Stoughton policy is to use papers that are natural, renewable
and recyclable products and made from wood grown in sustainable forests.
The logging and manufacturing processes are expected to conform to the
environmental regulations of the country of origin.

Hodder & Stoughton Ltd
338 Euston Road
London NW1 3BH

www.hodder.co.uk

For my darling Allegra

Who controls the past controls the future: who controls the present controls the past.

George Orwell, *1984*

1

Raffy watched silently as he, Evie, Linus and Benjamin were ushered into a large room by Thomas, their captor. Every so often he sneaked a little look at Evie, and each time it felt like a punch to the stomach because he knew that she would resent his gaze, knew that the only thing she felt for him was hatred and disappointment. She looked dazed, tired, desperate; she was staring ahead resolutely but he could see from her bloodshot eyes that she was having to work hard to hold herself together. And in a weird way it made him proud of her; she'd never let Thomas see her crack. She was too strong, too stubborn, too determined. It was what he had always loved about her, always been drawn to, those fierce eyes of hers, the way she was always so fearless even when she had so much to lose.

And now she had lost it all because of him. Now

everyone had lost. No one would meet his eyes, acknowledge his existence. No one except Benjamin, that is, who had put his arm around him gently as they walked into the room, whose sad eyes gazed at him in pure forgiveness, which Raffy found even harder to take. He knew he had let down the one man he would have done anything for. That Benjamin might forgive him just made him loathe himself even more.

'I'm sure you'll find this comfortable,' Thomas was saying, showing them around. Raffy could tell that everyone was doing their best to look unimpressed, unfazed, but the truth was that the place was incredible. It was huge, a sprawling apartment with floor-to-ceiling windows along one wall that were frosted so that they couldn't see out. Thick rugs covered the floor, and enormous sofas sat comfortably around the place. In one corner was a kitchen with gleaming black surfaces, on which sat a huge bowl of fruit and an even larger bowl full of cakes of some sort. There were two doors with glass panels, both closed; several solid doors were open and led into bedrooms, cavernous rooms with giant beds, private bathrooms and soft fluffy dressing gowns.

And then there were the screens. Large screens covered every wall, in every room, even the bathrooms. Screens that were divided up into ten, twenty moving images; other screens that showed just one. They showed people, walking down the street, laughing, talking, typing messages into mid-air that then miraculously appeared at the bottom of the screen. Most of them showed the same girl striding down the street, a purposeful look on her face.

Raffy tried not to look at them, tried to look nowhere, at nothing, but he couldn't help himself, couldn't stop himself from staring at the girl who beamed out from so many of the screens. A beautiful girl in a pale pink dress, she seemed to glow as she threw her head back and laughed.

'That's Frankie,' Thomas said with a little smile. 'I expect you'll get to know her quite well.'

'Who . . . who is she?' Raffy asked, needing to speak, needing to have his voice heard as though it might cut through the atmosphere, make things more normal.

'Frankie? She's the third most Watched person on the planet,' Thomas said lightly. 'A great ambassador for Infotec, although she doesn't know it. Everyone right around the world either wants Frankie or wants to be Frankie.'

Raffy stared at the screen. 'Infotec,' he said, his voice low, unemotional. 'This place belongs to your company?'

Thomas looked at him for a moment, then started to laugh. 'Raffy, you don't get it, do you? Infotec owns everything. Everything and everyone. Now, let me show you where you're going to be working. That is the point of this little holiday, after all.'

He walked towards the two glass doors and opened the first. In the room was a desk and a computer, which immediately said hello, making Raffy start slightly; on the wall was another screen.

'Linus, you'll be in here,' Thomas said. 'You have the latest technology at your disposal. Raffy, you're in here.' He walked out of the room and into an identical one next door. 'Linus, you will build the System; Raffy, you will check his code. My people will then check it again. If any discrepancies are found, any errors, any little worms or viruses, Benjamin and Evie will be punished. Do you understand?'

Linus looked around the room thoughtfully. 'Where are we, Thomas? Paris? Somewhere close to Paris?' Raffy glanced at him, suddenly realising why Linus had spent the journey here, by helicopter, with his face pressed against the window. Raffy had assumed travel sickness or anger, or both. It had taken them about two hours; in that short time they had travelled from a cave in the desolate scrubland outside the City to a civilisation that they had been led to believe had been destroyed many years before. Then again, they'd been led to believe a lot of things, and most of them had been lies.

Thomas nodded, smiling. 'Pretty good,' he said. 'So, let me introduce you to Milo. Milo, get in here please.'

Raffy didn't know who he was speaking to, but a few moments later the door opened and a man appeared, much younger than Thomas, his dark hair swept to the side, his face lightly tanned, his shoes shining. He was wearing a suit with a polo-neck jumper underneath; his teeth gleamed white.

'So, which one of you is Linus?' he asked, his face breaking into a grin that didn't reach his eyes.

Raffy stared at him sullenly. 'Which one do you think?' he muttered.

'I'm Linus,' Linus said then, stepping forwards, his voice soft, his expression unreadable. 'You're Milo? Nice to meet you, Milo. And how do you fit into this nice little set-up?'

Milo didn't answer; he looked at Thomas, who was staring at Linus, a strange look in his eye. 'This is him,' he said. 'This is the man who built the System. This is the man I created this world for.'

'No,' Linus corrected him immediately. The tone of his voice was still light, but there was no mistaking the seriousness in it. 'I can't take any credit for what you've achieved here. You didn't build any of it for me, Thomas. I didn't ask you to do any of this.'

'You're right.' Thomas shrugged dismissively, then his eyes lit up again. 'I did it all myself. And it's brilliant. Truly brilliant.'

'You've certainly been busy,' Linus said, nodding to himself as he gazed around. 'Tell me about the screens, Thomas. Who are these people?'

'Well, you've met Frankie,' Thomas smiled at Milo. 'The lovely Frankie, eh, Milo? She's Milo's girlfriend, lucky guy.'

Milo smiled bashfully.

'And the others?' Linus asked. 'They work for you?'

'Work for me? No, Linus. None of them work for me. Not even Frankie. No, they are just going about their lives, but everyone watches them. Well, not everyone. Only people like Frankie get watched by everyone. Only the most popular. Most people are just watched by us, by their friends and families, by ex-lovers, by prospective ones. But everyone is watched. All the time. It's part of the deal. And the best part is they love it. Everyone wants to build their numbers. The more Watchers they have, the more income they receive, but more importantly, the cheaper everything becomes. Restaurants give them money off because they're advertising their establishment. Clothes are virtually free. They get to the top 1000 most Watched in their country and they can get pretty much anything they want for free.'

'You're watching all these people? All the time?' Evie asked suddenly, her mouth hanging open as she stared at the screen next to Raffy's office, which had thirty or so images on it, ten of them Frankie. Raffy watched too; watched a man walk into a bathroom and urinate, watched a man undress a woman, kissing her breast.

'Me personally? Oh no. No, I don't have to Watch them. I can if I want to. If I sniff a problem. But mostly we just sit back. Because everyone else is doing it for us,' Thomas said, a little glint in his eye. 'Incredible, isn't it?' he asked, turning back to Linus. 'Fear got me through the door. I mean if it hadn't been for the Horrors, I'd never have convinced the governments of the world to install cameras on every corner, in every room of every building. But what I never expected is how much people like being looked at. The narcissist in all of us is quite a potent tool, you know.'

'It certainly is quite something,' Linus said, frowning as he looked at the screens. 'But this woman, she's at home?' He motioned at the image on the top left hand of the screen, a middle-aged woman drinking a cup of tea, carefully dunking a biscuit into it.

Thomas nodded enthusiastically. 'CCTV captures people outside the home, but ninety-four per cent of people now have cameras in their homes too and they're better quality generally.'

'People actually have cameras in their homes now?' Linus asked.

Thomas looked very pleased with himself. 'What can I say? People like them; won't stop installing them,' he said with a little shrug that belied the glint in his eye. 'They want higher Watcher numbers, and they like the security. And of course it makes updating much easier. Every fifteen minutes – that's the rule. Unless you're in sight of a camera, you have to manually update your status. So that everyone knows what you're doing, so everyone knows you're safe. Having cameras in your home makes everything much easier.' He laughed.

'How do people sleep?' Linus asked, curiously.

'Motion sensors on the bed capture DNA from the skin,' Thomas said proudly. 'People can switch them on and switch off the cameras if they want to . . . if they want some private time. Although people don't care so much about private time these days. Private time means that Watchers lose interest. Got to keep those numbers up. Got to be entertaining. Sometimes people share just a little too much for my liking, but what are you going to do when they're all chasing Watcher numbers? Far be it from me to get in the way.' He winked, and laughed again, like he'd just told the funniest joke. But no one else laughed.

'And these Watcher numbers,' Linus asked conversationally. 'How do they work?'

Raffy looked at him curiously, wondering how he could stay so calm. Because Thomas was no ordinary man. This man had manipulated a war so that Linus would build a computer system that was capable of controlling people's lives, capable of reading their thoughts. This man had made Linus believe, along with all the other survivors in the UK, that the rest of the world had been destroyed, that there was nothing left, that it was up to them to build a new civilisation. And this man had manipulated them every step of the way, bribing, corrupting, controlling them. All so that Linus would build his System, which, as he'd told Thomas years before, during a brief internship at Infotec, required an impossible situation: a small population who genuinely desired to be controlled, cut off from the rest of the world. He had said it as an off-hand remark, little guessing that Thomas would take him at his word and would spend the next ten years engineering exactly that.

Thomas grinned. 'Watcher numbers are ingenious – I know you'll agree. We don't have celebrities anymore; we just have people who are Watched and people who no one cares about. Each Watcher generates a penny a week in income. There are no benefits anymore, there's no state to give you money. If you need money, you earn it, by living your life on camera, by convincing people to Watch you every minute of every day. And it's not just income; with Watchers comes power, influence. If Frankie wants to buy a dress, the shop will virtually give it to her because she'll make it famous. For everyone else there's a sliding scale. Try to buy one when you've got Watchers in double digits only and it'll cost you a fortune. Which is why everyone wants to be followed. Everyone! See this girl?' He moved his hand; immediately every screen showed the same person, a girl with cropped white hair, wearing a pink dress and a black leather jacket, laughing, then embracing another girl. 'She's copying Frankie, hoping that some of Frankie's magic will rub off on her. Good luck to her.'

'And your hand. What's that? Some kind of chip?' Linus asked, his brow furrowing.

Thomas moved towards Linus, putting his arm around him and showing him his hand. In the fleshy area beneath his thumb, Raffy saw a flesh-coloured panel, barely noticeable. 'See this hardened skin? Look what's inside.' He tugged at the panel and it came out smoothly, like a drawer. Out of his hand. Raffy's eyes widened.

'Impressive, huh?' Thomas laughed. 'We tried getting people to just carry them in glasses, jewellery, that sort of thing. But they always took the things off eventually. This way, the chip's with them all the time. It's a simple procedure. The skin hardens over time so you can take them out and exchange them like an earring. And look what they can do,' he said, replacing the chip back in his hand and waving it around, watching for Linus's reaction as all the screens changed. 'Chips make everything so much more secure. Everyone has one – a tiny computer at their disposal 24/7. They can talk to their friends, and Watchers, download information, anything, all in front of their eyes, no screen required. And of course it's linked to the mainframe so we know where they are and what they're doing. They love it. And why wouldn't they? A chip that allows them access to everything.'

'And, presumably, denies them access when it suits you?' Linus asked, his voice deadpan.

Thomas laughed. 'So cynical, Linus. Always so cynical. Chips have revolutionised the world. Made it safer. World peace, Linus. That's what the people want. And that's what I've given them.' His voice was serious, but he winked as he spoke. 'Nothing like the destruction of a first-world nation to shake people up, make them review their priorities . . .' His eyes were gleaming as he moved away and stood next to Milo, both of them apparently scrutinising Linus's face for a reaction. Linus offered them nothing; he just looked right back at Thomas, his crinkly blue eyes giving nothing away.

Thomas frowned. 'But look at me, talking too much and forgetting my own priorities,' he said briskly. 'So. Here's the deal. This is where you live for the next three months. Everyone has their own room; there will be plenty of nice food, drink and screens to watch. As I've already told you, these two cubicles are for you, Linus, and you, Raffy. In three months the System will be delivered to me. If it isn't, Evie and Benjamin will be taken from here to somewhere . . . well, somewhere less comfortable. A lot less comfortable. And they will be filmed so that you can share in their discomfort as you rush to complete the System. After four months, one of them will die. After five months, the other will die. After that . . . well, I don't think it will come to that, will it Linus?'

Linus didn't say anything; he just stared back, his expression unreadable.

'You'll find clothes in the rooms, toiletries, everything you need,' Thomas continued. 'Oh, and I wouldn't try opening the windows. They're locked, of course, but they're also electrified. Touch them and you'll get a shock. Keep hold of them and the voltage increases until . . . well, sixty seconds and game over.'

Everyone regarded the windows warily. 'Seems you've thought of everything. And on about an hour's notice,' Linus said thoughtfully.

Thomas smiled bashfully. 'You know me,' he said. 'I like to plan ahead.'

'Know you? I wouldn't say that.' Linus shook his

head, his eyes suddenly very serious. 'I wouldn't say I know you at all, Thomas.'

Thomas appeared to consider this; then he laughed. 'You're right. But it doesn't matter, because I know you, Linus, that's the thing. I know you. I know everyone.' He turned to Benjamin, who looked at him stonily. Raffy tried to imagine Benjamin as the young boy who had worked for Thomas, the gang leader who Thomas had tried to recruit, who had eventually resisted. But he couldn't see it; he could only see Benjamin, brave, thoughtful leader of the Settlement that Thomas had destroyed, just like he'd destroyed everything else.

'Where's my room?' Evie said suddenly.

Thomas pointed to a door and she rushed towards it, opened it, then slammed it behind her. Raffy felt his stomach clench; he knew that she needed to be behind closed doors because the pain of what had happened, what was happening, was overwhelming her.

And it was his fault. It was he who had led Thomas to them, driven by anger, by envy, by jealousy. Of Lucas. Always his brother, Lucas. Lucas, who was so noble and strong. Lucas, who Evie loved. Lucas, who was now alone because Raffy had stopped Evie from escaping with him, making her hate him even more than before. Thomas knew how to manipulate, and he had manipulated Raffy. He had manipulated him to the point where Raffy had lost sight of who he was, of what he believed in. To the point where he had betrayed his friends, betrayed everything he thought he had stood for.

But he'd been a willing participant. He'd been easy prey.

'Teenagers,' Thomas said with a little sigh. 'So, Linus. What do you think? Bit better than that cave you were working in, right? I've even got you a kettle. Loose-leaf tea. I know how much you love your tea.'

'I do like a cup of tea.' Linus nodded, a little smile on his lips. 'So I guess it's just like the old days then.'

'Exactly!' Thomas said happily, his eyes shining. He was looking so pleased with himself, Raffy found himself thinking. Like a child. Were they all just like toys to him? Was all of this just some elaborate game? 'Well, I'll leave you to get to work shall I? The computer will talk you through the operating system. Obviously yours mirrors, but isn't connected to, the mainframe. Just in case you get any ideas,' he said lightly.

'Obviously,' Linus said.

'And you, Devil, what would you like?' Thomas asked, turning to Benjamin, using the street name he had shed many years before.

'My name is Benjamin, and I would like to leave this

place. I would like to go back to my people,' Benjamin said, his eyes thunderous.

Thomas looked pained. 'Yeah, I'm afraid that's not going to happen. So, second choice?'

Benjamin glared at him. 'You used me,' he said, his voice low and angry. 'Many years ago you used me, but I fought back. I escaped from your clutches, Thomas. And now you think you will use me again. You think that by threatening me, my friend Linus will do your bidding. But I will not be used, Thomas. I will not.'

Thomas raised an eyebrow 'No? And exactly how do you expect to escape from me this time, Devil? There are no police to run to, no prison that will protect you. You're in my world, Benjamin. I control everything. And I control you. The sooner you accept that, the better for us all.'

Benjamin appeared to contemplate this. He turned and stared at Thomas. Then he smiled. 'You like to control people, Thomas. You always have; that's all you've ever wanted to do. Manipulate, control, create order. You think so little of people, Thomas. You think we are all like you, that we are all susceptible to bribery or punishment of some kind or another, that our morals are changeable or even non-existent. You have never understood people who believe in something, who stand for something. We unnerve you; make you want to control us even more.

But a controlled life is not a life, Thomas. The human spirit needs more than what you can offer. You think you have control of the world but I can tell you that you don't. There will be pockets of people across the globe who are conspiring against you. Pockets of people right here, wherever we are. Little weeds pressing up against the concrete you have laid. And they will find a way through. They always do, Thomas.'

'Giving me a sermon are you, Benjamin?' Thomas sneered. 'What on earth makes you think I am interested in anything you say? You were a drug-running lowlife when I met you. In my eyes you still are. You're pathetic, Benjamin. You stand for nothing but self-preservation.'

'Self-preservation?' Benjamin laughed. 'Nothing could be further from the truth, Thomas. I stand for many things, but not that. I stand for freedom. I stand for allowing people to achieve their potential, for encouraging independence of thought. I stand for hard work and duty. I stand for loyalty. I stand for forgiveness. And I stand for making a stand. When required. To make a point. To remind people who they are, what they `are capable of.' He turned his gaze to Raffy, who reddened. 'You remember the Bible, Thomas? Remember you liked me to recite it to you? You like this, Thomas? "Because you despise what I tell you, and trust instead in oppression and lies, calamity will come upon you suddenly – like a bulging wall that bursts and falls."' Benjamin's eyes were flashing; Raffy had never heard him speak like this, like he'd been possessed, like his silence in the past few hours had all built up to this huge eruption. '"In an instant it will collapse"', he said, almost shouting now, '"and come crashing down. You will be smashed like a piece of pottery – shattered so completely that there won't be a piece big enough to carry coals from a fireplace or a little water from the well." That is what lies ahead for you, Thomas. That is what you have to look forward to.'

Thomas smiled uncomfortably. 'Don't tell me you've turned back to religion in your old age, Benjamin? You really think I'm going to be intimidated by something written thousands of years ago?'

Benjamin shook his head. 'I have never needed to follow the path someone else has set out for me,' he said. 'Nor have I ever needed to believe in anything to give my life meaning. But I do believe in redemption. And I do believe that sometimes, through death, can come life. From weakness can come strength. From an ending can come a beginning.'

He was staring at Thomas, but every so often he glanced meaningfully at Raffy, making it clear that the words were intended for him as much as Thomas. It brought Raffy out in goosebumps.

Thomas cleared his throat. 'All utterly fascinating, Benjamin. And I hope you felt the sarcasm in that comment because truly, you have none of the ability of your father. You are a very dull man. So, moving on . . .'

'I would rather be dull than a tyrant,' Benjamin interrupted him. 'And I would rather be dead than see you triumph. But you won't triumph, Thomas. I know that.'

He started to walk towards the windows, his eyes boring into Raffy's. Thomas watched him warily. 'Benjamin. Don't do anything you'll regret. I've told you, the windows are electrified.'

'I do not fear death,' Benjamin said, continuing to walk. 'And I do not fear you. But you, Thomas, what do you fear? Failure? Being revealed as the pathetic, insecure man that you really are? I have lived a full life. I have done what I set out to do. And now it is the turn of others.' He was still looking at Raffy. 'Now it is time for the prodigal son to return.' He reached out to the windows. 'I know he won't let me down. And I will be watching. From wherever I am, I will be watching.'

'Stop him,' Thomas shouted, but it was too late; Benjamin had grabbed onto a handle. Immediately there was a buzzing sound, which got increasingly louder.

'No!' Raffy screamed and rushed towards him, but it was too late; Benjamin's entire body was convulsing and there was a sickening smell of burning. Linus reached out and grabbed Raffy's arm, holding him back. 'Let him go,' he whispered. 'Let him escape what we can't.'

'Get him off,' Thomas was shouting, but Milo appeared frozen to the spot.

'I touch him and I'm fried too,' he managed to say, his eyes wide with confusion. 'Why would he do that? Why?'

The buzzing stopped and Benjamin's body fell to the ground.

'Because he was mad,' Thomas said, looking at his body in disgust. 'Get rid of him, someone. Get rid of him now.'

'He wasn't mad,' Raffy seethed, rushing forwards. He tried to wrap his arms around Benjamin, drag him away, but an electrical volt shot through him, forcing him back. Steeling himself, he reached out again and closed Benjamin's eyes.

He heard a sound behind him, a muffled cry, and he turned slightly to see Evie standing in the doorway, her face white, her eyes wide in shock. From the look on her face she had seen everything.

Linus crouched down beside him. 'He couldn't face prison again,' he said quietly. 'We all have to fight in different ways, Raffy. Benjamin wanted to go out shouting. And he did. He did.'

Raffy nodded miserably. 'He was talking to me,' he said, his voice choking up. 'I'm the prodigal son, aren't I? He still believed in me. After everything I've done.'

Linus caught his eye. 'Benjamin always understood people who got lost,' he whispered. 'Maybe he was hoping you'd find your way back.' He stood up and walked away, leaving Raffy to stare at Benjamin, a thousand questions circling his head, questions that he knew Benjamin could never answer.

'Get rid of him,' Thomas hissed at Milo, who was standing now, and immediately started talking into his palm, his face still white, his hands still visibly shaking. 'Get rid of the body now, do you understand?' Thomas continued. 'And you . . .' He stared angrily at Raffy and Linus. 'Both of you get to work. Now.'

'Whatever you want, Thomas,' Linus said quietly, as he walked towards his cubicle, leaving Raffy staring down at the father figure he had loved, respected; the man who had believed in him.

Benjamin would not have died in vain, he told himself as he slowly stood up. He would repay his trust, prove that he was worth a second chance. Like Benjamin had said, he wouldn't let him down.

2

Lucas felt the glare of the sun hit his face and he opened his eyes and squinted.

'You really should be getting up,' Martha said, her usual warm smile filling her face. 'I've brought you a cup of tea.'

Lucas looked at the mug on his bedside table. 'Thanks,' he said. 'What time is it?'

'Time to get going,' Martha said. 'Time to get up and eat some good food and go to work.'

Lucas raised an eyebrow. It had been his idea for Martha to move in to his old house with him; after Thomas had taken Linus and the others, he had taken it upon himself to go to Base Camp and break the news to Martha, Angel and the others. Angel had immediately gone north with most of the men to tell the people of the Settlement that it was time to come out of their caves, time to rebuild their township; Martha, meanwhile, had told Lucas she was coming back to the City with him. And at first he'd thought it was because she didn't want to be left alone, because she was afraid. But increasingly he was realising that in fact she had come to look after him; to make sure he ate well, that he slept, that he had someone to come home to. And he kind of liked it, but he also found it tiresome sometimes.

She always wanted to talk, kept telling him how strong he was, how lucky the City was to have him, like he needed building up or something. The truth was he didn't need anything. As the days went by, any hope that Lucas might have had was diminishing, any belief that Evie would come back, that life would resume. She was gone, and now there was no point to anything. It had taken him a long time to accept, to digest what Thomas had told him, but he knew the truth now, knew that the City was just a little experiment, a means to an end. Nothing was real. And Lucas suspected – no, was certain – that Thomas would want to destroy his little experiment before too long. Before anyone else found out. Before his little plan started to unravel. With Linus tasked with rebuilding the System, Lucas knew that things would unravel pretty quickly. Thomas had no idea what he was dealing with.

For a moment he allowed himself a little smile as

he imagined Linus stealthily pulling apart everything Thomas had built, those twinkly blue eyes of his revealing nothing of what was going on inside his head. Linus was the most infuriating person Lucas had ever met, but there was no one else he'd want on his side more.

Except Evie, of course.

But the truth was, he hadn't had a message from Linus in weeks. No signal at all.

And that's why his hope had gone. That's why he didn't care anymore.

He closed his eyes, felt his chest clench with desperate rage that she had been taken away from him yet again, rage at his brother for bringing Thomas to Linus's cave, rage at himself for escaping and leaving her behind. He didn't know what had happened; he had followed Linus's instructions faithfully, expecting Evie to follow . . . He should have made her go first. He should have held back, waited, watched. It had all happened so quickly, under Thomas's watchful eye, but he should have known, should have held onto her, should have been better, stronger . . .

He had failed her. And now, now he had no idea where she was. If she was even alive.

'Lucas, your tea is getting cold,' Martha said sternly, picking up his clothes from the day before and bundling them into the laundry.

Lucas pulled himself up. 'Leave those,' he said. 'I can do it.'

'You can lead the City, Lucas. Let me take care of the washing. Now, breakfast will be ready in ten minutes. Don't make me come and get you.'

Lucas heard her walking down the stairs, and let his head fall back against the pillow again. Lead the City. He'd dreamed of doing just that for most of his life, dreamed of leading it towards freedom, banishing the System, destroying all the lies that had held its people captive for so long.

And now? Now he was doing just that. Now people treated him like a hero; they looked to him to tell them what to do, tell them how they should live. The lies were behind them; the truth was known, and bit by bit the people of the City were rebuilding their lives, adapting to their new freedoms, to living without labels, without tyranny.

But they didn't know the biggest lie of all. They didn't know that the very world they lived in was a lie, that everything they'd ever experienced had been orchestrated by one evil, crazy man; that beyond the sea, the world lived on, that they were not survivors of a global war, because there had been no war.

They were nothing.

Everything was nothing.

There was no point even getting out of bed, because anything he or anyone else might do would be, in the end, entirely meaningless.

'I knew it!' Lucas looked up to see Martha standing in the doorway, a frown etched into her face. 'Lucas, you have to stop this.'

'Stop what?' Lucas sighed. 'Martha, I'm getting up. I will get up. Soon.'

'And what then? You'll wander into your office, stare into space, give no one any of the answers they crave, no vision for them to follow? Lucas, you have to pull yourself out of this. You have to, for the City's sake.'

'The City?' Lucas shook his head wearily. 'The City is a sham. The City is doomed. Thomas will come for us, and when he does, we'll be destroyed. You know that and I know that. He'll bomb us to smithereens just like he bombed the Settlement, only this time he won't leave any survivors, unless we're willing to hide in caves for the rest of our lives.'

He sat forward, looked Martha right in the eye. 'My father died for something he believed in, and I spent my life pretending to be something that I'm not, all for nothing. All for nothing.'

He felt a lump appear in his throat and he looked away, out of the window to the grey sky framed by heavy wooden shutters.

Martha walked towards him. 'So you've given up?' she asked quietly.

Lucas shook his head. 'I'm just seeing things how they are,' he said.

'You're just allowing yourself to wallow in self-pity you mean.' Martha shook her head. 'Honestly, if Linus heard you . . . if Angel heard you, for that matter, there'd be hell to pay. So there are more lies, so you have a new enemy. So fight him. Warn your people; give them a chance to defend themselves. Fight for us. Fight for yourself. Fight for Evie. Or have you given up on her, too?'

Lucas rounded on her angrily. 'Given up? Martha, he's taken her away and I have no idea if she's even alive. I let her down. I let him take her. And I will never forgive myself.'

'No, Lucas,' Martha said, sitting down on the bed. 'From what you've told me it sounds like Linus made sure you got away. And he generally does things for a reason, doesn't he?'

'He wanted us all to escape,' Lucas said miserably.

'And he thought Thomas would let that happen?' Martha's eyebrows shot up. 'Lucas, just think about it. Linus doesn't make mistakes. Nothing he ever does is random. It's all part of a plan. So if you're here and Evie isn't, chances are there's a reason for that. And chances are Linus hoped you wouldn't just go to bed and stay there. You said there was a signal. Said he was communicating with you.'

'He was,' Lucas said grimly. 'And now he isn't.'

Martha looked at him worriedly, then folded her arms. 'If something was wrong, he'd have let you know,' she said firmly. 'If he's gone quiet it's because he's being watched too closely. They're alive. I know they are. If Thomas wants his System, Linus is alive, and Evie too.'

'Alive for how long?' Lucas asked.

'Stop, Lucas,' Martha said then, a note of irritation in her voice. 'You can't give up. You can't. You know the System better than anyone else, except Linus. So use it. Find a way of communicating with Linus. Find out where Evie is. And prepare the City for Thomas's attack if you're so sure it's coming. The people here believe in you. Maybe you should start believing in yourself, too.'

She looked at Lucas meaningfully, then stood up and left the room. 'Breakfast is ready downstairs,' she called from the stairs a few minutes later.

Lucas closed his eyes for a few seconds; then he opened them again, jumped out of bed and headed for the shower.

3

'Hi, how are you today?'

Raffy stared at the screen uncertainly. It had taken him a week to adjust to this place, to accept that he was really here, that he wasn't going to wake up from this hideous nightmare, back in the Settlement, or Linus's cave, or even the City . . . But now he was ready to get on with stuff. And first he had to figure out how to use the computer.

He remembered Linus telling him about a computer he'd 'met' at the Informers' camp on the UK coast, before they'd known that the rest of the world was thriving, before they realised that they had all been pawns in Thomas's little game. The computer, Linus had told him, his brow furrowing, made no sense. It had told him it was made a few years before, that it had been made in the US. And Linus had searched for other explanations, a satellite civilisation that had somehow continued to develop technology secretly. Had he suspected the truth back then, Raffy thought now as he wondered whether he was expected to reply. Did he wish he had?

'Can I help you with something?' the computer asked in silky, flirtatious tones that made Raffy self-conscious until he reminded himself that it wasn't a real woman, that Thomas had probably programmed the voice himself. 'Would you like to ask me any questions?'

Raffy pulled a face. 'Maybe,' he said. 'Actually, yeah. How do I get out of this place?'

'Getting out of this apartment is impossible without the key and codes to the seven doors between your cubicle and the outside,' the computer said silkily.

Raffy took a deep breath. 'Do you have a face? It feels weird talking to a blank screen.'

'I can have a face if you would like me to. Do you have a preference?'

'A preference?'

'Young, old, male, female, attractive, unthreatening, blonde, brunette?'

'You'd look weird if you had a man's face and a woman's voice,' Raffy said.

'You can change my voice too, if you'd like.'

Raffy considered this, then shook his head. 'No, I like it,' he said. 'Tell me what's happened to Benjamin then.'

'Your friend Benjamin went to autopsy under Regulation 5:6:p and his remains were incinerated yesterday morning. His ashes are in locker room 6b.'

Raffy felt tears pricking at his eyes and forced them away. 'Just like that,' he said. 'Like he never even came here. Like he never existed.'

'Is that a question?' the computer asked. 'I am in start-up mode at the moment. If you would like me to switch into conversation mode, please just let me know.'

'No, you're okay,' Raffy said heavily. He wasn't ready to discuss the point or pointlessness of life with a computer. Particularly not one that was built by Infotec.

'So you work for Infotec,' he said, suddenly suspicious. 'Is Thomas listening to all of this?'

'I was made by Infotec; I am a computer; I work for the person using me,' the computer said. 'But there is a record function, which is operating at the moment, feeding through to a computer being used by Milo Gant. The cameras in this room are also being monitored by Mr Gant. Does that answer your question satisfactorily?'

'He hears what I say or he sees a typescript?'

'The feed records a typescript; the camera records your voice.'

Raffy digested this. 'I can't get away with much then,' he said eventually.

'Would you like to configure me instead?' the computer offered, helpfully. 'You can give me a name, choose a background colour or image, font type, search program, navigation bar, multiscreen hologram, and build your Watch List.'

'Watch List?' Raffy frowned.

'Who you'd like to Watch,' the computer explained. 'I suggest you start with the top ten and go from there, if you're new to the Watching system.'

Raffy nodded slowly. 'I thought I wasn't connected to the mainframe,' he said.

'You have viewer rights. You cannot send messages, or be Watched yourself,' the computer said. 'At least that's not strictly true. You can send messages. Try to, anyway. But I am duty bound to send any outward communication to the Infotec Hub to be . . . considered.'

'You mean censored?' Raffy asked.

There was a pause. 'Best stick to watching,' the computer said eventually. 'So, would you like to start by giving me a name?'

'A name?' Raffy let his head fall back against his chair.

'I can suggest some if you'd like. Give me a starting letter and I can give you a list of names to choose from. Maybe you could choose one from a favourite book?'

'A book?' Raffy asked, sitting up suddenly. Back in the Settlement it had always been Evie who was into books. She'd loved them, had joined a literature class with a guy called Neil. A guy who Raffy had punched because he had something Raffy didn't, because Evie listened to him rapturously, because Raffy was a stupid, jealous imbecile. And Neil hadn't even punched him back. He'd forgiven Raffy the next day, had offered to teach him, too. And Raffy had been so mortified he'd taken him up on his offer, had chosen a book from the Settlement library at random, promising to read it. And he had, some of it anyway; it was an old book written in a strange language, a weird book, full of stories of war and loyalty and deception. Benjamin had laughed when he'd seen him reading it, had told him he hoped he took the good from it and not the bad. The truth was, Raffy hadn't taken much from it really; it had confused him more than anything. But there was one story that he'd really liked, a story that he still thought about sometimes. 'No, that won't be necessary. I'll call you Cassandra.'

'Cassandra?' the computer asked. 'The doomed soothsayer?'

'No one listened to her,' Raffy said lightly. 'Maybe

they'll ignore you, too. How do you know that story, anyway? I thought you were in start-up mode. Does that include knowing about the *Odyssey*?'

'I know everything,' Cassandra said simply, no arrogance in her voice, no self-congratulation.

'Everything? Are you sure?' Raffy asked.

'I have never been found wanting so far,' Cassandra replied.

Raffy considered this. 'Okay then,' he said. 'In that case, Cassandra, let's get to work, shall we? I want you to show me the world. Everything you can. I want you to fill me in on what's happened in the past twenty-five years. I want all the facts. And then I want you to tell me how you work, all about the technology platform you're built on. Got it?'

A woman's image appeared: young, blonde, beautiful. 'Got it,' Cassandra said, winking.

Raffy held her eye for a few seconds, then shook his head. He needed to focus, not to be distracted. 'Twenty years older, please,' he said, his voice deadpan.

'Really? You're sure?' Cassandra sounded plaintive, disappointed; it made him think of Evie, think of every time he'd disappointed her.

He cleared his throat. 'Definitely,' he said quickly. 'Actually, on second thoughts, make it thirty.'

*

Gemma Malley

The apartment was big. Too big. Particularly with just the three of them rattling around in it. Raffy felt Benjamin's shadow everywhere and he longed for his mentor to still be alive, to walk over to him, those serious eyes looking right into his as he proffered advice that was always so welcome, so exactly right. Benjamin had been a good man, but he also knew what it was like to not be good; to feel anger, resentment, jealousy and envy. He knew what it was like to inhabit dark places, to allow the demons within to have free reign. He got it; Raffy could see it in his eyes. Had seen it in his eyes.

He missed him. Missed him more than he would admit to himself. Missed his very existence, not just his presence. If the world could forgive Benjamin, if Benjamin could be reborn as such a wise, just man, then perhaps Raffy could, too. Perhaps there was hope after all.

But for the time being, there wasn't much of anything. Linus may as well have been living somewhere else for all Raffy saw of him. He shut himself away in his little cubicle from morning until night, only emerging for comfort breaks and, occasionally, to eat. When he did emerge, he was monosyllabic, gruff; the only sentences he managed were platitudes that meant nothing. Bide your time. Be patient. Let's play the long game.

The problem was, it wasn't a game, not anymore,

and Linus didn't see that. He was so used to being several steps ahead of everyone that he couldn't deal with the fact he was now miles behind. Thomas had won the game; now it was real life. Now, if he didn't build Thomas the System he wanted, Evie was in danger. Raffy would put up with many things, but he wouldn't jeopardise one hair on Evie's head, and he kept trying to make that point to Linus. But he hadn't got through. At least he was pretty sure he hadn't.

He sat down heavily at the table where food was laid out, just as it was for every meal. Fish tonight, with roasted vegetables and couscous. Cassandra had told him what it was all called, told him how it was made. She hadn't been allowed to tell him exactly where they were in this place called Paris, or what else was in this building, but as soon as he asked her questions she was able to answer, she got super excited, rattling off a million facts about aubergines, about modern farming, about nutritional values and health measurement. She'd also told him the history of Paris, about how it had been a cultural centre before collapsing in the early twenty-first century, and how Infotec had rescued it, moving their head offices there when London had been destroyed, rejuvenating this great City and turning it into the capital of Europe. In many ways, capital of the world, now that there were no language barriers.

'That's what Infotec has programmed you to say, right?' Raffy had asked, his left eyebrow raised pointedly.

'That is fact.' Cassandra had pouted. 'It's in the history books. On Infopedia. I don't know why you're so suspicious of everything. There's no need for suspicion anymore because everything is out in the open. There are no secrets, no closed doors.'

'The door to this apartment is pretty closed,' Raffy had retorted, after which Cassandra had gone silent for a bit.

It had taken Raffy a while to get used to talking to a computer. But now, as he sat at the table, eating on his own, just like he always did, he was almost tempted to open up a hologram and have her sit on the table to keep him company. Evie had worked out some kind of rota so that she ate whilst he was working, then disappeared into her room when he ate, so the only time he ever saw her was through the glass door of his cubicle. He would watch her lying on the sofa, looking at the various screens, her nose wrinkled in irritation, or pacing around the apartment, gazing mournfully towards the opaque windows. And every time he saw her he longed to rush out, to tell her how much he hated himself, how sorry he was, how determined he was to make things right. But he didn't; he knew the look of scorn that he would be greeted with, knew that she would regard him coldly before walking away. And she'd be right to. What use were words? If he was sorry, he had to prove it. If he wanted to redeem himself, then he'd have to find a way.

Which would also mean finding a way out of this prison.

He looked over at Linus's cubicle, contemplated trying to talk to him, find out if he was plotting anything, if he knew anything Raffy didn't know. But he knew there was no point. Linus knew nothing. There was nothing to know. They simply had a choice: deliver the System or die. Probably painfully. Almost certainly after watching Evie being tortured. And now that Benjamin was gone, that threat was even more pressing.

Of course, to Linus there was no choice; he would choose the latter every time. And he'd be right to. The System would destroy lives, just as it had done in the City. The System was evil; it could not be recreated.

Raffy knew all this. He knew that Evie would hate him if he even tried, that if she was going to love him again he had to show her that he had changed, that he could be noble and self-sacrificing and team-spirited.

But he also knew that he'd do anything to keep her safe. Even build Thomas his System.

Heavily, he picked up his fork and started to eat.

4

'So you like Frankie, do you?' The door opened suddenly and Raffy swung round to see Milo striding towards him, his glossy hair pushed to the side, his eyes and teeth shining as they always did, his dark suit and white shirt hanging beautifully off his broad shoulders.

'I was just . . .' Raffy started to say, awkward suddenly. It had been Cassandra's idea for him to watch Frankie; his computer had insisted that through Frankie he would learn all he needed to about the world. And since the alternative was desperately watching Evie every time he was able to glimpse her through his glass door, he'd reluctantly agreed. And actually Frankie was almost diverting in her own way. But she was Milo's girlfriend and it felt a bit weird being caught in the act. Luckily Milo didn't seem to be too upset; in fact, he grinned.

'It's fine,' he said. 'Everyone watches her. That's the point of her. To be watched. I'd be insulted if you didn't. But she's quite something, isn't she?'

Raffy shrugged. 'I guess,' he said noncommittally, not wanting to flatter Milo by saying anything nice about her, but not wanting either to tell him that Frankie was, to him, just something to distract him from his desperate need for Evie, his self-loathing, his devastating regrets. Fortunately Milo didn't care.

'Quite something,' he breathed, staring at her for a few seconds. 'And all mine.' He folded his arms and stood, his legs shoulder-width apart, as he stared at the screen proprietorially. Then he turned back to Raffy. 'Of course, she'd be nothing without me,' he winked. 'But no one needs to know that. It would ruin the magic, don't you think?'

Raffy didn't know what to say, so he just shrugged again.

Milo's eyes narrowed slightly. 'So,' he said. 'You've had a while to acclimatise. Ready to do some work now?'

Raffy nodded. 'I guess,' he said. 'I mean, I don't really have a choice, right?'

Milo considered this. 'Everyone has a choice,' he said. 'But you have chosen to work for us. And now that you've made that choice, it's incumbent on you, for your own health, sanity and satisfaction, to do a good job. That turns this into a win-win. Makes us all happy. And happiness is no bad thing, Raffy. You should try it some time.'

He was smiling again and Raffy wondered how much Milo believed his own words.

'I wouldn't know much about happiness,' he said carefully. 'You know, having been born into the City, into a country that doesn't exist apparently.'

Milo scratched his chin. 'What's happened is in the past, Raffy. We can't change it so we would be foolish to dwell on it. It's done. It's old news. What's ahead, though . . . That's up to us. How we approach it, that's up to us too. We can choose how we look at the world: through a screen of resentment, or through a screen of optimism. It's time to draw a line in the sand, Raffy. This world, the real world, you're in it now. It could all be open to you. You're young; you've got everything to play for. Do your job, do what we are asking of you, and you can be part of this world. You and Evie can make a life for yourselves.'

'Me and Evie?' Raffy raised an eyebrow. 'I don't think so. Not anymore.' He managed to keep his voice light, even though inside it was like someone was stabbing him over and over again.

'Okay, so then you and someone else. Someone who

appreciates you. Someone who wants *you* to be happy. Look around. Plenty of pretty girls you can watch. In your own time, of course. When you've done your work.'

Raffy forced a little smile. 'Of course.'

'So,' Milo said, looking pleased with himself. 'You have just been sent Linus's first batch of code. You will review it, improve it where you think it can be improved, and you will search it for bugs, for errors and any other problems. Two heads are always better than one, aren't they. And whilst you're not the genius that Linus is, you have more to lose from things going badly, more reason to check that Linus is really . . . focused on the task. Do you understand?'

'Sure,' Raffy said.

'Good.' Milo reached his hand out and put it on Raffy's shoulder. 'It's good to have someone with your energy as part of the team, Raffy,' he said. 'You've got promise. You could really have a future here. Remember that. See this job as an audition. See it as a gateway to a real future. I was like you once. And look at me now.'

'You were like me?' Raffy asked uncertainly. 'You mean your father was murdered by a corrupt regime, you hated your brother for pretending to be someone else, not knowing he was doing it to protect you? You mean that you betrayed the people you loved and then got kidnapped by the very person who was responsible for all your pain?'

Milo looked at him quizzically. 'What?' he asked.

'Nothing,' Raffy said. 'Just making conversation.'

Milo cleared his throat. 'Okay then. So, head down. Work hard. Yes?'

Raffy nodded slowly. 'Absolutely.'

'I know you will,' Milo said, squeezing Raffy's shoulder. 'Good man, Raffy. And we'll need the code back the day after tomorrow, when the new batch should be arriving. See you then!'

He turned and left as abruptly as he'd arrived, his smart, shiny shoes clipping across the apartment; he didn't acknowledge Evie, who was pacing around the sofa as he left. But he did turn, and smiled when he saw that Raffy was watching him, gave a little wave, then opened the door with a flourish of his wrist, and disappeared.

Raffy stared at the closed door for a few minutes, then let his eyes move back towards the sofa where Evie was now sitting, her eyes glazed. Her face was expressionless, but Raffy could read it, just as he had always been able to read it when they'd glimpsed each other in the City, or, rather, when he had glimpsed her. He'd made a point of glimpsing her whenever he'd had a chance – in the street, at work, at the weekly Gathering. He used to dream of having her with him all the time; even a few months ago he'd probably have jumped at the chance of being locked in a prison like this if she was with him, away from everyone else, his and his alone. Only now that he had what he thought he'd wanted, he realised that he had nothing. Because she no longer loved him. Because he had hurt her; because his jealousy had pushed her away not brought her closer; because he had let her down. Just as he'd always known he would. Just as he'd always been so afraid of doing. And now, as he looked at her, he could see her desperation, could feel the hollow building inside of her and it made him ache. Because he could no longer fill it. Because he could no longer give her what she wanted, could no longer bring her the happiness or joy she so deserved.

But he would. One day. He would redeem himself. He would turn everything around. For her. For Benjamin . . .

She moved, glanced over at him, then looked away again. Raffy did the same, his cheeks hot as he turned back to Cassandra's screen, where Linus's code was all displayed, had been displayed for a few hours now. And as he looked at it, he felt his heart sink just as it had when he'd first clapped eyes on it. Because it was barely code, and certainly wasn't code that would build Thomas the

System he so desired. It was . . . gobbledegook. It was utter rubbish. No, not rubbish. Gibberish. It was littered with errors, full of weird symbols that meant nothing.

Maybe Linus thought that he wouldn't notice. Thomas certainly didn't seem to realise that Raffy could virtually write the System himself if he wanted to, and Raffy was hardly going to tell him. He was happy being underestimated. It was the story of his life. But it put him in a difficult position. Because he knew now that Linus had absolutely no intention of even pretending to build the System. Which meant that Raffy had to make a choice: he could rewrite the code completely, pretend it was Linus's work, and keep Evie alive. Or he could tell Milo what Linus was doing, and let Linus face the consequences. Or he could pass on the gobbledegook, wait for Thomas to find out, and then watch helplessly as Evie was first starved, then tortured to death.

It wasn't a choice. It was a joke. He looked furiously at the wall that divided his cubicle from Linus's and cursed the man for his defiance, his determination, his ability to take all emotion out of a situation. Linus didn't think about individuals; they were an irrelevance to him, just as his own health and wellbeing was an irrelevance. Which was admirable and impressive sometimes. But was mostly just highly irritating. And right now it was much worse than that.

Raffy drummed his fingers on his desk.

'Everything okay?' Cassandra asked.

Raffy glowered at her. 'Just dandy,' he said, his voice low.

Cassandra's face appeared, still very attractive but more maternal now, with fine lines around her eyes and some grey hair framing her face. 'You're not happy with the code,' she said. 'You can't be. You've been in a bad mood ever since I brought it up and you haven't typed a thing.'

Raffy shook his head. He was not discussing this with a computer. Especially one built by Infotec. Even more especially since his every move was being watched, his every word being listened to.

'I'm just envious of the code,' he said eventually. 'Just working out how I can improve it. You know, add value.'

'Right,' Cassandra said, dubiously. She seemed to peer at Raffy. 'Really? You're sure that's all it is?'

'Really,' Raffy said irritably, then, realising that if Cassandra was suspicious, whoever was watching him would be too, he started to scroll through the code properly, trying to look impressed instead of utterly lost.

And then, suddenly, he frowned. Because in amongst the garbage was a line of code that he recognised.

Something Linus had used over a year before when he had been teaching Raffy how to dismantle the System, back when they were planning their attack on the City, believing it would change things, that it would make a difference. It wasn't code. It was something else. It was a language.

Raffy stared at it for a few minutes, but it made no sense; he figured Linus had just put it in because he was bored, because he could, because sometimes coming up with meaningless junk is actually quite difficult. But then, as he scrolled on, he saw something else, another line that stood out to him as though there were a light shining behind it. It was the language of the System but it wasn't in code that would build anything. It was spelling out words. Words that only Raffy would be able to read. Words that only Raffy would even be able to recognise. They could communicate. Secretly, away from the cameras, away from everything.

Raffy moved his chair forwards and started to read, deciphering phrases and words to create sentences. And as he read, he felt his heart begin to thud in his chest. 'Your computer has a blind spot,' the message started. 'You can communicate with the outside world as well as me.' As he read on, Raffy felt his eyes widen and his temperature rise. It was audacious, what Linus was suggesting. Impossible. Dangerous. But what hit Raffy most of all was the way Linus was trusting him. When all he had ever done was to prove himself untrustworthy.

He took a deep breath. He was going to repay that trust. He was going to make this work.

'Cassandra,' he said thoughtfully a few minutes later.

'Yes?' She looked excited to have been called upon; Raffy had to remind himself that she was just a computer.

'Would you mind doing some research for me? I'm trying to rework some of Linus's code but I need to see the latest Unix, see how it's changed over the past couple of decades.'

Cassandra nodded vigorously. 'I'll have to go into archive mode.'

'Whatever,' Raffy said. 'Just quick as you can.'

'It means I have to restart, I'm afraid, but it won't take me a minute.'

'Go for your life,' Raffy yawned.

'See you in a minute!' Cassandra closed her eyes and started to close down. Quick as a flash, Raffy typed a line of code. And there, as if by magic, was what Linus had told him about. His very own Trojan Horse. A corner of the screen that Cassandra wouldn't see, couldn't see, that couldn't be reported on, couldn't be censored. The screen went black, then Cassandra started to reboot. And Raffy waited.

5

She was running, running so fast her heart felt like it was banging its way out of her chest; she was gasping for air but still she ran, not towards anything, but away, away . . . They could see her. See her every move. They had always seen, always been watching, waiting. But they would not get her. They would never get her. She would run, run until death took her, if that was the only way of escaping them. And as she ran, all she could see was his face. His pinched, knowing, evil face. And he didn't even know he was evil. He didn't even know what that meant . . .

Evie woke with a start, just like she always did, a judder, a gasp, sweat-drenched sheets, the sickening realisation that she was still here, in this place that Lucas wasn't, the immediate, devastating knowledge that he was somewhere else, that she had no idea if she would ever see him again.

She pulled herself up, got out of bed. It was a huge bed, way too big for her, covered in soft white sheets, softer than anything she'd ever felt back in the City, the Settlement, the two places she'd called home in her life. The two could not be more different: the City, a paranoid world of rules, of labels, of a System that controlled everything and everyone; the Settlement, a place of learning, of building, of freedom of expression, of community – and yet now she was in a place more different still. And all she wanted to do was go home. To Lucas. To Lucas . . .

Was he still alive? Was the City still there? It seemed impossible somehow, impossible it should still exist now that she knew this place existed also; impossible that Lucas should be alive knowing what Thomas was, knowing what he had done. They had been here for five days; Evie felt like she had counted every second, every minute, every hour as she waited for it to expire. She wanted the weeks to go by, for Linus to fail to deliver his System, for Thomas to starve her, torture her, kill her. He would never return her to the City and death would be infinitely preferable to this no-man's land, this purgatory of nothingness, of isolation, of imprisonment. Evie had been imprisoned before, not physically but emotionally; back in the City, where the System controlled everything, she had spent her days paralysed, fearful, empty. But then she had experienced freedom, had understood what it felt like to take responsibility, to challenge, to fight, to believe, to hope, and she wasn't going back. She couldn't. She would rather die.

At least . . . She closed her eyes. If Lucas was alive, then she could at least cling on to the thought that he might come. No, not come. They would kill him. That he was safe, then. That he was back in the City, left alone by Thomas because he was no longer of any interest to him. If Lucas was alive, then the world was not an entirely dark and vile place. If Lucas was alive, then there was still a light glowing somewhere.

Just not here.

She closed her eyes, took a deep breath, then opened them again and walked to the bathroom. Her bathroom. Her own bathroom with a shower that jetted warm water over her, soaps that smelled of roses, soft fluffy towels to dry herself with, mirrors to educate her on how she looked. Evie had never seen so many mirrors; they adorned every wall, reflecting themselves back at her, creating walls beyond walls, a thousand Evies trapped behind them, staring at her, pleading with her, take me home . . .

And there, in the corner, a camera. Keeping watch. Checking up on her. She resented it, loathed it, but it was better than the System. At least she could see it; at least she understood how it worked.

In the City the System had been a terrifying thing; people had believed it could see everything, possibly even their thoughts. It had been all powerful, deciding whether citizens were good or bad, labelling them accordingly and striking terror into their hearts whenever their label changed for the worse. When the System had been destroyed, Evie had thought it was over; she and Raffy had escaped and moved to the Settlement, where they had been almost happy for a year. But that was before they knew the truth, about the City, about the System, about everything. And now they were back in a new prison as Linus built the System again, this time for the whole world.

She got dressed, covertly; she'd quickly worked out how to protect her modesty from the camera, draping a towel over the shower enclosure, wrapping another around her as she got out, getting dressed without removing the towel until the last minute. Thomas assured her many times that no one was interested in seeing her naked – he said it with a sneer, she guessed to humiliate her – but she didn't trust a single word he said, and anyway, she assumed the worst of people these days. Even Raffy.

Especially Raffy.

Evie slipped on her shoes; then she left her bedroom. In the kitchen area, as always, the table was set for breakfast, which was barely touched; instead there were two empty coffee cups, which she knew had been left by Linus and Raffy.

They were both getting thinner; she noticed it day by day. Even though there was more food here than they'd ever experienced before. She understood why; she had no appetite either, had no desire to eat the food that Thomas presented to them. She longed for the fresh vegetables of the Settlement, food that had been worked for, food that nourished the soul as well as the stomach.

But the Settlement had been destroyed; its people would still be hiding in caves, waiting for Benjamin to return. She wondered if they were still hiding, wondered how her friends were, wondered if they knew the truth about their world.

Evie felt a tear prick at her eye and she blinked it away; she would not cry, not when Thomas would be watching, smiling to himself. Not when Raffy or Linus might catch a glimpse too. She didn't want their pity; didn't want them to think about her at all. Because if they did, they might build the System for Thomas. She wanted them to think nothing of her, so that Thomas had nothing to bargain with, no hold over either of them.

She poured herself some coffee and started to drink, planning her day minute by minute, a strategy that she had developed on the first day and which was helping her cope with this horrible, sterile confinement.

And as each day had gone by, Evie had found it a little bit easier. Bit by bit, she had created a routine for herself, of nothingness punctuated by activity, of mealtimes, of particular sitting positions, which now felt familiar, felt almost bearable. She had resisted the screens at first, determined to allow the Watched their privacy, as she would prefer her own. But eventually she had been sucked in; had realised that without watching she would have only her own mind for entertainment and that it would quickly drive her mad with unhappiness and anger. And so she had begun to watch strangers, watch their every move, hear their every thought, read their messages to and from their friends, their loved ones. She saw images, words, people laughing, crying, shouting, sleeping; strangers telling the world everything and nothing, all the time, constantly. They were talking to no one, to everyone, to the wind, to the sky.

They had appeared alien at first; they spoke so quickly, rushed everywhere, used words she hadn't come across, confronted each other, ignored each other in ways that she found shocking. But gradually she became accustomed to their way of life, realised that they were not aggressive, antisocial monsters, but were people, like her, people with dreams, with fears, with worries, with hopes. And whereas in the City such things were kept hidden from view, here they were shouted out, exposed, communicated. And which was worse? Which was better? Evie didn't know. Didn't feel able to judge.

'Good morning.' Linus appeared in front of her; he had come to pour himself more coffee.

'Good morning.' She forced a bright smile. 'How are you?'

'Good, good.' Linus smiled. Their conversation had been stilted since they arrived here, since they understood that their every word was being listened to.

'Great,' Evie replied.

'You should eat. Get your strength up.' Linus pushed some cereal boxes towards her, a jug of milk. She frowned, about to protest, then saw something, something in his eye, something that disappeared the moment she'd seen it, making her wonder if she'd imagined it. But she knew she hadn't, so she chose some cereal, poured it into the bowl in front of her and added some milk.

'Good idea with the walking,' he said, adding some sugar to his coffee, stirring it then smelling it before taking a gulp. 'There are exercise channels if you're interested. They're fun, if you're at a loose end.'

He grinned, then turned and walked back to his cubicle. Evie stared after him. Exercise channels? Was he insane? What next? Watch some of the weird people who talked about nothing but clothes, or hair, or make-up? Did he not know where they were? Did he not get . . .

Then she stopped herself. Of course he knew. Of course he got it. And he wanted her to do some exercise.

Mentally she made a note to add it to her routine. An hour before lunch. Did he want her to get strong for a purpose or just to take her mind off things? Either way, it didn't matter. If he wanted her to do it, she would.

Silently she finished her cereal, and then ate some fruit and two eggs just for good measure. Then, just as she had done at this exact time for the past five days, she moved over to the central sofa, sat down and started to watch Frankie.

6

Frankie pulled open her wardrobe. 'So,' she said. 'I'm thinking . . .' She moved her hand in front of her and an image appeared of a clothes rack. She flicked through the virtual version of her closet, then chose a black tee-shirt. Immediately it whizzed to the front of the image, presenting itself on a hologram of herself, turning around to show all angles. 'This.'

She waited a second or two for her watchers' comments, which flooded the space in front of her eyes in bright yellow, green and orange.

'Love it Frankie,' Dib 1 said immediately. 'Maybe with your black skinnies?'

'With grey skinnies,' chimed in Sarah H. 'Much more flattering. They make your legs look sooooo long.'

Frankie scrolled through the rest of the feedback and grinned.

'Grey it is,' she said, flicking through the virtual rail again to pull out her trusty dark-grey moleskins. 'And . . . how about these?'

She hit an icon and then moved her finger to pick out the black studded ankle boots. The virtual her strutted around in the proposed outfit. 'Nice, huh?'

Again she was flooded with endorsements of her choice. But that wasn't surprising. Frankie was flooded with endorsements every time she made a choice, every time she so much as sat down in a café. Everyone wanted to be her. Everyone Watched her; globally she was number three, after the US president and Emile, the latest boy band heart throb. Until he'd released his latest track, Frankie had been number two and she was fairly confident she'd return to that position within a month, when the song had lost its sheen. No one was as good as her. No one.

Outfit decided on, she picked out the actual items from her real closet and put them on, applied a slick of lipstick to her wide mouth, and drew some kohl around her dark brown eyes. She stared at her reflection for a few seconds, trying to remember her face before she'd become Frankie, Number Three Watched in the Whole World, when she'd just been Frankie, Watched by some of her friends and family when they could be bothered. Then she quickly looked away. Contemplation didn't attract Watchers. Nor did vanity. Or doubt . . .

And anyway, what did any of that matter? She was Frankie. She was on top of her game. Life was good. Life was excellent.

'And I'm out,' she said cheerily to the camera in her bedroom. 'Café Honore here I come.'

As she walked, more and more comments appeared. Some just checking in, some admiring her look, some wishing her a good morning, saying that they'd try and get to the café if they could.

And some would. Some would get there. But not many. Most of her 23,589,704 worldwide Watchers would be at work, sleeping, eating, doing whatever it was they did day to day. Her role was to make them feel part of things, to be their friend, to cheer them up and entertain them. It would make them feel like Paris wasn't so far away after all, that they were virtually there.

'That's why people follow you,' Milo had explained. 'Because they want to feel like they're part of things, that they're involved, even if they live thousands of miles away. You owe them. Keep it upbeat.'

Keep it upbeat. Frankie smiled as she left her building and walked down the narrow Paris street. As she walked, she saw her image on several screens outside cafés, outside shops, drawing people in: you can watch Frankie while you shop! While you eat! People stepped aside as she walked towards them; some lifted their hands in greeting, high-fiving her as she walked past.

And all of them looked so excited to see her, so happy. Milo had been so right. She couldn't believe how much things had changed since she'd met him. Back then she'd just been a blogger, covering politics one day and fashion the next, going wherever her curiosity took her. Her writing style was confident, inviting and humorous; she had a few thousand regular readers and her pieces were often forwarded on. But nothing more. Nothing like this. Then Milo had taken her under his wing, taught her how to work it, put her on the Infotec 'We're Watching' page, made sure she was at every party, every event, and her Watcher numbers had started to rise. And Frankie had messaged them all, responded to them, name-checked them whenever she could, just like Milo had told her to. That's when she'd been promoted on the 'Top Ten New Faces to Watch' Infomercial that had accompanied the launch of the latest chip. That's when her numbers had really gone up. No, that was an understatement. That's when her Watcher numbers had gone through the roof.

She was on Honore Road, formerly Rue Honore. That's back when there were loads of languages, when communication between people was hampered by governments desperate to divide and rule, determined to stop any kind of world peace because peace didn't bring them power, peace didn't make them any money. Frankie shuddered at the thought. Her father, before he died, used to tell her about Paris in the old days, about the poverty, the anger, the in-fighting after Europe fell apart. Infotec had chosen Paris to be its centre because of its culture, its beauty and its location, but also because it knew that they would be welcoming. Not like the Americans, or the Chinese, who expected Infotec to be grateful to them, who put restrictions on them, made things difficult. Paris knew a good thing when it saw it; knew that this was the chance it needed to get up off its knees. Infotec could have chosen any European city; they were all in the same boat. And so Paris bent over backwards, agreeing to all of Infotec's demands and requests because it needed the jobs, needed the money; because its people were grateful. And they still were, he used to say, raising a glass of wine to the 'I' that was hologrammed onto the wall in their living room. '*Merci*,' he would grin before taking a gulp of Bordeaux.

The café she was going to was on the corner; as she walked towards it she passed a group of girls busy preening in front of a street camera, performing a little dance, apparently in a bid to improve their Watcher numbers. When they saw her, they stared open-mouthed, hostility and awe both visible on their faces. She ignored them and walked on; like Milo often told her, other people's jealousy really wasn't her issue. As she approached the café, she could see that someone had hastily erected a 'Café Honore welcomes Frankie!' sign and that a group of people were hovering outside waiting for her. She smiled, waving at them. 'Hey, I've got a welcoming committee. How nice!' she said, the words immediately appearing in front of each of her followers, courtesy of some new software that she was trialling for Infotec. The group of people cheered.

'Have a coffee on me,' one of her followers messaged immediately. 'I'm thinking of you over in hot Kentucky!'

'Will do!' Frankie said, before several thousand more messages appeared. She couldn't answer them all; couldn't even scratch the surface. But she always commented on the first one or two she received, always replied like they were old friends. And in many ways they were; they knew everything about her. She just knew nothing about them. Nothing except the messages, the constant dialogue right in front of her eyes.

'Oh my God! It's her! Frankie! Over here! Over here!' The screams rose in pitch as she walked towards the cluster, mostly girls, as always, all desperate to be caught on camera with her; the image would be sent to everyone they knew in the desperate hope that it would be circulated more widely, that they would attract a few more Watchers. Some were very young, some were maybe a year or two younger than her; a few were in their twenties, thirties.

'It's me!' She smiled, gave a little self-deprecating shrug. 'I can't believe you're all here already! So great to see you all!'

Immediately another stream of messages and status updates swam in front of her. She high-fived as many of the group as possible then made her way into the café, where a table was waiting for her.

'So, what shall I have?' she mused out loud. Immediately several million suggestions appeared. She considered a few of them, then picked up the menu. A waiter hovered over her.

'I think . . .' she said, hesitating for a second, 'that I'll have eggs over a bagel and a coffee. Thanks, Paul. Great suggestion!'

It was a trick she'd learnt from Milo, to scan quickly, zoom in on one comment, memorise the name, the exact suggestion. It made her millions of followers feel like it could be them, that they were really in this together. Made her one of them. It had felt cynical the first time she'd done it; she'd felt uncomfortable. She knew what it was like to look up to people, to watch them, to want to be like them, and she wanted to be able to get back to people properly, answer their questions, thank them for their nice comments. But it was impossible with these numbers; Milo was right, as always. And his technique worked; people felt like she was really listening to everything they said, so maybe it was okay that she was just performing a little trick, the same way Milo had taught her how to make her eyes all shiny and sparkly when she was on camera. 'Tricks of the trade,' he'd told her with a little shrug. 'Welcome to being famous.'

The food took a few minutes to arrive; all around her people were updating their status, mentioning her, taking photographs of her or purposefully moving close to her so that the café's surveillance cameras could pick them up with her, beaming their image across the globe and updating their status simultaneously.

She saw a waiter walk past her towards the corner of the café, where a man was sitting hunched over a coffee. The waiter leant down, pointed to the cameras; the man ignored him. Frankie frowned as she watched the waiter shrug and point to his watch. He had missed the fifteen-minute deadline; at least she assumed he had. You didn't have to say much, didn't have to do anything much at all. But you had to update every fifteen minutes unless you were in direct sight of a camera or unless your bed sensors could verify that you were asleep. Most computers could be set to auto-update; in most places you just had to look up at a camera to update. If you were at home, you just needed to install a camera and be clocked by it every fifteen minutes. Worst case, you had to stop what you were doing for a few seconds to write a quick update for your Watchers: 'I'm in the café'. 'I'm in the park'. It really wasn't that hard; most people updated way more frequently to keep their Watchers interested, and for those who didn't, it was totally worth the small inconvenience. It meant everyone knew where you were, what you were doing; it meant that there were no secrets, meant that everything was out on the table. It was a small price to pay for world peace, for a world free of crime, free of pain. If people knew you were sad, they could cheer you up; if they knew you were hungry, they could feed you.

The man had been drinking; Frankie could tell from the way he was lurching slightly. Like her uncle used to when he'd been on the beers. He hadn't liked the modern world either; unlike his brother, he had found it terrifying, intrusive. He'd insisted on speaking French until the day he died and had regularly missed updating his status, in spite of the threats, in spite of his wife's pleading. Some people just can't adapt, Milo had said dismissively when she'd told him about it. Some people don't want progress.

The waiter stepped back; moments later the café doors opened and two men appeared in grey suits, a large 'I' emblazoned on their lapels, the same 'I' that everyone else wore on their palms where their communication portals were embedded. They walked towards the man, who seemed not even to see them. They stepped behind him, lifted him up, hooked an arm each under his shoulders.

And then, not sure why she was doing it, Frankie found herself standing up, rushing towards him. 'Hi!' she said. 'Hi, I'm sorry I didn't see you there.'

She looked at the men with a rueful smile. 'Sorry, it's my fault he didn't update. I told him to wait for me. Look, we'll do it now!'

'*Mais . . .*' the man began in French, his expression one of incomprehension. '*Mais . . .*'

She stepped forwards quickly, turned around so that she was next to him. Then she held up her palm. 'Say hello to my friend everyone,' she winked, then turned to the Infotec men, a big smile on her face. 'Now let me get you all a coffee for the inconvenience.'

They looked at her hesitantly, then shrugged. Immediately the waiter appeared with coffee to go; no café wanted Infotec Inforcers sitting at their tables scaring everyone off. The men took their coffees, took one last look at the drunk man, who Frankie was now holding up, her arm clenched around his waist, then left.

Frankie put the man back on his chair.

'*Qu'est ce que vous faisez?*' he was saying, but his words were drowned out by Frankie's shouts to the people around the café; a 'Hey, how are you?' here, a 'OMG I love that top,' there. She deposited him on a chair, then sat down opposite him, trying to look relaxed, normal.

'Don't forget to update again in fifteen minutes,' she said brightly.

He stared at her, blue watery eyes seeming to look right through her. Then he shrugged. 'They want to know what I'm doing, let them take me,' he muttered, his accent thick; then he reverted back to French, a language that she knew from her uncle's emotional outbursts, from her parents' arguments when they hadn't wanted her to understand. 'They can go screw themselves. All of them.'

'You don't mean that,' Frankie said, laughing theatrically, looking around to check that no one had heard him. 'You're so funny.'

'Am I? I don't feel funny.'

He flopped back against the back of his chair. Frankie

leant over, closed her hand so that no one could hear. 'Sober up,' she hissed. 'Back home you've probably got someone who loves you. So love them back. Update your status. Every fifteen minutes. If I can do it, you can do it. Okay?'

Her father had never got over seeing his brother taken away by the Inforcers, never to return. Her cousins and their mother had left soon after; the shame had driven them away, her own mother explained sadly. Infotec had offered them the chance of a new life in Madrid, and they had taken it. Two weeks later, Frankie's own father was diagnosed with a heart condition and died soon afterwards.

The man's eyes widened; he looked genuinely surprised. '*Mais . . .*' he said, but Frankie moved closer.

'No buts,' she said. 'No excuses, no making out like it's not your fault. Drinking is your fault. Go home, or I'll make sure the Infotec Inforcers get you next time, understand?'

The man looked at her belligerently. Then he drank his coffee in one, stood up and staggered out of the restaurant. Home to his wife and children, Frankie found herself hoping. Children who wouldn't be left without a father, like she was.

She felt a tickle and opened her palm again. 'Hey

gorgeous.' A face appeared in front of her, a special border around the image denoting a personal contact.

'Milo!' She started; found herself walking quickly back to her table, her forehead suddenly covered in a thin veil of sweat. He wouldn't have seen what had just happened; it was out of the café camera's reach, otherwise the man's status would have been updated automatically. And even if he had seen, it was okay. She hadn't done anything wrong. And Milo was her boyfriend. He loved her. He just happened to be the head of Infotec's Paris division.

'How's my hot girl?'

Frankie reddened. She still hadn't entirely got used to holding all her very personal conversations in front of so many people, but that was the price for being so popular.

'I'm good. How're you?'

His image appeared on the larger screens; someone, somewhere had realised who she was talking to. Or maybe Milo had told the mainframe himself. Immediately a thousand messages appeared in front of her: 'He's so dreamy!' 'Oh, Frankie, so happy for you,' 'Wowzer, I love that guy. If I didn't love you so much too I might go after him myself!'

She blinked, looked back at the image in front of her eyes, a bonus of trialing Infotec's latest software – a bonus of having Milo as her boyfriend. 'So I was hoping to take you out to dinner tonight,' he said. 'Somewhere special. What do you think? Can you squeeze me in?'

She raised an eyebrow. 'I think I can probably manage to fit you in after the prize-giving at the Ritz,' she said with a wink. 'Does 8.30 p.m. sound okay?'

Words in front of her eyes. 'Somewhere special – he's going to propose!' 'Hey Frankie, he's got it bad,' 'I hear wedding bells!' She did her best to ignore them, but managed a little smile for the camera.

'Great, I'll pick you up outside the Ritz.'

He mouthed a kiss then disappeared, but she saw a message left behind, a private message just for her eyes: 'I love you. Can't wait to see you later.'

She smiled secretively, pleased for a second that the cameras didn't have to see everything.

She ate quickly, drained her coffee, then thanked the staff, waved her hand over the payment machine, added a generous tip – essential now that she had so many followers, but expensive – then walked out onto the road again, down towards the Info Palace, then across into Louvre Street and finally into the Library on Rivoli Road, where she quickly updated her status before shutting down her communication portal. 'Out of respect to people trying to study,' she explained to her disappointed followers. 'Back in 15 minutes!'

7

The Library was where Frankie worked, where she wrote, researched, where many of the City's bloggers came to work, to see each other, to compare notes. Blogging was a dying art; they all knew that. Images were far more popular than words and reader numbers were dwindling. But still the bloggers came, to think, to write, to rant. A lot of the time they wrote blogs on the sad implications of the demise of the blog, ever-diminishing circles that were chock full of irony, but written anyway. And Frankie knew why. She didn't need to write a blog anymore; the income she received for it was peanuts, utterly inconsequential. But she'd never give it up.

Milo didn't get it at all, could not see why she would spend so much time writing stuff that no one read when she could be out and about gathering more Watchers.

The problem with the Library, he'd say with a shrug, was that there were no cameras there. She could still update her status, but if she wasn't visible, people would switch off, would watch someone else. Words didn't matter anymore; people wanted visual stories, not boring text. And she owed her Watchers, after all. They needed her.

He was right, of course he was. But there had to be a balance. Frankie hadn't decided to be a blogger because she'd thought it would bring her fame and fortune. She'd done it because she'd always done it, because it was her way of pausing the world, of figuring out what she thought about stuff. She'd started when she was a teenager and had got enough people reading it to make it vaguely financially viable. Now there was no need for her to do it, but she just couldn't give it up. It was as though the blog kept her on the ground; without it, she was afraid she might just blow away with the wind.

Plus it meant she got to hang out at the Library most days, and if she was completely honest, she rather enjoyed a few hours out of the glare of being watched; being like she used to be, anonymous, a person known for what she wrote rather than for what she looked like, what she did, the minutia of her day. It still amazed her how many comments she got from complete strangers following her decision to have cereal for breakfast or a chicken sandwich for her lunch. Until recently, such comments had come only from her friends and family – or, rather, her extended network of friends-of-friends and acquaintances built up over her life. Fifteen hundred or so Watchers; respectable by most standards.

Now, though, it was something else; now she had followers in America, in China, Africa, the Middle East. Now she was a role model; a beacon of the new world, inspiring and engaging people everywhere. And she loved it; loved the knowledge that she was making people happy, that they were rooting for her, that in some way she was giving their lives meaning. Because, as Milo had pointed out, not everyone lived in Paris; if you lived in a village in the middle of nowhere, reading about the life of someone in the metropolis would help you to feel connected, part of the whole. But it was still a little overwhelming. Still a bit terrifying sometimes when someone from Kazakhstan commented on the toothpaste she was using.

So Frankie's balance was that in the mornings she worked. In the afternoon, she'd be out and about, shopping, partying, going to launches, whatever; being visible. But from nine to one, she got to focus on her blog. Her blog that barely anyone read. Her blog that was, according to Milo, utterly pointless.

She walked in through the grand entrance, past

the download terrace and through to the work bank, where fifty or so people sat, typing furiously onto keyboards, hologram screens in front of them. The room was silent, one of the few places such a thing was possible; no audio or visual updates were allowed.

She sat down in front of a screen, then opened a hologram keyboard by opening her hands and choosing a tab button.

'You made it, then.'

It was a message from Jim, her old comrade in arms, her friend since she was . . . well, since always as far as she could remember. She scanned the line of people, clocked him and gave him a little wave. He pretended to ignore her.

'Hey, some of us have work to do,' appeared in front of her eyes. She grinned. Jim was about the only person nowadays who didn't treat her like a superstar, who wasn't intimidated by her, who didn't fawn over everything she wrote or said. If anything, he judged her for being a celebrity; he preferred to keep a low profile, only updating his status every fifteen minutes, when his chip reminded him, avoiding cameras where he could and refusing to follow anyone. Which was why, she regularly told him, he was such a social outcast and couldn't get a girlfriend.

She sat down, took her keyboard out of her bag and unfolded it; when she was properly writing she liked the satisfying click of an old-fashioned physical keyboard rather than a VR one. Then she moved her hands to bring up her screen and opened the investigative report she was working on.

But before she could type, another message appeared.

'Hey, gorgeous. I'm missing you. What are you up to?'

She smiled. Milo. She instinctively moved to turn on visual, but remembered where she was in time and stopped herself. 'Hey yourself,' she typed back. 'I'm working. I want to get this blog done.'

'The party girl strikes again?'

Frankie raised an eyebrow then remembered that Milo couldn't see her.

'Not today. And I don't party all the time. I want to write something interesting.'

'You want me to go, is that it?'

She smiled. 'Milo, you've got a big job. Shouldn't you be doing it right now?'

'I can't help it if you're irresistible. You're definitely meeting me for dinner later?'

'I wouldn't be anywhere else,' she promised, and the message box disappeared. He was super keen, she found herself thinking. But whereas that might put her off another guy, with Milo it just made her more excited. She'd never met anyone like him. So intense, so interested in everything she did, everything she thought about.

She frowned as another message pinged into her inbox; a personal message sent to her blog but with no name attached, no return address. A total stranger had sent it and it wasn't the first time; she'd seen and ignored the same message several times already that morning. And sure, the world was full of total strangers and it was the fact that they followed her that made her who she was, but this kind of persistency still irritated her, particularly when it was obviously a crazy person peddling some made-up conspiracy theory,

'Communications blackout over UK. Haven't you noticed? Why? Radioactivity doesn't require it. We have been lied to.'

Another crazy kook. She got all sorts of drivel sent to her; kind of came with the territory. She rolled her eyes and deleted it, then started writing that day's blog, a rather deep piece, she thought, about how the world was now so similar that the only divisions were down to weather and terrain; people were united by common language, common aspirations, and had more in common these days than at any time in history. She wrote three hundred words, re-read it, and was about to publish it when another message arrived. 'You think I'm crazy so why not look into it for yourself? As far as your systems are concerned, there is no UK. Don't you want to know why?'

Frankie looked at it in irritation. What was it with people and their conspiracy theories? They were so pointless, so damaging. Only desperate bloggers took them seriously. Her blogs were considered, thoughtful, carefully researched. Like that one she did on wheat rationing in sub-Saharan states.

Of course, her reader numbers had dipped to an all-time low after that blog. Like Milo kept telling her, it was new dresses that people were interested in, parties, kissing Milo for the cameras. That's why the vast majority of her followers had deselected her blog when they'd subscribed to Watch her. Which hurt a little, if Frankie was honest, but she understood why. Kind of.

'Gorgeous,' Milo had explained patiently, 'it's not that you're not a great writer. You are. But no one reads your blog because people don't care about serious things. They have enough of that stuff in their own lives. They want you to take them away from that. They want to know where you've been, what you've been up to.'

Maybe a conspiracy theory piece wasn't such a bad idea after all, she found herself thinking, then shook herself. She wasn't that desperate. Instead, she forwarded the email to Milo with a quizzical face. Maybe she should write the story, she found herself thinking, but with a damning indictment of the whole conspiracy, warning against anyone taking such stupidity seriously.

To her surprise, Milo messaged back straight away.

'Total loon. Frankie, don't get sidetracked by crazy people. And whatever you do don't give them oxygen. People won't respect you for it. You'll lose social capital.'

Frankie pulled a face. Milo was always using phrases like 'social capital'. Everything was business to him; everything was about on-message branding. But he was right. He was always right.

The weird thing was, though, that him telling her not to cover the crackpot theory somehow made her want to write about it.

'I was thinking about writing about it, but not giving it oxygen, more talking about the way that all those conspiracy theories over the UK just refuse to go away and why that might be?' she asked him.

'Absolutely not,' Milo messaged back right away. 'Don't do it. You don't want to upset people. People will have relatives who died over there. Don't go reminding them. That's an order, Frankie.'

Frankie stared at the words for a few seconds. An order? What the hell did that mean?

She took a deep breath. He meant it tongue in cheek. He had to. He'd never give her an order seriously.

She re-read the message. Of course, he was right about reminding people. People never talked about the UK; it was the world's elephant in the room; it quashed most arguments for letting people do their own thing, for not worrying if people didn't update regularly enough. A whole country annihilated because a few extremists got too powerful, because the government didn't act quickly enough to stop the inevitable retaliation and escalation. A whole country destroyed by a nuclear bomb that should never have been activated; no one was even quite sure who controlled it. According to those who had been alive at the time, it had been life-changing, world-changing. No one felt safe anymore; no one took anything for granted afterwards.

She closed the stranger's email and turned back to another blog she'd started the day before – a piece on how information sharing was the latest development in human evolution, about how for billions of years humans had developed tools like language, the written word, the telephone, the television, to communicate ideas with each other, and that now InfoSharing meant that humans were almost like one, ideas being communicated instantly across the globe, total openness meaning that genuine equality was becoming more and more achievable. It wasn't great, but it was better than the piece she'd written today. It would do. She read it over once more, then felt her stomach clench as another message popped up from the stranger.

'If you want the truth, don't expect to get it from the people who lied in the first place. I thought you were an investigative blogger. So investigate.'

Frankie could feel her heart thudding in her chest. How did they know she'd spoken to Milo? Then she shook herself. Of course they didn't know. They were guessing. Milo was her boyfriend after all.

But it still irked her. Still made her feel hot and uncomfortable.

Another message appeared. 'What if I'm not crazy? What if I'm telling the truth? Just dig a little bit, then ignore me if you want to. Because your interest is piqued, isn't it? And you're your own woman, right?'

Frankie stared at the screen, feeling the blood drain from her face. Her own woman? It was like this person had seen the message Milo had sent her. And taken it seriously.

'How about if I say please? And smile flirtatiously? You can't see it, but I'm doing it, right now. My most charming smile.'

The messages were coming through thick and fast; Frankie leant forwards to read them all again.

Her heart was thudding in her chest. Who was this? He wasn't like the usual conspiracy theorist, who would write long diatribes full of assertions that had no evidence to back them up. This guy ... he was different. And it was a 'he'. Frankie was sure of it. She frowned.

'You're wondering if maybe there's something in it after all, aren't you? I know you are. Frankie, you're cool, and hot, but you're also clever. So do something brave. Do something a bit more exciting. Please?'

Frankie bit her lip and did her best not to smile. The stranger was totally flirting with her. If Milo knew he'd be furious.

But he'd said 'please', which was better than 'That's an order.'

Even if Milo had been joking, the words still rankled. Which was no reason for listening to the stranger. No reason at all. But then again, people *had* been talking about the UK all her life; theories abounded of how there were still people there, that the talk of radiation was a conspiracy to stop people investigating. And she knew it was all just conjecture and gossip; knew that test after test had been done to confirm the devastation, but what if the stranger was onto something? What if there was something real underpinning the rumours? What if there was something that they weren't being told?

And as if the messager knew what she was thinking, as though he was sitting right there with her, another message appeared from the same untraceable address. 'Don't be an Infotec Stooge. Think for yourself. Look into it before you dismiss me out of hand.'

The smile disappeared from her face immediately. Infotec Stooge? How dare they? How dare someone say such a thing? She would sue. She would tell Milo and get him to track them down and . . .

Her eyes narrowed. Not Milo. She didn't need Milo and his Infotec army. That would play into this person's prejudices. She was so not an Infotec Stooge. She was totally her own person.

She folded her arms in irritation; whoever this person was they had hit a nerve. She'd ask Jim to track him down instead, she decided. Then she'd write back and make it absolutely clear that the reason she wasn't following up on his message was because he was obviously mad and delusional, that's all.

'Try sending a message to the US and follow its path. You know how to do that?'

She stared at the message in front of her eyes. The audacity of it! Of course she knew how to do that. But she was busy. She was pissed off. She wasn't doing anything just because some mad person wouldn't leave her alone.

She exhaled angrily. Then her eyes narrowed. Maybe she could send one message. Just one. Just to see. The message would whizz straight to the US and that would be the end of that, she reasoned. Conversation over.

Quickly she sent a few messages to the US and traced their path. Then she watched uncertainly as everything bypassed the UK, zigzagging round it, which was strange because nuclear fallout might be bad for humans but, to her knowledge, there was no reason wireless signals should avoid it.

Then again it didn't mean anything. So the network was complex. There would be a reason. A perfectly good reason.

Suddenly Frankie had an idea. She went into the 'Questions Worth Answering' section of her blog, and wrote about what she'd done, asking if anyone had any suggestions.

Straight away her palm started to tickle; it was Milo. 'Milo?' she whispered. 'I'm in the Library. Can't really talk.'

'What's with the question?' he asked immediately.

'The question?'

'The one you've just posted. Frankie, I thought you understood that you're in a powerful position. You can't go repeating crazy theories because you'll give them credence. You'll get people worried. And you'll put my career in jeopardy. Take it down. Now.'

Frankie cleared her throat. 'Take it down? Milo, it's just a question on my blog. I doubt anyone's even seen it. No one's interested in my blog, remember?'

'I've seen it,' Milo said. 'And I want you to take it down. It makes you look foolish. It makes me look foolish.'

Frankie felt her jaw harden. 'Then why don't you answer the question?' she said, her temper beginning to flare as it always did when people tried to hem her in.

'You really want me to?' Milo sighed. 'You know, I don't really know. But I suspect the protective barriers that were erected around the UK after its civil war, after the devastation of the nuclear attack, have probably got something to do with it. And I'd love to double check it, love to go over there just for you so I can clear up any uncertainty, but I'm not so wild on nuclear contamination, if it's alright with you. Not so keen on sending anyone else over yet either. But just as soon as the United Nations has given the all-clear for their envoys to visit the islands and test their radioactivity levels, I'll be sure to ask them to look into zigzagging communication lines. For your blog. Because you got a message from some weirdo. Okay, Frankie?'

His tone was more sarcastic than she'd ever heard it; Frankie knew that she'd riled him, knew that everything he was saying made sense.

She sighed. 'I guess I just wanted to write about something important,' she said quietly.

'So do that,' Milo said impatiently, 'but make it properly important. Write about how much happier people are now. Write about how safe they feel, how protected, how unified the whole world is. Please delete that stupid question. Please do it right now.'

'Yeah,' Frankie said. 'Yeah, okay.'

'And leave some time to get ready for tonight. I'm planning to ask you something important. I'm kind of hoping the focus could be on us. Not some technological hitch that may or may not exist. Think about us, not some freak.'

Frankie reddened in pleasure. 'I will think only about us,' she promised. 'I'm sorry, Milo. Okay, see you later. Can't wait . . .'

She closed down the conversation, then sat back against her chair. An important question. Was he seriously going to propose? That was a bit out there. Really lovely, but still quite bonkers. She was only nineteen after all. She wasn't sure she was ready to get married. Was she? She shook herself. Of course she was. She loved Milo; was definitely ready to commit to him. He was everything she'd ever wanted. But being a Mrs? Freaky. Seriously. Maybe he was going to suggest they live together? She could be moving into his a.m.a.z.i.n.g flat in St Germain. Hell, that was definitely worth a blog.

But as she started to delete the question on her blog, another message popped up. 'He called pretty quickly. And seems very keen that you don't write anything. I wonder why? And I wonder if you're going to do what he tells you to? I hope not. You're better than that.'

Frankie stared at the screen indignantly. Who the hell was this person? How did he hear her private conversation with Milo? And how dare he suggest he'd called to shut her up. Milo was her boyfriend. If he gave her advice it was because he wanted her to do well, because he understood the social market, because he was in love with her. He often made suggestions about what she wore and which parties she should go to; why shouldn't he give her advice on what she wrote, too? He was a smart guy. That's why he was head of Infotec Paris; he knew how to make things good, how to make things successful.

And, frankly, she could blog about whatever she bloody well liked.

She closed the message. Then she opened it again. Then closed it. Then she stood up. This was making her really mad. Milo was right: the messager was obviously a freak. But she didn't want the freak thinking that she was a stooge when she was absolutely not. She was her own person. Always had been. Infotec didn't tell her what to write, but nor did she let freaks dictate to her either. She hadn't asked Infotec to put her on its Top Ten New Faces to Watch. She hadn't gone out of her way to fall in love with the head of Infotec.

She sat down again. And then she made a decision. She would leave the question on her website. But she would also write a short blog about it and, in doing so, would close the question down, demonstrate that it was stupid. In one fell swoop, she would prove she was her own person and show Milo that she was able to tackle crazy ideas without appearing crazy herself.

At the thought of Milo and his big question, butterflies appeared in Frankie's stomach; she enjoyed the sensation for a few seconds, imagined herself looking into Milo's eyes, the world watching as he asked her to marry him, move in with him, or something, something big . . . Then she briefly turned on the camera on her computer to update, steeled herself, and started to write.

8

'Working hard?'

Jim's face popped up in front of Frankie and she looked at him awkwardly.

'You know. Pretty hard,' she said, shooting him a quick smile before turning back to her work.

It was already 11 a.m., she realised; 11 a.m. was when they used to stop for coffee. Every day for a long time. But lately . . . lately she hadn't really had time for coffee. Or time for Jim. He was a nice guy. Really nice. It was just that her life had changed; he had to realise that she didn't have the same amount of time as before.

'Too busy for coffee then?' He looked disappointed. Or rather, he looked like he was trying not to look disappointed, which amounted to the same thing. She sighed, telling herself not to feel bad. She'd been his friend for a long time; at school she'd done her best to hang out with him, even though she was the popular, pretty one, and he was a nerd that no one really had any time for. He was a geek, after all. A geek who liked to question everything and be difficult about everything and make life incredibly hard for himself. But he'd also lived in the same apartment block as her, and he was kind of funny and weird and Frankie had always had a soft spot for him; she'd always been able to see beyond the angry-young-man act to the clever, thoughtful friend who always used to know what was wrong before she'd even opened her mouth to speak, who saw through the crap that fixated everyone else, who always gave her the best advice, who never demanded anything of her. Except for coffee, of course.

But that was before she became . . . Well, before she became famous. Before she met Milo. Now, his smart little jokes and his sarcastic humour didn't seem so funny. Now she resented the way he liked to think he knew what she was thinking, particularly because he got it so wrong these days. And he was so anti Infotec, so anti Milo. It was unfair. She'd never be rude about his girlfriend. If he ever got one. If he ever took his nose out of his screen long enough to notice there were girls around.

The fact of the matter was that they moved in different worlds now, and Jim had to get with the programme. It would probably do him some good.

'You know what, I'm kind of in the middle of something,' she said with an apologetic shrug. 'Maybe another time?'

Jim raised an eyebrow. 'I guess writing about parties does take some concentration,' he said.

Frankie's eyes narrowed. 'And writing your inciteful blogs for an audience of two must really take it out of you, too,' she said archly. 'No wonder you need coffee to keep yourself awake.'

She stared at him, waiting for his comeback. They both knew that he was the brilliant one; he always had been. But it wasn't her fault he'd failed spectacularly to make anything of himself. After school, he was headhunted by Infotec; they offered to put him through Oxford University (now situated in Lille) and guaranteed him an amazing job afterwards. But Jim being Jim, he turned them down, refused to take the funding, refused to consider working for them. To the surprise and dismay of all his teachers, he self-funded himself through a distance-learning degree, then set up a blog that aimed to awaken the world to all the terrible things going on. But the trouble was, there were no terrible things going on, not really, and other than a handful of equally nihilistic nerds, no one ever read his blog. What Jim failed to grasp was that things were okay. Better than okay. Infotec was a force for good. Then again,

Frankie often thought to herself, if he had grasped that Infotec wasn't the megalomaniac evil corporation he made it out to be, it just would have made him more depressed. Ultimately, Frankie had realised long ago, Jim didn't want to be happy. And he didn't want to write things that made people happy either. In a world where happiness was a big priority, that kind of made things difficult for him. But he didn't seem to care; he just kept on writing his gloomy blog full of stories of poverty, of invasion of privacy, of fear and loathing for anything new, or anything that seemed to make Infotec yet more money. Milo called him 'deranged' and she totally saw why, but a bit of her was also jealous because he never pretended to be something he wasn't, never seemed to care that no one was interested in Watching him or even reading his blog.

She realised Jim wasn't looking at her; he was looking over her shoulder at what she'd written. And he was smirking. Frankie moved herself in front of the screen.

'I thought you were going for coffee,' she said. 'Shouldn't you be going instead of reading my blog? Unless you want tips on how to get a few more Watchers, that is?'

Jim shook his head wearily. 'You know, Frankie, you used to be a really good writer. I just hate seeing all that promise go to waste.'

Frankie turned around. 'It isn't going to waste,' she

said, angry now. 'I have a zillion Watchers, in case you'd forgotten. And anyway, you should like this particular blog. I'm investigating just the sort of conspiracy theory that you love.'

'Investigating? Is that what you call it?'

Frankie felt herself flush. Why had she ever defended Jim? Why had she ever thought it was a good idea to be nice to him? 'Yes, actually,' she said. 'Why, what would you call it?'

'I don't know,' Jim said, folding his arms. 'But as far as I can see, you're raising the question about a blackout over the UK and then answering it with Infotec spin. I mean I get why – this isn't stuff anyone wants to read about, not least your boyfriend. It's much more my territory. But if you're not going to do it properly, why cover it at all?'

'I am doing it properly . . .' Frankie said irritably. 'It's a whole load of bullshit and I'm treating it as such.'

'Whatever,' Jim said. 'Look, I really need some caffeine. I'll see you around, okay?'

'Suit yourself,' Frankie said stiffly, refusing to even turn around. She was incandescent with rage. How dare he? How dare Jim with his poxy little blog that no one cared about criticise her, when she was Watched by so many people? Sure, barely any of them subscribed to her blog, but she still had way more readers than him, even if the stats suggested that people clicked on her blog, read the first sentence then closed it down right away.

The point was, she was no way going to be lectured by Jim. No way at all.

She re-read her blog. It was fine. It was more than fine. It raised the questions the anonymous messager had posed about the UK, then it dismissed them all as complete nonsense. Quoting Milo, mainly. Or rather, quoting Milo and no one else. But that was okay. Milo was the spokesperson from Infotec.

But as she read it again, she felt herself getting hot and bothered. Because Jim was right; what she'd written was pointless, meaningless. Maybe Milo was right; she should just stick to writing about the party she went to last night, the gossip currently doing the rounds. That's what people wanted to read; that's what would cheer them up.

And yet she didn't want to write about any more bloody parties. She wanted to be taken seriously. She wanted people to know there was more to her. She wanted to convince herself of the same thing.

She felt someone walking towards her and swung round – to her surprise it was Jim again, two cups of coffee in his hand.

'What?' she barked.

He put one of the coffees on her desk and pulled an

apologetic face. 'I've come to say I'm sorry,' he said, crouching down next to her. 'I was rude and patronising and insulting and I'm sorry. I have nothing to write about, no one reads anything I write anyway, and I let myself get bitter about the fact that I'm a total loser. But I shouldn't have taken that out on you. Your blog is great. Please ignore everything I said before.'

He stood up and started to walk away, but Frankie's hand shot out and grabbed his arm, stopping him in his tracks.

'Liar,' she said, standing up. 'This piece is a total load of rubbish and everything you said about it is right. But that doesn't mean I will ever forgive you for being such a shit.' She shot him a meaningful look.

'Understood,' Jim said.

'Particularly since you could have stepped in just now to say it wasn't actually that bad.'

'Also understood,' Jim nodded awkwardly. 'And if it isn't too late, I'd like to add that it really isn't that a total load of rubbish at all.'

'It is too late,' Frankie said, then sighed. 'So what do I need to do to it?'

Jim took a slurp of coffee. 'Seriously?'

'Seriously,' Frankie said, drinking some coffee then leaning forwards.

Jim's face changed, like it always did when he started

talking seriously, when he allowed his sarcastic front to melt briefly. It reminded Frankie of when he used to help her with her maths homework. 'Seriously, I think you should delete it. All of it. Write about something else instead.'

Frankie looked at him indignantly. 'Why? Because you think I should be writing about parties instead?' she said, her tone cutting.

'No,' Jim said quickly. 'Of course not. I just don't think writing about this is a good idea. You start writing about information blackouts, even made-up ones, and you're getting yourself into deep water. Infotec don't like people writing about stuff like that.'

Frankie raised an eyebrow. 'I think I'll be alright, Jim. They'll be fine with it. And anyway, someone keeps sending me messages, asking questions about it. So I'm answering them.'

'You're writing this because some conspiracy nut wants you to?' Jim asked incredulously. 'Why aren't they writing about it themselves? Just think about it, Frankie. Tread carefully.'

Frankie stared at him uncertainly. 'You'd write about it,' she said. 'If the lead had come to you.'

'Maybe,' Jim shrugged. 'But maybe not. I don't want the Inforcers banging on my door, thank you very much.'

'They wouldn't bang on your door,' Frankie said

immediately. 'You're not influential enough to cause them concern.'

Jim caught her eye, saw the little smile playing on her lips, then looked down at his coffee cup. 'You're right,' he said. 'But still. You're up for a prize today, aren't you? Inspirational woman of the year, isn't it? Or is it of the century?'

Frankie kicked him. 'Year,' she said. 'Stop taking the piss.'

'I'm not,' Jim said, quickly. 'I'm trying to make you see sense. Things are good. Don't go pissing people off for no reason.'

Frankie looked at him thoughtfully. If Jim was trying to dissuade her, he was doing a very bad job. She knew full well she was winning the award for being pretty and going to parties, not for doing anything meaningful. 'And if I decided to ignore your advice and publish the story? What would you say then? What do I need to do to make it better?'

Jim took a deep breath, then looked her right in the eye. 'You really want to know?'

'I really want to know,' Frankie nodded.

'Okay,' Jim said with a sigh. 'Do the same thing you'd do for any other story. Question everything. Question the assumptions, question the questions, question the answers. That's it, really. That's all I've got. But think

95

carefully, Frankie. Please think before you start writing this. It could get you into trouble.'

Frankie nodded thoughtfully. 'Thanks Jim,' she said, looking at her watch then shooting him a little smile. 'I think I'd better get back to work.'

9

Frankie sat down and started to type. The words flowed out of her, just like they always did when she was on a mission. It had been too long since she'd written like this, hunched over her keyboard, eyes staring at the screen, all her senses cut off from the world outside, unaware of sound, of movement, of anything but the words, sentences, interrupted only by an alert every fifteen minutes to update, which she did with a very perfunctory 'writing'. And what she wrote, mainly, was questions. She didn't have answers; every search she had made ended with a brick wall, with a dead end, with a polite dismissal. Just like Milo had dismissed her questions, she thought as she typed. Just as he had cleverly side-stepped them, put the focus back on her. But now it was time to demand proper answers. And thanks to Milo and her growing 'social capital', she had the platform to do it. He would be irritated, she knew that. But she'd be able to talk him round. He loved her; he would understand why she'd written what she had. He had a job to do, but so did she. She might have forgotten that recently, but not today.

She read what she'd written, changed a few words, read it again, and then, before she could change her mind, pressed Publish.

A message arrived, not even a second later, not even a nanosecond, and it sent a jolt of electricity through her. It was as though whoever had sent it could see her, even though that was impossible; even though the Library was the one place on earth they couldn't see her, where visual images weren't beamed out to the world. Unless the stranger was in the Library himself, of course, but that was impossible too. No one could see what she was writing and even if they could . . . No, it couldn't be.

Frankie looked around furtively, but there were only the usual suspects here, all bloggers. None of them would ever give her a lead or information; they'd be all over it themselves if they discovered something interesting. Scoops meant readers, who might become Watchers, and Watchers meant that life became easier. Much easier. They were friends, but friends in competition with each other; that's why their smiles were rather more insincere now than they had been, before Frankie was so popular, before she was famous. She had been one of them; now, her celebrity made them feel self-conscious; now, her success made their achievements seem microscopic.

One of them, a girl called Honey, met her eye and shot her a little raised eyebrow, code for 'I'm stuck, too. Sucks, doesn't it?' At least that's what Frankie had always assumed it meant. That's what she always meant when she shot a raised eyebrow back. But today, she almost forgot the code, only remembered to offer a rueful smile when she noticed Honey's face harden slightly. 'She thinks she's too good for us,' was emblazoned across her face. Or was Frankie imagining it?

She looked over at Jim, who was head-down, and felt a small lump appear in her throat. All the bloggers loved Jim. Because he was brilliant. Because he was funny, and warm and self-deprecating. Because he could be the most successful one of them, but chose not to be. Whereas she was the most successful one, but didn't deserve to be.

She wanted to tell him about the message she'd just got, the message from the stranger who had apparently already seen her blog seconds before she published it.

But he was hard at work, headphones on. And anyway, he'd just tell her he'd told her so.

She read the message again. 'Well done. Nice start. But you've only just started. There are people here from the UK. Prisoners of Infotec. You need to keep asking questions.'

Was this stranger watching her? How? Who was this person?

She deleted the message; whoever had written it was obviously beyond help. People from the UK? Brought here as Infotec prisoners? It was a sea of radiation out there. No one could live there. It was impossible. And secondly, why on earth would Infotec keep them prisoner if they did get here? It was completely loopy.

Her blog appeared suddenly, officially published. She re-read it, smiling as she got to the end: 'What remains, though, are some unanswered questions that simply won't go away until Infotec play by their own rules and open up their information to public scrutiny.'

The stranger might be loopy, but they were right about it being a good blog, she thought triumphantly. It was the best thing she'd written in ages.

She heard a little beep and moved her head; immediately she heard Milo's voice. He wasn't happy.

'Are you mad? I told you. I warned you.'

Frankie took a deep breath. 'So you saw the blog then?' She used her more coquettish voice, hoping it would mollify him before he could really get started. It didn't work.

'Of course I saw the bloody blog. I can't believe you wrote it. What were you thinking?'

'I—' Frankie said, but Milo wasn't finished.

'You weren't thinking,' he said, speaking over her. 'You weren't in your right mind. You can't have been. And that's exactly what you're going to say when you retract it.'

'Retract it?' Frankie's eyes widened. 'I'm not going to retract anything. It's a good blog. I've already had great feedback.'

'Oh yes you are,' Milo said, his voice cutting, harsher than she'd ever heard it before. 'You are going to retract it now. Say it was a joke. Say that someone hijacked your account. I don't care what you say, but you do it right now.'

People were looking at Frankie in irritation; the Library was supposed to be a place of work and she had broken the rules by talking. Pulling an apologetic face, Frankie turned to her keyboard instead.

'Milo,' she wrote, trying to stay calm and rational. 'Milo, you may not like what I wrote in my blog, but it's really no big deal.'

'No big deal? You think it's no big deal to suggest that Infotec is hiding things? That it's involved in a major cover-up? Really, Frankie?'

Frankie hesitated for a second, then steeled herself. 'I

think,' she said carefully, 'that I have a right to ask for answers. All Infotec needs to do is explain itself. Open up the files on the UK. It was a long time ago, Milo. People can handle it. And Infotec is so big on being open . . .'

'You have five minutes to retract it, Frankie. Five minutes. After that, there's nothing I can do,' Milo cut in.

'Milo,' Frankie wrote pleadingly. 'Milo, don't be like this. Let's talk about it later . . .' But it was too late; he had disconnected. Frankie stared at their conversation for a few seconds; her head spinning, her mind whirring. Then, in a daze, she stood up.

She could retract the blog; of course she could. But she didn't want to. For the first time in a long time she actually felt proud of something she'd done. And she knew that she would never be happy if she did what Milo had asked. This wasn't about the UK; wasn't about some crazy conspiracy theories. This was about her, what she did, who she was and who she wasn't.

She looked at her watch. It was 1 p.m. Time to go home, get changed, prepare herself for the afternoon's various events. Milo would get over it. He was going to have to.

Picking up her bag and closing her screen, Frankie made her way uncertainly out of the Library.

It took her about six minutes to get home; she walked straight there, only scanning through the first few of the thousands of messages she'd received whilst in the Library. None of them were about her blog; most were related to what she was wearing now, what she had worn the night before. One or two asked if they could come to the wedding if she and Milo got engaged; one of these was from a man living in India, she noted with a slight shake of the head.

She got to her building and walked through the door, reminding herself to smile as a comment appeared in front of her 'Hey, Frankie, looking stressed out. What's wrong hun?' It was from Budapest, a girl called Nia.

'Hey, Nia,' she said brightly. 'I'm not stressed. Just, you know, excited about tonight!'

She winked and immediately more comments flooded in. 'Ahhh, Frankie. It's so romantic!' 'Don't think too hard – you'll get wrinkles!' 'Wear the pink dress tonight! The one you wore the first time you went dancing with Milo. Pleeeeaaaaseeee!'

'Okay people, having a shower now!' She winked again, this time at the camera in her hallway, then she put down her tablet and bag and headed straight for her bathroom, with its carefully positioned camera that she could avoid if she wanted to. And she wanted to. The truth was, she wanted all the cameras to disappear for an hour or so. She felt shaky. Felt really strange. And she knew why. It was Milo's voice. The way he'd spoken to her. It was like he was someone else. Like a stranger. She was supposed to be in love with him; he was supposed to be in love with her. He was. She was. But not with the person who called her eight minutes ago. Not the person who'd issued her with an ultimatum.

She turned on the shower and kicked off her shoes, then leant against the window ledge, letting her head fall back for a few seconds. She steeled herself and started to take off her top. It was no big deal, she told herself. Milo had been angry. He had overreacted. But also, she'd kind of betrayed him and she knew it. Had done it on purpose. And as she unbuttoned herself she suddenly knew why she'd done it. To see how he'd react. To test him. And now she knew.

She took a deep breath. What had she expected? A wry smile? An indulgent shake of the head? He worked for Infotec. He had helped her. Helped her hugely. Had asked her to do something for him. And she had effectively put two fingers up at him. Just like she always did when people tried to get close to her. This hadn't been a test. It had been sabotage. And this time, she knew deep down, she'd really screwed up.

She thought for a moment, then called up a number,

using her private channel; she didn't want the world listening in on this conversation.

'Hello?'

'Milo, I'm sorry. I wasn't thinking, like you said. I just . . . I wanted to get a reaction, I guess. It's what I do. I push people until they push me back and then I tell myself it would never have worked out. But with you, I want it to work out, Milo. I really do. So I'm sorry. I was stupid. I'll . . .' She heard a bang and frowned. 'Oh, wait, there's someone at the door. Jeez, calm down. You'd think the building was on fire.' She started to button herself up again; wanted to look half-decent before opening the door. A bit of her hoped it might be flowers, an apology from Milo for flying off the handle. 'Look, Milo,' she continued, walking out of the bathroom. 'I'll retract the blog. I'll do whatever you want if you'll . . .' There was an almighty crash and she stopped in surprise as her front door fell forwards and two men walked into her apartment. She screamed in fright, then edged backwards. There was no need for hysterics. The men were on camera. They'd be stopped in moments. 'Milo,' she said, trying to keep her voice calm. 'There are two men here. You'll see them on camera. They have just broken down my door and they're coming towards me. Milo? Are you there?'

There was a pause. Then she heard Milo sigh. 'I wish you'd retracted it within the five-minute timescale I gave you,' he said, sadly. 'Then none of this would have happened. I'm sorry, Frankie.'

'Sorry?' Frankie asked uncertainly. She was pressed against the bedroom door; the men coming towards her looked relaxed, unafraid. They were twice her size, dressed in nondescript khaki. Behind them was a girl, a girl who looked like her, wearing the same clothes she had on. She was hallucinating; she had to be.

'Sorry it had to come to this. Goodbye, Frankie.'

The line went dead; immediately the men lunged at Frankie, one of them pressed his hand around her mouth, whilst the other grabbed at her hand and wrenched her chip out of her palm. 'Won't be needing this,' he said gruffly as Frankie's world went strangely silent, and with one swift movement, they carried her out of her apartment.

10

Frankie was dragged out of her apartment, down the stairs, out into the street, where she was bundled into a van. No one was around to see; the road had been cordoned off by an Inforcer van. But even if they'd seen, she had no chip; there would be no record of what was happening, and so it wouldn't have happened. Frankie felt disoriented; there were no messages in front of her, no one empathising with her, telling her that she looked amazing. There was nothing. It was like she didn't exist.

The van started; she was in the back, half lying, half sitting. It was dark, but she could see that the van was empty except for a couple of old blankets. It smelled terrible, of rancid food. She felt all around; found a spanner in the corner, an old carton of juice. She pulled her knees into her chest and breathed through her mouth. She was shaking; she knew she had to calm down, had to think. But her mind seemed incapable of rational thought; it flitted around in starts, her heart thudding, her stomach lurching every time she thought of something else uncomfortable. Milo. He had known about the men. Sent them, even. No one had seen; the cameras must have been shut off. This had been orchestrated. She had no idea where she was going; no way of contacting anyone. Where would they be taking her? What would the men be doing with her? Meting out some kind of punishment? For daring to publish that blog?

Had that been what she and Milo were all about?

Had she really been that stupid, that naïve?

No, impossible. Milo wouldn't . . . She felt her stomach constrict. Wouldn't what? Send two men in a van to pick her up? Shut down her communication?

The van stopped and she lifted her hand to bang on the wall. 'Help,' she shouted out as loudly as she could. 'I'm suffocating here. Please, help me.' She shifted down towards the doors. Moments later the door to the van opened and one of the men looked in.

'You shut up,' he said menacingly, but was immediately caught off guard by a foot kicking out at his face followed by a spanner being swung at his forehead. He stumbled back, swore, waved his arms around before falling to the ground. Frankie didn't wait to see if he was okay; wrapping one of the blankets around herself, she started to run. She recognised the street immediately; the van hadn't got too far, just a few blocks from her apartment. She crossed the road, ran around the corner, and then she stopped. Because in front of her was a screen. And she was on it. Only it wasn't her. It was someone else. Someone else who looked just like her, wearing her clothes, or clothes just like them, sauntering down Honore Road, smiling. And underneath was her latest message, only she hadn't written it. 'OMG, can you believe some criminal gang hacked my accounts and put out that awful blog in my name? Terrifying. Well if they're trying to make us scared, or trying to persuade us that Infotec have anything to hide, it won't work. They won't stop me that easily! Xxx'

For a moment, Frankie froze. As she stared, responses started to appear underneath it. 'Wow, Frankie, that's so scary. UR amaaazing.' 'Didn't think it was you . . . forget the idiots, Frankie. We love U!'

'Thanks you guys.' Another message from 'Frankie' popped up on the screen. 'Better get to my lunch now!'

'Move. Now.' It was someone behind her, grabbing her hand, pressing something into her palm. A new chip. Communication, thank God. She turned quickly but whoever it was had gone; she could see the men from the van running towards her. But she didn't move; she waited. They were on a busy road now; they couldn't do anything, knowing that she would cause a scene.

'You need to come with us,' one of the men said, approaching her cautiously. 'Come nicely and everything will be fine.'

'Don't.' The message flashed in front of her eyes, jolting her. This new chip was empty – no contacts, no history, nothing. Nothing except for this message. Which, frankly, was pretty unnecessary. She had no intention of going with those men again.

'You mean you'll shove me back in your van,' Frankie said, her voice low. She was doing her best to stay calm; they were very visible here. The men couldn't drag her away here, she told herself. Not without drawing attention. 'Who the hell is that girl up there pretending to be me?'

'Pretty isn't she?' the man said, pointing at the screen. 'That's Frankie now, you understand? Not you. You're no one. But come with us and you'll live. Otherwise . . .'

'Otherwise?' She stared at him icily. 'Otherwise, what?'

Frankie didn't wait for an answer. She turned and she ran, along the road, into an alleyway, pounding down the pavement. She barely recognised the streets;

felt naked with her chip utterly empty, no contacts, no messages, nothing.

'Turn left.' A message appeared, but Frankie ignored it. She needed to get back to her apartment. Needed to work out what was going on, what she should do. She felt strange, unbalanced, like the ground was moving underneath her feet as she walked on autopilot, her pace picking up as she got nearer to home until she was running; never had she been so desperate to get home, to close her door, to take a shower, take a bath, clean this day away, allow her space to think. And finally she was there, outside her building. She couldn't believe what had happened; it was like a bad dream, like some strange aberration that made no sense. And yet it had happened. The police van had gone, but she still had the blanket wrapped around her to prove it. She dropped it, kicked it away. Then she lifted her hand to the door fob.

The door didn't open.

She tried again, but the door stayed resolutely closed. She tried banging, but it was no good. Of course it was no good. She wouldn't get through the door without her chip.

'You know you're not getting in there. Stop wasting time, you have to hide.'

Frankie took a deep breath, then took a few steps back. And then, without thinking, she ran at the door, pounding it with her fists, shouting at it to open. People were staring at her but she didn't care; it was her apartment. She needed to get in.

'This is where I live,' she shouted, to no one in particular. 'This is where I live.'

A man stopped, looked at her kindly. 'Maybe your chip is damaged,' he said. 'Call the Infotec helpdesk. They're very friendly.'

Frankie stared at him, then she started to laugh. 'Friendly? You have no idea.'

She turned back to the door, ran at it, gave it a kick.

'Excuse me,' a terse voice came over the building's speaker. 'Please desist from your activities. This is a five-minute warning.'

'Run, Frankie. Please. I'm trying to help you here.'

The man shrugged at her and walked away. A five-minute warning. Five minutes until the police were alerted automatically by the camera software, which had registered some kind of vandalism or threatening behaviour.

Frankie knew all about five-minute warnings, but had never been on the wrong side of one. They had always been a reassuring sound, a voice of reason reminding some foolish person that their aggressive behaviour would not be tolerated, reminding them that they were being watched, monitored. Now the voice sounded menacing, terrifying. Was Milo watching her?

Was he watching her right now? She felt tears pressing against her eyes and looked up at the camera.

Then, her chest heaving, she dialled a number, a number she knew from memory.

'You do not have clearance for this number. For Infotec head office please dial 0.'

She tried the number again.

'You do not have clearance for this number. Please do not retry. We have your number. Thank you.'

She shut down the line, looked back up at the camera. 'You bastard,' she mouthed.

'He's not going to take your call. The two guys chasing you are at the bottom of this road and they will kill you if they get you, so please will you get moving now?'

Frankie shook her head. 'I'm not running anywhere,' she wrote, seething. 'Who the hell are you, anyway? Just leave me alone.'

Angrily, she turned, walked across the road towards the café where she often bought breakfast. She would wait there, watch her apartment, see who went in, who went out. Her stuff was in there. Her whole life was in there. If Milo wanted to punish her, to show her how tough and powerful he was, then fine. Whatever. But this was going too far. He couldn't lock her out of her home.

She walked up to the door. But as she pulled it, she heard a sound she hadn't heard in a very long time. A low beeping sound. The door stayed resolutely closed. She stopped, took a deep breath. This was crazy. She banged on the door. 'Will someone let me in please?' Through the windows she could see a screen with the Frankie imposter on it. 'OMG, late for my next appointment,' she was saying. 'Can't wait to get my award later!'

Frankie's eyes narrowed and her heart began to thud in her chest, but she took a deep breath, forced herself to calm down. No one had noticed. No one had noticed it wasn't her. All her adoring fans, all her millions of Watchers, loved her so much they had no idea that she'd been replaced by a total stranger.

A waiter rushed towards her, smiled, pulled open the door. 'Hi!' he said brightly. 'Sorry, must be a problem with our machine. Would you wait there? I'll get the manual processor.'

Frankie smiled sweetly; a minute later he returned with the processor, which he held up against her hand. And then his smile faded. 'I'm sorry,' he shrugged. 'You have no credit logged. No access.'

'No access?' Frankie stared at him angrily. 'But I come here all the time. You know me. I'm Frankie. You know I'm Frankie.'

He looked at her uncertainly. Then he turned to look back at the screen where other 'Frankie' was rushing into a swish restaurant across town, her trademark leather jacket draped around her shoulders. He looked back at her, his face a little harder this time. He trusted the screen, Frankie's chip, more than he trusted his own eyes. 'I'm sorry, but the machine says you have no credit. It shows no link to a bank, a card, nothing. Maybe take it up with your bank?'

'My bank,' Frankie said, raising an eyebrow. She could feel someone behind her; the men were closing in, tight smiles on their faces. They wouldn't want to cause a scene, but then again, she couldn't get into a bar; no one would be surprised if the Infotec Inforcers dragged her away.

'Could be a technical fault?' the waiter said with a tight smile. 'Now, have a nice day!' And with that, he retreated; the door closed behind him. Frankie held her hand up to the reader again and heard the low beep. Access denied. She left it there, heard the beep again. Then she kicked the door.

'Please desist from your activities. This is your second and final warning.'

Another message popped up. 'I thought you were clever, Frankie. Stop acting like an idiot and get the hell out of there.'

She stared up at the camera. 'Screw you,' she mouthed, then she started to run.

11

'Turn left.'

Frankie shook her head and continued to run. Her head, usually full of messages from a million strangers, was strangely clear, and it made her feel disoriented, dizzy.

'How the hell did you track down my new chip anyway, stranger?' she messaged back as she panted. 'Do you work for Infotec or something?'

'No.' The message came straight back. 'Where are you going? To the Library? You're going to the Library aren't you. You know that's the first place they'll look? Please, follow my directions. I can see them and you. I can get you somewhere safe.'

Frankie rolled her eyes. 'It's thanks to you that I'm in this mess,' she said, irritated that the stranger had read her mind so easily. She *was* headed to the Library; it was the only place she had to go. She loved the Library; was so proud that her parents had been among the people who had fought to keep libraries open to all, no cameras inside, no chip restrictions allowed. Her parents had joined the protests for knowledge to be available to everyone, even the drunks, the destitute, the outcasts, and had instilled in Frankie the importance of learning, of knowing the truth. Anyone who had a chip could enter; activity was monitored via chips but no cameras were allowed. Critics had said that libraries would be overrun, that they would be taken over by the destitute, by those who wanted to avoid being seen, who were determined to wreak havoc on those who lived peaceably.

But it hadn't happened. Every so often someone was found asleep under a bench; every so often the old and confused wandered in with no barrier to stop them. But mostly things stayed pretty much the same. Same people, same activity. And it was about the only place she was sure she could get into.

'Bad idea. Very bad idea. Turn left here, then right, straight away. It's a small road with no cameras. Run down to the bottom and there's a tiny alleyway on your left. Turn onto it.'

Resentfully, Frankie read the message in front of her eyes.

'Why should I listen to you?' she asked. 'Assuming you're who I think you are, you're the reason this is happening to me.'

'I'm not the reason. Infotec is the reason. I'm trying to help you. So please, turn left.'

Frankie hesitated, then, hearing footsteps behind her, she did as the stranger told her, keeping her head down. When she got to the alley, another message appeared immediately.

'Go into the café on your right and ask to use the bathroom. It's in the courtyard behind. You need to jump over the back wall, and there's a path. Follow it.'

Frankie paused again, wondering what the hell she was doing, then reluctantly followed the instructions. This time the chip allowed her into the café; evidently it was less fussy about its clientele. She ran through it mumbling something about ordering a coffee, and escaped into the courtyard. The wall was five feet tall and not the easiest thing to get over in super skinny jeans that didn't give much at the knee, but she managed it after a few attempts and staggered down the path that greeted her. She was hot now, hot and angry.

'Where the hell are you taking me?' she demanded.

'You don't recognize it? Turn left at the bottom of the path and wait there for a few minutes.'

'Wait? For what? For Milo's friends to come and pick me up?'

'No, for something else. Someone else. Just wait.'

'Just wait? No please this time?' Frankie asked, her eyebrow raised. Who was this joker, she wondered to herself. And how did she end up taking instructions from him?

She stopped for a moment and caught her breath; the truth was that it was a relief not to be running, just for a short while. But as she stood there, the enormity of what had happened, what was still happening, started to overwhelm her. She couldn't trust this stranger. It was his fault she was in this mess. She had to get away, had to find Milo, explain herself. Those men had to be a mistake on his part; he couldn't have known what they'd do to her. It was all a big mix-up and by running she was just making it worse. By running, she was getting herself into serious trouble. She was going to get out of here. She was going to go to Infotec's offices and straighten this mess out.

But just as she started to move again, she heard someone behind her, heard a voice say 'Frankie?', and it made her freeze. It was Jim's voice; he touched her lightly on the shoulder and she nearly jumped three feet in the air.

'Jim?' She turned, saw him looking at her uncertainly. 'Jim, thank God you're here. Look, things have got really weird. I need to get in touch with Milo . . .'

'No, you don't,' he said firmly. 'Here, have some water.'

He pressed a bottle into Frankie's hands; she took it gratefully. 'Jim, we need to get out of here. There's been this huge mix-up. Milo – he . . .'

He clasped her arm. 'Frankie, you're shaking.'

She looked down; sure enough her whole body was trembling.

'How . . . how did you find me?' she asked, falteringly.

'I got an anonymous message,' Jim said. He looked at his watch. 'When did you last update your status?'

'My status? Are you kidding me? I don't have a bloody status. Some bitch has taken it.' Frankie's voice started to wobble as she talked.

'You have a new chip, and that means you are registered on the mainframe, so you need to update your status. Quickly,' he said. 'Do it now.'

'You're serious? You, the phobic updater, are telling me to . . .'

'Just do it,' Jim cut in. 'Say something apologetic. Something meek. Just in case.'

Frankie raised an eyebrow. 'Meek? I don't even know what that word means.'

'Don't joke,' Jim said. 'Not now. Say you're thinking things over. Coming to your senses. Something like that.'

Frankie opened her mouth to tell him where to go,

but realised she didn't have the energy for a fight. 'Fine.' She opened a hologram keyboard, talking the words as she typed: '"Walking around, thinking things over. Have acted rashly. Am really sorry." There. That meek enough for you?'

Jim nodded. Then his expression changed, became sadder. 'Frankie, I'm so sorry. So, so sorry. But right now, we have to get you somewhere safe. Look, I brought you these.'

Frankie frowned as Jim took some clothes out of a bag. Jeans, a sweatshirt, trainers.

'You're joking aren't you?' she asked incredulously. 'I'm not getting changed. I'm not wearing this stuff.'

'I'm afraid you are, Frankie,' Jim said, his voice low. 'You have to understand, you're in danger. Everything has changed. So you need to put these on. Do you understand, Frankie?'

She nodded vaguely; she didn't understand, not at all. But something told her to do as Jim said. 'Turn around,' she said quietly, then quickly pulled on the clothes. 'There's a hat in there too,' Jim said. Frankie took it out; like the clothes, it fit her fine but felt utterly alien. Still, she supposed that was the point. Jim took the other clothes and put them in the bag, but she refused to give him her leather jacket.

'Fine,' he relented. 'But give me your hand.'

'Another chip?' Frankie asked. Jim nodded. She gave him her hand and winced as he took it out and replaced it with another one.

'It's a blank one,' he said, noticing the flicker of disappointment on her face as he put it into her palm. 'It just connects you to the mainframe, allows you to walk around. And now that it's active, you have to update like any other chip, otherwise the mainframe will be alerted and . . . Well, you don't want that. Just keep your updates simple, nothing that will attract attention, And do it regularly, okay?'

Frankie looked at him mutinously. This wasn't Jim's fault, she knew that, but he was here. 'You carry spare chips with you?' she asked, her tone sarcastic. 'What are you, a secret terrorist in your spare time?'

Jim managed a rueful grin. 'Not exactly,' he said. 'But I know some people.'

Frankie stared at him. 'What people?' she demanded.

'People,' Jim said. 'Just people. People who can help you. Come with me and you can tell me what's happened. Please?'

'I suppose,' Frankie said, her tone still dubious. 'So where are we going? Who are these people you apparently know? What's going on, Jim?' She felt tears pricking at her eyes and did her best to blink them away.

Jim took a deep breath. 'Look, we have to keep

moving. Make it as hard as possible for them to keep track of you. I don't know where your chip comes from; it might be a six-foot man for all I know. If the biometrics don't add up, the mainframe will notice a discrepancy soon enough. So we'll get you another one soon. And in the meantime, we need to keep moving. I'll explain more when we're . . .' He hesitated, looking around nervously. 'When we're where we're going,' he said eventually.

'And where is that, exactly?' Frankie asked, pushing her hair back and pulling her hat down. But Jim didn't answer; he just waited for her to follow him.

'We walk quickly,' he said. 'But not too quickly. Pretend we're talking to each other. Make sure you smile a lot. We're sharing a joke. Okay? Now, just wait here one second . . .' He ran off and immediately bumped into a group of girls, who shouted at him. He apologised profusely and ran back to Frankie. 'Okay, and we're walking again.'

Frankie stared at him uncertainly. 'What was that all about?' she asked.

'The chip I just removed from you,' he shrugged. 'Infotec will be following those girls for at least a few minutes, giving us a chance to disappear.'

'I see,' Frankie said, her brain trying to process this strange world she seemed to have fallen into where no one was what she thought they were.

'Good,' Jim said, then walked towards the main doors and out into the road. 'This way,' he said, tugging her arm. 'Remember. Smile. And stay with me whatever happens.'

Frankie had thought she knew Paris; thought she knew every road and café, no matter how off the beaten track it was. But as she walked with Jim, down alleyways she'd never even noticed before, she realised that there was a whole underbelly she'd never encountered: tiny roads with barely one camera covering everything, no screens, no personalised adverts jumping out at her as she walked. It felt like she'd gone back in time; the feeling was enhanced by the fact that she had no communication with anyone. Well, no one except the stranger, anyway, and even he had gone pretty quiet. She kept checking her instinct to update her Watchers, to make little wry comments about what she was doing, what she could see. And it made her realise how little she ever really observed her surroundings, how little thought she gave to her environment, to her thoughts, to her life. Instead, she had spent her days viewing everything through the lens of Watcher numbers, reducing every event to a sound bite to be sent out into the ether and read by people she'd never met. Now, for the first time in a very long time, she was really here, in the present, experiencing, looking, seeing. And in spite of her anger, her fear, her indignation, she realised that it felt good.

'This chip,' she said. 'How can it be blank? How come there aren't messages? For the person it belonged to, I mean. And where are they? How come they don't need their chip anymore?'

Jim frowned. 'As far as I know, your chip will have been wiped clean of everything except its code, which is what connects it to the mainframe. There's no address book, nothing. Every time anyone sends a message to someone else, it's recorded and makes it easier for someone to join the dots. So it's better if your chip is empty. And better if you don't try communicating with anyone. Okay?'

Frankie digested this.

'So the mainframe thinks I'm whoever this chip belonged to before?'

'It should do now, yes. But these clean chips usually come from people who have died, or sometimes they've been smuggled out of one of the chip manufacturers. Either way, the chip is an anomaly and will soon be ringing bells somewhere. That's why we keep changing them.' Jim caught Frankie's expression and stopped walking for a moment. 'You're still the same person Frankie. You just don't have your chip anymore. It feels like you're naked, I know. But you'll get used to it. And hopefully soon you'll get your own chip back. Okay?'

Frankie bit her lip. 'Okay,' she said, as Jim started to walk again.

Eventually Jim ducked under an archway into a little cobbled cul-de-sac, then into a café where, to Frankie's distress, the chip reader emitted the same low beep she'd received before, only this time the waiter saw Jim and ushered her in anyway.

It was a tiny café with room for just three tables, all decked out in old Parisian style with red checked table cloths and a zinc-topped bar. The lights were dim and the blinds at the windows let in minimal light. Jim and the waiter conferred silently, then the waiter nodded and walked towards Frankie. 'Hold out your hand,' he said.

Frankie stared at him, but she did as she was told. Deftly he took out her chip yet again and pressed a new one in.

'Now you need to go for a walk for a few minutes and return via the other entrance around the back.'

'But . . .' Frankie frowned. 'But why?'

'Because Infotec can backdate its tracking,' Jim said. 'They will have had every camera searching for you, every Informer looking out for you. We can't afford to take any chances; once they home in on this chip, they'll be here in minutes to take you away. We have to stay a few steps ahead. Even with a new chip they'll have historical tracking and camera footage that they'll study. You have to be caught on camera walking away because they will know soon enough the time at which you swapped chips, then, if your new chip doesn't move away, they'll put two and two together, check the cameras, find us on it, and they'll raid this place. So. Say goodbye to me, look at me like I'm giving you directions, then rush off, okay? Pierre here will deal with the chip. We want them hunting in as many different directions as possible.'

Frankie did as she was told, taking a convoluted route along several streets and alleyways before arriving at the back of the café, where she slipped inside a tall door that opened in front of her; Jim was waiting there. 'Come on, downstairs,' he said.

Frankie hadn't realised there was a downstairs, but Jim quickly opened a door that revealed a stone staircase down. Tentatively she followed him, the door clunking firmly behind her as she made her way down the steps. At the bottom was a small wine cellar with another door to the right; Jim opened it and walked through, beckoning for Frankie to follow him.

'Where are we?' she breathed as she found herself walking into a small room with stone flooring, stone walls and two low sofas covered in cushions. A small gas light flickered in the corner and a man sat at a table under a tiny window, which let in a dim glow of light. There was a small pile of vintage books by the sofa, a large blanket folded up behind them and an old-fashioned rowing machine in the corner.

The man looked them both up and down, then stood up. He was tall, but his posture seemed stooped; he was in his sixties, his face grey, his eyes watery. 'Jim,' he said. 'Good to see you. So this is Frankie? Or rather, *was* Frankie, should I say? I don't think I've ever met a socialite before.' His voice was gravelly, dry; Frankie regarded him uncomfortably.

'I'm still Frankie,' Frankie said pointedly. 'And for the record, I'm not a socialite. I'm a blogger.'

The man smiled. 'I see.'

His expression was incredulous, his tone patronising and Frankie bristled. 'Do you?' she demanded. 'What is this place anyway?' She could feel her anger building up, her frustration, and she needed to vent it. She rounded on Jim. 'Where have you brought me? What am I doing here? We should be at Infotec, demanding my chip. We should be telling someone what Milo did. We should be shouting from the rooftops that the girl running around in my clothes is not me.'

'Isn't she?' the man said gently. 'Who are you, if not the messages you send and the picture everyone sees?'

Frankie's face creased with irritation. 'Who am I? I'm

me. I'm the thoughts in my head. I'm this arm. This leg. Who are you, anyway? What is this place?'

The man held out his hand. The light was behind him, making his whole face shadowy. 'My name is Sal,' he said. 'It's very nice to meet you.'

Frankie hesitated, then shook his hand. She owed it to Jim to be civil at least; owed it to him to give this Sal person a chance.

'I need to let everyone know what they've done, what Milo's done. The men he sent round, this girl who looks like me. She's an imposter. People have to be told. They have to know.'

'But they have to know what?' Sal said with a little smile, motioning for Frankie and Jim to sit. 'That the flesh and blood of their favourite blogger has changed? If they are in the Yemen what do they care? What do they know of your flesh and blood anyway? They know your words, your images. These continue, therefore you continue, whether it is truly you or not. You see, that is what the world is now. We are interchangeable. We are no longer essential to anything.'

Frankie frowned. This man was beginning to irritate her. 'This is not helping,' she said, turning to Jim. 'You said you knew people who could actually help me.'

Jim pulled a rueful face. 'Frankie,' he said slowly. 'Frankie, what I was trying to tell you . . .'

He trailed off; Frankie looked at him in frustration. 'What?' she said. 'What did you try to tell me? Will someone please tell me what the hell is going on?'

'This place,' Sal said, 'is the Safe House, the only place in Paris that is not logged, tagged, linked in.'

'Except for the reader at the door,' Frankie said, unable to keep the sarcasm out of her voice.

Sal nodded. 'There is a reader, just as there has to be. But your chip has now left the café, and been taken by car into the centre of Paris. It will be updated every fifteen minutes and passed from person to person to make it as hard as possible for the Infotec thugs tasked with your murder to track you down. Eventually they will find your chip in a pile of rubbish and will start hunting for you, but by then you will be out of the country with a new identity.'

Frankie laughed. 'You're joking, aren't you? I mean, you have to be joking. Because I'm not going anywhere. I'm going to get my apartment back. My blog back. My Watchers back.' She stood up, marched to the door and tugged it open. 'Thanks Jim, but this really isn't what I had in mind. I'll leave you conspiracy theorists to your little safe house if that's okay. I'm going to . . .'

'Here. Watch.' Frankie heard a voice that sounded a great deal like hers and she turned. Sal was holding up a screen; on it Frankie could see herself. Only it wasn't her. It was her doppelganger. The imposter. She was holding her award up in her arms. The award that Frankie was supposed to have got. There were tears in the imposter's eyes. 'This is just the best day of my life,' she said. 'And I couldn't have done any of it without Milo. My true love.' She turned and Milo was there, next to her, grinning proudly. 'And I can't believe that in a few months I'm going to be his wife!' There was rapturous applause.

Frankie's eyes widened and the blood drained from her face. He had proposed? At the prize-giving? Milo was marrying this imposter?

'Tell us why you love Frankie so much,' someone was saying.

Milo smiled. 'That's easy. There are many pretenders to Frankie's throne, so many people who would love to be her. But Frankie's the real deal. Frankie's the only one who comes close.' He smiled into the camera and Frankie felt her stomach turn.

'He's lying through his teeth,' she whispered, stepping backwards and letting the door close again.

'Yes,' Sal said simply. 'And you, Frankie, are in grave danger.'

12

'You're kidding me, right?' Frankie looked at Jim uncertainly, forcing a smile, telling herself that there was some joke that she wasn't getting, that maybe this whole thing was some weird set-up and any minute now someone was going to jump out and tell her it had all been engineered, for entertainment, for . . .

For what?

Jim's face was deadly serious. And Jim wasn't the sort of person to get involved in publicity stunts.

'Frankie, you have to understand that everything has changed,' he said.

Frankie nodded slowly, trying to suppress the bile that was coming up the back of her throat. She felt a huge urge to run, to get out of this place. But she knew, deep down, that there was nowhere to run to. And it made her more angry than she'd ever thought she was capable of feeling.

'How do you even know about this place?' she said eventually, her voice choked. She couldn't look at the other guy. At Sal, the man who hid in the shadows. 'How do you know all this . . . stuff?'

Jim exchanged a glance with Sal, who nodded what Frankie took to be his consent. 'Some of us . . .' Jim stopped, corrected himself. 'There are people, of whom I am one, who find our current society oppressive and intrusive, who believe that Infotec's hold over us is . . . unhealthy. It's impossible to discuss with anyone because we're being watched all the time, not just by other people but by Infotec themselves. If they hear something that alarms them, that they don't want to hear, they move in, cut you off, reduce your credit rating, deny you access to places, to people. That's what happened to me. And Sal found me. Sal and the . . . others. We meet here, sometimes. It's a safe place. Our feeds are updated for us upstairs but here, downstairs, there are no cameras, no one watching, no one listening. Infotec doesn't know it exists, otherwise they'd be in here like a shot.'

Frankie digested this. 'So what, you come here to talk? To complain about Infotec?'

She sounded more patronising than she'd meant to; she could see the hurt in Jim's eyes. But she needed to lash out at someone, and he was there. He was always there, she thought heavily.

'To complain, yes,' Jim said carefully. 'But also to help others. To identify others like us. To eventually . . .' He trailed off again. 'It doesn't matter. What matters is that you are in deep trouble and we're going to help you.'

Frankie exhaled loudly. 'To eventually change things?' she asked. 'To show everyone what bastards Infotec really are?'

Jim didn't say anything. There was a knock on the door; the waiter, Pierre, appeared.

'I have this for you,' he said, walking towards Frankie; she gave him her hand and watched silently as he inserted yet another new chip into her palm.

'Thank you,' she said quietly. 'They used me, didn't they? I mean, that whole thing with Milo. It wasn't real, none of it. He just wanted to turn me into a performing seal. He pretty much did. And I'd have married him too. I'm such a sap.'

She stared up at the tiny window, through which the faintest trace of sunlight could be seen. 'And how about you?' she said, turning to Sal suddenly. 'You live here, right?'

Sal raised his eyebrows. 'Why do you say that?'

'The rowing machine,' Frankie said with a shrug. 'And it makes sense. You're obviously the boss. So what, you started it up? This place? This . . . movement? Why? Did what happened to me happen to you?'

Sal smiled. 'I'm not the boss,' he said. 'I'm just a communication midpoint. But yes, I live here.' He moved a little and Frankie saw how pale his face was; she guessed he didn't get out all that much, if at all. 'And yes, I pretty much went through what you have. Not being made the most Watched person in the world, just the bit where the men turned up at your apartment and dragged you away.'

Frankie's eyes narrowed. 'So what happened then?'

Sal sighed heavily. 'They took away my chip. That's always the first thing they do. Your chip is your identity, it has every record, every message you've ever sent, all stored in it. Your number, all your contact details are on it; without it you can't go anywhere, can't contact anyone, and no one can get hold of you. Not the real you. Infotec put a stooge in my place too, just long enough to alienate all my friends, and to build a believable story about what had happened to me.'

'They really do that?' Frankie breathed. 'I mean, a lot?'

'When they want to,' Sal shrugged. 'Sometimes that's enough. Losing your chip cuts you off, stops you talking to people, stops you getting into your home, your workplace, wherever. Stops you causing problems. They say that you did it yourself, that you've gone off the radar, that you're dangerous and have committed some crime or other. Then they start to hunt you down, make you run, make you hide, make you steal to feed yourself, force you to accost family members, old friends, begging for help, looking and sounding like the crazed criminal they've made you out to be. That's when you're labelled highly dangerous, your image shown on every screen. Of course sometimes people are just taken away. If there's nothing complicated about them, if no awkward questions are likely to be asked. But they can make mistakes. Your uncle was just taken away. And then your father started to dig for answers. That was a complication.'

Frankie's eyes widened. 'My father?' she asked. 'What do you know about my father? He died. He died of a heart condition.'

'That's what they told you?' Sal shook his head. 'Your father was a bright man. A tenacious one. But he was also naïve. He thought he had a right to ask questions, thought that Infotec would be grateful. He had no idea what he was up against.'

He studied Frankie's face; Frankie shrank backwards. 'He isn't dead?' she whispered.

'He's dead,' Sal said gravely. 'As is your uncle. But don't go thinking that heart attacks had anything to do with it.'

Frankie blinked back more tears. She had seen those

people, flashed onto her screen, hardened criminals that Infotec wanted to protect everyone from, renegade citizens who had taken out their chips and gone on the run. 'They killed my father?' she asked, her voice breaking as she spoke. 'They killed my uncle and my father? Did Milo know that? Was he the one behind it?'

Sal was pacing around the sofa. 'The final stage is when you go missing,' he said quietly, ignoring her questions. 'By then no one cares. Even your own family are relieved. You're either dead, or you've escaped; either way, you're not their problem anymore.'

Frankie cleared her throat, tried to look like she was listening, like she hadn't been transported back to the apartment they'd lived in, the men in dark suits coming to tell her and her mother about her father's fatal heart attack at work. 'And what . . . you end up here?'

Sal laughed, a dry, dirty laugh. 'The lucky ones do. The ones we can get to. The ones we know about. I ended up here, but that was because I was prepared. I had this place all ready for me just in case. Most people . . . don't.'

'My father,' Frankie managed to say. 'So where do . . . the others . . . where do they end up? What does Infotec do with them?'

'Taken away to be disposed of discreetly,' Sal shrugged. 'Or there's always the bottom of the Seine.'

Frankie's eyes widened. 'They jump?'

'Sometimes. But more often they're pushed.'

Frankie began to shake again. 'Milo wants me dead,' she whispered, 'doesn't he? This isn't a punishment. This isn't him showing off his muscle. He actually wants me dead. But why? Because of the blog? Because I didn't do what he said?'

'Because you struck a nerve. Because you reported on something that Infotec doesn't want anyone knowing about. And I suspect he doesn't want you dead quite yet. You're a more complicated case. Too high-profile. So he got your replacement all ready; I suspect he's had one waiting in the wings for a while now. But what he really wants is your contact, this person who put you in touch with us, sent us to help you. He'll be hoping that they contact the new Frankie instead, that he can trace them. But after that, you're just a loose end. And that is why you are in such grave danger. That's why we've got to get you out of Paris as quickly as possible.'

Frankie stood up. 'This is bullshit,' she said angrily. 'This is just bullshit. They can't do this. Milo can't do this. Who the hell does he think he is?'

'He doesn't think, he knows,' Sal said seriously. 'He's the most powerful man in Paris. In Europe.'

Frankie shook her head. 'Wait a minute,' she said. 'So this imposter. This girl. She knows what's going on. All I have to do is get to her, make her tell the truth. I'm not leaving Paris. I'm going to let everyone know what an evil bastard he is. Show him that he can't bloody well mess with me.' She walked towards the door, opened it, then closed it again and turned around. 'You have to help me,' she said to Jim. 'I can't get in anywhere. I can't even get into my apartment. You have to take me to Le Bon Pain tonight. That's where we're . . . that's where Milo and this girl will be having dinner. We have to confront them. You have to get me in there. You have to . . . What? What are you looking at me like that for? Stop shaking your head. Stop looking at me like I'm stupid or something.'

Jim stood up. 'You're not stupid,' he said gently. 'But do you really think Milo's going to let you anywhere near him or the new Frankie? He'll have people everywhere looking out for you. The new Frankie will have been told that you've gone mad, or bad, that you've been corrupted by evil forces, that you need protection, that you're dangerous.'

'People will know it's not me,' Frankie said, her voice choking because she knew it wasn't true. Her parents were dead; she had no close friends other than Jim. Had Milo known that? Had he chosen her knowing that one day he would dispose of her?

'Anyone who suspects something will be strung a line

too,' Jim said, reaching out, holding her arms. 'They'll be kept at arm's length, told you're too busy. Maybe an argument will be initiated. Something. They control everything, Frankie. Every message. Every post, every image. No one has noticed have they? No one has noticed it's not you.'

'But they will eventually,' Frankie insisted desperately. 'This new girl can't go to the Library or hang out with any of my real friends, can she?'

Jim looked at Sal; a silence hung in the air. 'What?' Frankie demanded. 'What aren't you telling me?'

Jim bit his lip. 'The new Frankie . . . The likelihood is, she'll have an accident pretty soon,' he said quietly. 'Something tragic. Something where the body isn't . . .'

He trailed off; Frankie pushed him away, walked over to the sofa and sat down, letting her head fall forwards into her hands. She wanted to cry; needed to cry. But now no tears would come.

'So that's it?' she managed to say. 'He's won?'

Sal moved his chair round to face her; Jim joined her on the sofa. 'No,' Sal said. 'He hasn't won because you're here. You're safe. And we'll get you out of Paris tonight and out of Europe by tomorrow. You'll have a new identity. They won't find you. You'll be fine.'

'A new identity?'

Sal nodded. 'We have friends around the world. You can go to Australia. Somewhere far away. You'll be fine, Frankie. We'll make sure of that.'

Jim put his arm around her. 'I'm sorry, Frankie. But Sal's right. You'll be fine. You'll have a new life. And so long as you lay low, so long as you . . .'

'As long as I don't stick my head above the parapet?' Frankie cut in. 'As long as I mind my own business and forget all about my life here, you mean?'

Jim pulled a face. 'Better that than the alternative,' he said awkwardly.

'No,' Frankie said, shrugging off Jim's arm and standing up. 'No, I'm not doing it. I'm not going.'

Sal looked at her archly. 'You're going to stay here?' he asked. 'There isn't a lot of room for two of us.'

'I'm not hiding. And I'm not running,' Frankie said, folding her arms defiantly. 'This all happened because of what I wrote about, because Infotec were afraid. So I'm going to make them even more afraid. I'm going to expose what they're hiding, expose what they're doing. I'm going to tell the world what they did, what they did to my father, my uncle. I'm going to write about everything.'

'No,' Sal said sharply. 'No, you can't do that, Frankie. It's no good going up against Infotec. They're too powerful. You can't win. You don't know who your source is and now they've got no way of finding you.'

'Maybe I can't win,' Frankie said. 'But I can land a few punches. I know I can. And you're going to help me. You've got to help me.' She looked at them imploringly. 'Please?'

Sal and Jim exchanged a glance. Then Sal exhaled slowly and turned back to Frankie. 'You really don't want to go to Australia? It's lovely there, I hear. Beaches, sunshine . . .'

Frankie shook her head. 'Either you help me, or you let me out of this place and I'll do it myself,' she said. 'I just need access to a computer.'

Sal regarded her dubiously. Then he looked over at Jim. 'In that case she should probably meet Glen,' he said with a little shrug.

'Who's Glen?' Frankie demanded.

'Glen . . .' Jim said, thoughtfully, then looked over at Sal, who smiled opaquely.

'We should eat,' he said. 'I'll go talk to Marco, get him to rustle something up. Actually, Jim, you go up and talk to him. And then leave. We don't want your chip here too long, don't want to draw any unnecessary attention to this place.'

Jim nodded and pushed back his chair. 'I'll see you later,' he said, giving Frankie's shoulder a squeeze. 'As soon as it gets dark.'

'And then we meet this Glen guy?' Frankie asked.

'And then you meet Glen,' Jim said, then left the room.

'So,' Sal said, a broad grin revealing large, yellowing teeth. 'You play cards? I do hope so, because there's really not much else to do around here.'

13

It was late. Frankie had spent hours in the café basement playing cards, watching the one screen on the wall, trying not to feel like she'd been punched in the stomach when she saw images of Milo and her doppelganger laughing as they came out of the restaurant she should have been at, their hands entwined, a blush spreading across her cheeks as people rushed up to see the rock on her finger.

What line had they fed her, Frankie found herself wondering. Did it even matter? How was it that no one noticed? Couldn't they see it wasn't her? Couldn't they just . . . tell?

She had posed the question to Sal, but he had dismissed her with a shrug. 'Seeing is believing,' he'd said. 'And believing is seeing. There is no truth in what we see, just information that we can accept or reject.

Mostly we accept. If things follow a correct order, we make assumptions, fill in any gaps and move on. Infotec knows this. Your followers weren't following you. They were following the image of you, the idea of you. And those two things remain.'

'But . . .' Frankie had started to say, then stopped, because she'd known he was right. For a few days, anyway. The new Frankie wouldn't go to the Library again, and no one would suspect anything; it would just confirm their suspicions that Frankie thought she was too good for the Library, especially now that 'she' was marrying Milo. Close-ish friends could be dropped easily; anyone who would spot that Frankie wasn't Frankie could be avoided, expunged from 'her' life. And no one would really care. Perhaps no one ever had.

The door opened; Jim appeared and Frankie looked up at him, immediately having to suppress the tears that had been absent for hours and which now threatened to flood out of her eyes like a child whose mother had just appeared to collect her from school, all the pent-up frustrations and adrenaline of the day immediately unlocked.

But Frankie couldn't cry. Wouldn't. Not over Milo. Not over what had happened. What she'd worked out that evening, her mind whirring as she played cards on autopilot, was that she'd allowed this all to happen; had allowed herself to get swept away. Had allowed that bastard to manipulate her. Because she'd liked the fact that Milo had liked her. Because she liked all the attention.

Because she'd been a sap.

She pushed her chair back and stood up. Her muscles were tight from sitting down for so long and she got a rush to the head as her blood failed to circulate quickly enough; grasping the table, she steadied herself.

'You okay?' Jim asked.

She nodded quickly. 'Are we going to meet Glen?' she asked.

'Yeah,' Jim said. 'Put this on.'

He threw something into Frankie's hands; when she picked it up she saw that it was a wig. A dark crop with a fringe. She raised an eyebrow, then put it on. Sal gave her the thumbs up.

Jim looked at his watch. 'Ready?' he asked. 'We need to give you another new chip upstairs. You know. Just in case.'

'Ready,' Frankie said grimly, and put on her leather jacket – the only thing that connected her to her former life. 'You coming?' She looked over at Sal, but he just smiled and shook his head.

'Where you're going . . . it's not for me,' he said with a knowing shrug, then turned back to the cards in front of him, picking up Frankie's hand and folding it into the pack. 'Look after yourself, won't you?'

Frankie nodded, then glanced over at Jim, who was holding the door open.

'Okay?' he said.

'Okay.' She nodded, and followed him up the stairs.

They walked silently through alleyways, down quiet roads, their hands in their pockets, their heads down. Jim had briefed her before they left the café: her new chip, he told her, had belonged to an unremarkable girl of a similar age from Toulouse. When Frankie asked him how they had got hold of it, he shot her a look that suggested she didn't need to know. 'No one was hurt, no one's in danger,' was all he'd say. She was to stick with him, draw no attention to herself. And that's exactly what she did, walking through the streets of Paris. It was like she was walking through a new city: it looked the same, but underneath it was different, with depths that she hadn't known before and threats that she'd never had cause to imagine.

Every time someone looked at her she felt her heart clench; every time a camera swivelled in her direction she froze momentarily. But after a while she started to enjoy it, started to feel slightly lighter than she used to as she glanced up at the large screens hanging across the roads and saw not herself, but the other Frankie. Earlier that day, Frankie had loathed this girl, this pretender. Now, she just felt sorry for her, felt sorry for the girl who had taken on her straightjacket, who lived within her prison.

'In here.' They were in the Marais district; Jim pulled her down a narrow staircase towards a dingy-looking club. Frankie followed uncertainly. Two bouncers were on the door. They opened it and nodded Jim and Frankie in; a deafening beat suddenly filled the air. Frankie followed Jim in, her chip allowing her access, drawing no attention from anyone, and immediately the heat, dry ice and smell of sweat hit her like a wall, the trance music so loud she felt disoriented for a moment or two. Then she saw Jim waving at her and followed him through the throng of moist, dancing bodies, skimpily clad, moving in virtual unison to the heavy beat, their arms in the air, their faces uplifted. The place was packed, full of beautiful, strange-looking people who would stand out in the street, their necks adorned in collars, the girls wearing shorts, trainers and bikini tops, the men wearing baggy trousers and little else, their torsos gleaming under the flashing lights.

She looked around; there were screens but the darkness of the room combined with the strobe lighting meant that the images couldn't be seen properly. There were cameras, too, but Frankie immediately realised that they would see nothing because they were covered in condensation. Nor would the microphones be able to pick up anything other than pounding beats.

She took off her jacket and tied it around her waist, then walked quickly after Jim, suddenly not caring about the sweat dripping from her neck, down her back; she almost enjoyed the wet bodies brushing against her, the elated smiles, the shining eyes. She felt like she had died today; these people were alive, and their energy was infectious. She longed to join them, to lose herself in dancing, in the heavy beats, the strobe lighting. But she had to follow Jim, and he was walking towards the bar, where bottles of water stood waiting for whoever decided they needed to hydrate. He walked straight past it, over to the left, then down two steps and through a door that was invisible except for a small handle. Frankie ran to keep up with him; as soon as she'd walked through the door, it closed behind her and Jim locked it.

'Down here,' he said, walking down a narrow corridor with a stone floor and rough brick walls. They passed what looked like a store room, then a small kitchen, and finally reached another closed door. Jim was about to lift his hand to knock when Frankie stopped him.

'What?' he frowned.

She looked at him intently. 'How?' she asked, her voice a whisper. 'How do you know this place? And Sal? I had no idea. How did I have no idea?'

He returned her gaze for a second or two, then his face crumpled into a half smile. 'You didn't need to,' he said with a little shrug. 'You were living the dream.'

Frankie's eyes narrowed. 'Stop it,' she said. 'And anyway I was only with Milo for a few months. Seriously, Jim. All these people, chips, underground rooms . . .'

Jim breathed out slowly. 'You remember when I turned down the university funding from Infotec? The guaranteed job at the end of it?'

Frankie nodded.

'Not such a good idea as it turns out,' Jim said, with a sort of half smile. 'They don't like to be turned down. Gets them suspicious. They started messing with me. I thought I was imagining it at first. Contacts would disappear, Watchers stopped following me, my grades were always lower than expected. Then, when I left university, my blogs were discredited, companies stopped giving me contracts.'

Frankie stared at him. 'You should have told me,' she said, slightly hurt that he hadn't.

'I didn't want you to worry. You were doing so well. Anyway, I didn't need to. I got an approach. Turns out it wasn't just Infotec who were interested in me. You make an enemy of Infotec and you make other friends. These friends. Come on, they're expecting you. Glen's expecting you . . .' He took a deep breath. 'He's the guy.

The one who started it all. He's . . . he's the most wanted man in France, possibly the world. He started all of this.'

Frankie looked at Jim curiously, at the way his eyes were shining and darting around all over the place. 'You like him,' she said, quietly. She had totally underestimated Jim, she realised. Had made so many assumptions about him, so many judgements. Just because he didn't broadcast his life to everyone like she did, she'd assumed he didn't have one.

Jim raised his eyebrows. 'I've never met him,' he said, looking slightly awkward suddenly. 'Only a handful of people have. He moves every two days. Probably changes chips more often than you do.' He grinned and Frankie managed a small laugh. 'He . . . People like me don't get to meet Glen.'

He knocked on the door, then knocked again, a strange kind of rhythmic knock that Frankie knew she would never be able to replicate. Immediately the door opened. Jim turned to Frankie. 'In you go,' he said.

Frankie frowned. 'You're coming in, right?' she asked uncertainly.

Jim shook his head. 'I'm just the delivery boy.' He forced a smile, a note of sadness in his eye. 'Send my best to Glen.'

'But . . .' Frankie stared after him open-mouthed as he walked back down the corridor. 'But . . .'

'No buts,' Jim said, turning briefly before unlocking the door in front of him and disappearing back into the club. Frankie took a deep breath, turned apprehensively and walked into the room in front of her.

She didn't know what she was expecting, but Glen, the number one enemy of Infotec had to be something special. Someone impressive, someone strong, dynamic, even tortured or strange; Frankie was prepared for all these things. What she wasn't prepared for was the middle-aged man in a business suit sitting on a rather cheap-looking office chair.

She smiled at him. 'Hi,' she said. 'I'm Frankie. I'm looking for someone called Glen.'

The man looked at her thoughtfully. 'You've found him,' he said. 'Please, sit down.' His accent was American; his expression was one of vague impatience.

He motioned towards another office chair, the swivel broken, the blue fabric stained with coffee in several places.

Tentatively, Frankie sat down. 'You're Glen?' she asked.

He nodded. 'Not what you were expecting?'

She reddened; Glen laughed. 'I rarely am,' he said with a little shrug. 'But then again, it's rather useful not to meet anyone's expectations. You see, Infotec relies on us being clichés, easy to categorise and group, easy to manage and package up. It can't see everything, not even close, but if we all behave in expected ways, it doesn't have to see everything, it just has to look at the right things at the right time. The unusual things. You know that your name gets an alert next to it when you change your brand of toothpaste? We're creatures of habit; when we change something, there's usually an underlying reason, a general dissatisfaction. Possibly with our toothpaste, but more often with our life. Infotec doesn't like dissatisfaction, doesn't like change. It's a threat. You start thinking about your toothpaste enough to make a change, you're probably going to look at other things too. So they watch you. Just in case.'

Frankie opened her mouth to speak, but for the first time in her life she found that she had nothing to say.

Glen laughed again.

'Your mind has gone blank because you're processing what I'm saying whilst taking in all the visual clues and trying to package it together into some kind of scene that you understand, that you can make sense of. But none of it makes sense; I don't look like a hero, or a villain, or a damaged victim, or even a clever genius, and we're in a shabby room with chairs that are supremely uncomfortable, and I look like a low-level white-collar worker who's close to retirement and yet I'm in the back office of a just-legal trance club. You came here looking for answers and instead you're feeling vaguely claustrophobic, very uncertain and possibly like you've made a big error of judgement. Or your friend Jim has. You're wondering why he had to leave you here. Wondering whether I'll let you walk out of this room; where you'd go if I did. Am I right so far?'

Frankie stared at him blankly. Then she mentally kicked herself. She had to get it together.

'I guess,' she said. 'About some of it. I'm not planning to leave. Not yet.'

'Glad to hear it,' Glen said warmly. 'Would you like some wine? I've got a lovely Chateau Margeau I was planning to open tonight. And some delicious cheese to have with it. You like camembert?'

'Of course,' Frankie said.

'Good.' Glen clapped his hands together and pulled out an old rucksack that was standing against the wall, barely visible because of the coats piled on top of it. He shook his head ruefully. 'I know,' he said, 'it's a mess. But that's what happens when you go offline. I need a filing system. And someone to file stuff. But I don't have either, so . . . Ah, here we are.'

He took out a bottle and two glasses, then walked over to the corner and took some cheese out of a bucket, shaking water off it and putting it on top of a small bureau.

'Much better than a fridge,' he said. 'Bucket with cool water. Perfect for cheese. Allows it to ripen without becoming . . . *de trop*. You know? I don't need much. But my friends are very generous. They keep me well fed wherever I am. Keeps the spirits up.'

Frankie nodded, staring in wonderment, and Glen opened the bureau drawers to reveal plates, oat biscuits, fig preserve. He poured her a glass of wine then carefully filled her plate and handed it to her with a knife. '*Bon appétit.*' He smiled.

Frankie ate hungrily but savoured the wine; her grandfather had been a traditional Frenchman and had ensured that wine was treated with respect by all his grandchildren. When her plate was empty, she looked up at Glen, who had eaten only a quarter of what was on his but appeared to be finished also.

'So,' he said, stretching his legs out. 'How does it feel to be on the "wrong" side, Frankie? How does it feel to be hunted? Scary, huh?'

Frankie shrugged noncommittally.

'You can admit it,' Glen said. 'I was shit scared the day it happened to me. But then again, I kind of knew it was coming. Knew the enormity of it.'

'The enormity of what?' Frankie said, putting her plate down and doing her best to sit back against the broken chair.

'Of what it means to be on the wrong side of Infotec,' Glen said, moving his chair towards her and looking her right in the eye. 'Of what it means to have crossed the line. Because you, Frankie, have crossed the line. And what you need to know, really know, is that there's no going back.'

The words hit Frankie like a blow to the head, although she didn't know why because it wasn't news. Except it was. Having someone else say it like that . . . She felt her head start to spin and gripped her glass of wine more tightly. Glen leant forwards.

'I know,' he said, his face full of concern. Frankie noticed his eyes suddenly; they were grey, clouded; they looked older than the rest of him somehow. 'I know how you're feeling, Frankie. Angry. Frustrated. Indignant. Disbelieving. You want to wake up from this horrible dream. You want me to tell you everything's going to be fine. I can't do that, Frankie. But I can tell you that you're not alone. That you'll be supported, helped. That we're on your side. It won't mean much now, but it will, I promise you.'

'It does mean something,' Frankie said, her voice brittle, higher than usual. 'It does.'

'Good.' Glen pushed his chair back and finished his wine.

Frankie took a sip from her glass, closed her eyes,

then opened them again. 'So tell me how you got here,' she said then, partly because she wanted to know, but more because she needed to have him speak, needed to have something else to focus on, something to stop her brain from whirring, from panicking, from self-destructing.

'Here?' Glen smiled ruefully. 'I came through the club just like you. Wearing the chip of a twentysomething accountant. You think I live here?' He chuckled. 'No. I'm not Sal. I choose to live above ground. But we have meeting points and this is one of them. But I'm being facetious. You wish to know why I am here, with you. What I did to anger Infotec. Why I am on this side instead of that?'

Frankie nodded. 'Then we are going to need more wine,' Glen said, picking up the bottle and pouring himself a glass, then pouring some more into Frankie's. 'To understand all of this, you need to take yourself back eleven years.'

14

'Eleven years?' Frankie asked, frowning. She was a child then. 'What happened eleven years ago?'

Glen pulled a face, like even now the memory was uncomfortable. 'What happened,' he said carefully, 'was that I found something out. Something I wasn't supposed to know. Something that . . .' he hesitated. 'That . . . caused me some uncertainty.'

Frankie stared at him. 'What was it?' she asked, leaning forwards.

Glen smiled. 'You're impatient, aren't you?' he said.

Frankie raised her eyebrows. Then she stood up and moved towards Glen, leaning down so that their faces were just inches apart. Up close she could see that his forehead was covered in small beads of sweat from the heat of the room, could see that his hair was combed across his forehead to disguise a receding hairline. She moved her face so that her eyes were looking right into his. 'Impatient?' she asked, her voice low but firm. 'I've been in a room all day with your friend Sal, hiding because the guy I thought was in love with me tried to kill me and had me replaced by some imposter. I have been cut off from everything and everyone, some girl is running around town marrying my pig of a boyfriend and my best friend Jim isn't even allowed into this room with me. I also discovered that apparently my father didn't have a heart attack; he was murdered by the same people who are now after me. So forgive me if I'm coming across as impatient. I just don't want to waste any more time, if it's all the same with you.'

She stood up again, walked back to her chair and sat down, feeling much better for having asserted herself. And to her relief, Glen didn't get angry and dismiss her or leave in disgust. He just nodded, slowly.

'You're right,' he said. 'And I'm sorry. You want answers. I know that. The reason you're not getting them right away . . .' He hesitated. 'There's a lot to get to grips with. To understand. To . . . accept. People don't usually accept major change without resisting it first, denying it, getting angry, getting depressed. We don't have time for all that; but it has to come out so I'm hoping it'll come out relatively quickly, whilst I'm telling you what lies ahead, what happened to me and what's going to happen to you. But let me start by saying that I know what it feels like. Exactly what it feels like. You see, eleven years ago I was working for Infotec.'

'You? Really?' Frankie asked in surprise.

Glen smiled. 'Really,' he said. 'Actually I was a big player. I headed up the network department; I deputised for the chief executive. I was responsible for screen maintenance, for story selection. Everything you see walking around – the people being beamed out at you, that was me. And I believed in what I was doing, too. All of it – the low crime rates, the way the world was united, sharing everything, communicating everything. It was a buzz. We all felt it. We all wanted to do our bit.'

'And then?' Frankie asked, leaning forwards. 'What did you find out? If I'm not being too impatient?'

She shot him a sort of smile and he returned it. He cleared his throat. 'I saw something very strange, that seemed almost unbelievable,' he said. 'But you'll know all about that. You see, what happened was that one day I was reviewing the network and I saw something. A flicker of activity in a place there shouldn't have been any.'

Frankie felt her heart begin to thud more heavily in her chest. 'The UK?' she asked, her voice almost a whisper.

'The UK.' Glen nodded. 'There was someone communicating with someone else, using old satellites to do it, but the signal passed across our networks. I saw it with my own eyes.'

'And what did you do?' Frankie asked.

Glen raised an eyebrow. 'I did what anyone would have done. I went to my boss. I was excited. I told him what I'd seen, waited for him to send out the search parties. I expected him to be amazed, just like I was.'

'And instead he told you to forget about it?' Frankie said, seething as she remembered the look on Milo's face when she'd told him about her contact, that she'd been told there were people alive in the UK. He'd looked at her with pity that she'd been so gullible. He'd made out it was the most ridiculous thing he'd ever heard, like saying there was a human colony on the moon.

Glen nodded. 'Ordered me to. Said it was a mistake.'

'And you didn't forget about it?'

Glen breathed out slowly. 'Actually I did. At least, I accepted what my boss had told me. He got it from Thomas. The guy in charge of everything. I figured he would know. He knew everything, after all, and he wanted the world to be a better place just like I did. That's what I thought. That he would know best. Only I guess Thomas didn't trust me to keep my mouth shut. Next day, what happened to you happened to me. The men, the van, the chip. I wasn't replaced; that wouldn't have worked. I was just discredited. Money appeared in my account to suggest that I'd become rich through illegal activity; it was announced that I'd disappeared, that I'd defrauded the company and gone on the run. I couldn't get into my apartment, couldn't get into a single bar. I went to my brother but he had already been warned by Infotec that I'd changed, that I was unwell, that I was paranoid and dangerous. He called the police whilst I was sitting in his front room trying to explain what had happened. I managed to escape and I went on the run. That was the last time I saw any of my friends or family. That was the last time anyone called me by my real name.'

Frankie stared at him. It was like the rest of the room didn't exist; there was a tunnel between her eyes and Glen's face, with blackness all around. She felt sick. Felt like she was falling. Somewhere inside she'd convinced herself that this was all a blip, a story she'd be telling people in a few weeks' time. That she'd prove herself, reveal the other Frankie as an imposter, get her life back. Now . . . now she was finding it hard to breathe.

'Is that what happened to my father too?' she asked, her voice barely audible.

Glen nodded slowly. 'Your uncle kept asking questions, got involved in groups who were questioning Infotec. There was lots of dissent in China, Korea,

Japan, where they felt like their whole culture had been stolen, discredited, crushed. There are still lots of groups wanting change, although naturally Infotec is pretty good at wiping them out. Your uncle got involved with these groups. Wouldn't give up. And one day he disappeared. Your father was a clever guy. He put two and two together, started to dig around a bit.'

'So they killed him too,' Frankie said, a lump the size of a golf ball blocking her throat.

'I'm sorry,' Glen said. 'I know you wanted reassurance, action, answers. And what I'm giving you is none of those things. But you have what I didn't have. What your uncle didn't have. Support networks. Places to go. I realised back then that I couldn't be the only person this had happened to, that I wouldn't be the last person either. So I set up my own network, hid it so carefully no one would be able to track it down. And I waited for people to contact me. Didn't take long. Soon we had our own little community. A circle of trust that gradually grew, that started to attract the disaffected, the people who dared to question Infotec. I didn't get to your uncle, I'm afraid, but we are continually monitoring the system to find sympathisers and people who need our help. There are over three thousand of us in Paris alone; more across Europe and all over the world, some of them like your friend Jim, helping to monitor, keeping their ears open; others are in powerful positions and can offer more strategic help. We can get people out of Europe, get them a new passport, another clean chip. The one you have right now you're borrowing, you see. That's how we do it, swap, swap swap so that by the time Infotec catches up and marks your chip it's back where it belongs. But let's say you go to Australia to start a new life. Once you're there we'll get you a permanent chip, a new, safe identity. We'll fill your chip with work experiences and references, friends you can trust, all the help you need. And you can start again, build your Watcher numbers, be completely normal. You'll be okay, Frankie. I promise you that. You won't be famous anymore, but you'll be fine.' He looked at Frankie reassuringly, reached out to give her arm a squeeze. 'So what do you think?' he said.

'What do I think?' Frankie asked, her brow furrowing. She took a deep breath. 'What I think is that I'm not going anywhere. I'm not running away. Those bastards are going to pay for what they've done.'

Glen sucked his lips between his teeth. Then he fixed Frankie with a stare. 'They want you dead. You know that? They are looking for you right now. You're a loose end. A dangerous one.'

Frankie didn't say anything.

Sighing, Glen opened a laptop and pressed a button;

immediately the screen was filled with a picture of people weeping. She stared at it uncertainly as Glen turned up the volume.

'So devastating,' someone was saying. 'She was in the prime of her life, engaged to be married . . .' The screen was filled with images of Frankie – the real Frankie, laughing, dancing, walking down the street. Then of her imposter being put in a car by Milo, reaching out to give him one last kiss. She was wearing Frankie's favourite pale pink dress and studded biker boots. She was wearing the engagement ring. Then the image changed again to a pile up, the car crushed, Frankie's body being taken from the wreckage. An image of a man appeared on the screen; the voiceover described him as a loyal driver who had momentarily lost control of the vehicle. No one else had been involved in the crash. But both driver and passenger were dead. Glen closed the laptop.

'Poor girl,' he said with a little shrug.

Frankie didn't say anything. She was still trying to process what she'd just seen. Jim had been right. She felt her stomach clench. 'They . . . they killed her?' she managed to say eventually. 'When?'

'These images were released an hour ago,' he said. 'So you see there is no Frankie. Not anymore. Just you. They won't stop looking for you.'

Frankie shook her head desperately. 'No,' she whispered. 'No.' She let her head fall into her hands.

'I'm sorry, Frankie.'

They sat like that for a while then Frankie looked up. 'So what's going to happen now?' she asked.

Glen leant around and picked up a bag from behind his chair, then handed it to Frankie. 'Inside here,' he said, 'is everything you need to know about your new identity. You'll be leaving Paris tonight, going to Munich then Bern. From there we'll transfer you to Australia the day after tomorrow. You'll have a week staying in a safe house while we check that you haven't been followed, that nothing has gone wrong. Then you get your new life and story and you're set. We'll contact you once a year to check everything is okay, but other than that you're on your own. No getting in touch, no checking in, nothing. It's too risky. I suggest you study this pack – it will give you everything you need, answer every question. But memorise it because the minute you land in Australia we'll destroy it as a precautionary measure.'

Frankie listened and as he talked she felt like she was somewhere else, watching what was happening. Most of what had happened over the past few hours felt like it had to be happening to someone else, but this was the first time she actually felt like she was on the outside looking in, watching herself as she nodded attentively, watching Glen as he flicked through the pack like it was the induction information for a new job or something.

And then something happened that forced her right back into her chair, that sent a jolt through her that felt like at least forty volts of electricity. A message flashed in front of her, a message so unexpected she jumped up in the air. A message that simply said: 'Don't run. You're close to the truth. Expose it. Glen can help you. I'll help you . . .'

Glen looked at her oddly. 'Are you listening, Frankie? Is everything okay?'

Frankie shook her head. 'The stranger's found me again,' she gasped.

'The stranger?' Glen looked at her strangely.

'The guy who told me about the UK in the first place. My source,' Frankie said. 'He's just sent me another message.'

Glen's face went white. 'That can't be. There is no way anyone could track your new chip.'

'There is a way,' Frankie said hurriedly. 'There has to be because he's found me. He knows your name.'

'How did he find you?' Glen asked, the whites of his eyes visible. 'What is he saying?'

'Tell Glen I never lost you,' flashed in front of her. 'Tell him I know the truth. Tell him what he saw was real.'

In a daze Frankie repeated the message. Glen's eyes started to dart around the room. 'This can't be happening,' he said, standing up. 'No one could track you here. We changed your chip twice, three times, right? No one knows . . . Who is this person? How did he find you? What have you done?'

'I haven't done anything!' Frankie said indignantly. 'And I've got no idea how he found me, but he saved my life and led you guys to me, so don't get all paranoid. He's on our side.'

Glen shook his head. 'In eleven years, no one has found me,' he said, his voice low. 'Not since I went underground. No one has ever done this . . .'

And then there was another message. Only this time Frankie suspected that it was flashing in front of both their faces because of the way Glen was staring right ahead, shaking his head in fear and wonderment.

'You have to trust me,' the message said. 'Frankie's right – I'm on your side. I need your help. And you need mine. I'm from the UK; I've been brought here by Infotec. What they're doing needs to be exposed. You have to get to the truth, and you have to show the world. Otherwise Infotec will never be brought to justice. Otherwise everyone I love will be murdered, and no one will even know they existed.'

'Who is this? Who are you?' Glen asked, looking

around the room desperately as though hoping to find the answer to his question on its walls.

'Me? My name's Raffy. Good to meet you. Now, can we get on with the task at hand please? I need you to organise a car. Actually I need you to organise a few things. Are you ready? Because what I'm about to tell you might well blow your mind . . .'

15

Evie stared at the screen in front of her and tried to ignore the fact that the restlessness had left her, that she no longer drummed her fingers violently on any available surface, no longer jumped up several times an hour to pace around in circles muttering to herself. She was able to sit still, stare at the screen. She had given up.

No, she told herself. She had not given up; she would never give up. She had just adjusted. She was surviving. To do anything else would be foolhardy.

She hated this place, this claustrophobic space with its white walls and fresh coffee and food that appeared regularly so that she never even had to think about whether she was hungry or not, never had to actively do anything at all. And yet she was used to it now. She had slipped into a kind of rhythm, a way of living. And she despised herself for it as she reached out to the plate of pecan pie in front of her and took another bite.

She looked around the room. Raffy and Linus were in their own little capsules, where they were beavering away, or not, she barely cared anymore. She saw them briefly, once or twice a day; they seemed to live parallel lives, not daring to look each other in the eye in case the pretence was shattered, in case they lost their ability to survive, to ignore, to forget.

She looked at the full plate of food in front of her and pushed it to the side. She used to eat at the table, but now that she was largely on her own, she had taken to eating on the sofa; the large, sprawling leather sofa that had become like a second home, a despised, suffocating womb that sucked her in and would, she knew, eventually spit her out again.

She glanced up at the television. Frankie was being driven through Paris to her final resting place and the world was crying.

Weirdly, Evie found herself crying, too. Not right now, but whenever she saw her death reported, whenever she found herself watching long reels of Frankie alive, various commentators talking about the tragedy of such a young life cut short.

Evie did not think much of Frankie, of the socialite who promoted Infotec, whose entire life seemed to revolve around clothes and make-up and talking to the millions of people who Watched her every day. She was a product of Thomas's Infotec; a doll who enjoyed being stared at, who never once asked what she was doing, what everyone was doing. She was vacuous; she was probably quite stupid. And yet, since she had been in this prison, Frankie had been Evie's constant companion. And now she was gone.

As she watched the people lining the roads, watched them cry out, watched them hold their pictures of Frankie aloft, signs that read 'Frankie, we'll never forget you', she found her eyes pricking with tears again, real tears that soon flooded her eyes and cascaded down her cheeks.

Was she really crying for Frankie? Or was she crying for someone else, someone who had been a true companion, who she missed with such an ache she sometimes gasped at the pain. What was Lucas doing? Where was he? Was he even alive?

Evie watched the casket as it reached the patch of grass in a cemetery near the Seine. And then the camera panned away, to Milo, to the man who had loved Frankie, the man Frankie had hoped to marry. The man who hung around with Raffy, who smiled patronisingly at her, who worked with Thomas. He had a badge on his lapel, the 'I' that made Evie shiver. But he and

Frankie had seemed happy; he had looked so broken the day they found her. She would do her best not to be happy that he knew what it was like to have the person you love wrenched from you.

'It's strange for me, standing here,' he said, 'talking about Frankie. Because I know that whilst what we had was irreplaceable, I also know that I never had Frankie to myself, because I shared her with you, because all around the world, there are people who are sharing in my pain, who wish as much as I do that Frankie could come back. And to all of you, I say thank you, because I know that Frankie loved you, loved each and every one of you, just as she loved this city, loved this new world that we have all created . . .'

There was a cheer; Milo wiped his eye distractedly.

'But today,' he continued, 'I don't want to talk about Frankie the icon, or Frankie the freedom fighter, Frankie the blogger who argued tirelessly for openness, for sharing of information, for everything, frankly, that Infotec hoped for and is so proud to now be a part of. No, what I want to talk about today is Frankie the girl, the girl we all loved, the girl I will miss forever.'

And then suddenly there was a ripple in the crowd as someone rushed forward. 'What about the UK, Milo? What about the blog Frankie posted about it? What do you have to say about that?'

Evie's chest tightened. The person speaking was wearing a monkey mask; as soon as the cameras panned in on them, they ducked down. And as they did, the crowd rippled as suddenly black jumpers and I badges could be seen moving around; the Inforcers who had been so inconspicuous in the crowd, who were now moving inwards in a pincer movement.

Milo's face hardened. 'Whoever that was,' he said coldly, 'I think we all know that Frankie had her accounts hacked from time to time by terrorists who weren't brave enough to speak in their own name, the sort of terrorist that comes to a funeral wearing a mask with the sole intent of causing trouble and anguish.'

Another ripple, and the masked terrorist was captured. 'Frankie was killed because she was getting close,' the man shouted as he was dragged away. Milo shook his head sadly but his eyes were like steel.

'This is the danger that has infected this City,' he said then. 'But we will not let these terrorists achieve their goal. We will not dwell on them, we will not give them the attention they crave. This is a day for celebrating Frankie, not for indulging the crazy whims of those who wanted to destroy her, to use her to further their own anti-progress ends. The UK was a great country but, as Frankie was only too aware, it is a wasteland, a nuclear wasteland and it's not getting any safer – there are significant fears of drift of nuclear waste to our shores, in fact. If it wasn't for that, I would send a team across to the UK to lay these insane claims to rest for the last time, but I am not going to put anyone's life in danger simply to stop conspiracy theories from proliferating.'

Evie watched, open-mouthed, waiting for someone to argue, to question Milo. But instead, the crowd was deathly silent. *Someone ask*, she begged silently. *Someone say something, please. Someone say something that makes the crowd demand a search party goes right now and finds Lucas and . . .*

She closed her eyes. What was she even thinking? Of course no one would say anything; of course there would be no search party. She had got so caught up in Frankie's death, in the funeral, that she'd almost believed that Milo's grief might transcend his badge, his allegiance to Thomas.

She sighed heavily, pulling her knees into her chest and holding them there for a few minutes. This place. This grim, comfortable, insidious, despicable place.

Evie pulled herself up off the sofa and did her best not to look back at the screen, at the many screens around her that did their best to draw her in as they flashed images of desperate fans with tear-stained faces, of the grim stoicism of Milo as he watched Frankie's casket being lowered into the ground.

Slowly, she reached forward, took another bite of pie, then sat back and closed her eyes.

16

'You've called your central base Cassandra?'

Raffy looked at Milo defensively. 'So?'

'So it's a weird name.'

Raffy pulled a face. 'I guess,' he said. 'Just seemed kind of apt at the time. She's tricky.'

Milo laughed. He'd taken to hanging around Raffy's cubicle for an hour or so most days; officially he was there to monitor Linus's work, but in reality he didn't seem that keen on spending time with the man tasked with building the System; only with the younger one who was supposed to be checking it. Raffy didn't mind. They were getting on pretty well. And he knew Milo would be useful to him at some point soon. 'All women are tricky. You should have had her change into a man. Much more straightforward.'

'Yeah, I'll stick with Cassandra if it's all the same

with you,' Raffy said with a shrug. 'Not exactly a hit with the girls right now, if you know what I mean. Cassandra's the only woman who's actually talking to me.' He looked meaningfully out of the glass door of his cubicle; Milo followed his gaze to where Evie was lying on a sofa, her eyes fixed on the screen ahead.

'Still not talking to you?' Milo asked sympathetically.

'Not even looking at me.'

'Well, plenty more fish in the sea.' Milo winked. 'Let's have a look shall we?' He leant in towards Cassandra and moved his hand towards the screen. 'How about her,' he said, pulling up an image of a blonde girl walking up some steps. He tapped the screen and some text came up.

Hi, I'm Vanessa. I have 43,689 Watchers. I'm a student right now but I want to be an actor some day. I like dancing, eating out and sexy lingerie. Follow me and I can promise you a good time!

Raffy stared at her; Milo laughed. 'Your pupils are dilating like crazy,' he said. 'There are loads of them. Here, what about her?'

A brunette appeared. *Hi, I'm Sara. I have 506,782 Watchers. I work as a receptionist but my first love is winter sports. Watch me bomb down mountains, then join me for some après ski in the hot tub!*

'She's nice,' Raffy said, his cheeks reddening slightly.

Then he sighed. 'Thing is, Milo, you're out there with these people. I'm not. And if Thomas has his way I'll probably never be.'

Milo pulled a face. 'I wouldn't say that. If he gets his System, he might release you into the wild, you never know.'

Raffy turned sharply. 'You think?'

Milo shrugged. 'I don't know. But I don't see why not. He likes loyalty. Are you loyal, Raffy?'

Raffy held his eye for a few seconds then looked down. 'I wasn't loyal to Evie,' he said quietly.

'Thomas won't mind about that.' Milo grinned.

'These girls . . . they're really real? I mean, they're actually out there?' Raffy asked then. 'Girls like this? Beautiful girls in hot tubs and dancing in their underwear?'

'They're actually out there,' Milo nodded, peering at the screen. 'Sara there is in Nantes if I'm not very much mistaken. Not so far away. And she's got great tits.'

Raffy spluttered. If anyone had said that in the City, or in the Settlement . . . Well they just wouldn't. Not ever. Just absolutely never.

'What?' Milo asked incredulously. 'She has got great tits.'

'But you're . . .' Raffy cleared his throat. 'You and Frankie. You were in love, right?'

Milo's expression changed slightly. 'Frankie? Yeah, we were. Of course we were. I'm just trying to move on, you know?' He moved his mouth to one side, then sat back on his chair, his arms cradling his head. 'Trying to ease the pain a bit.'

He didn't sound entirely convinced, but Raffy played along anyway. 'Must be hard,' he said. 'So you reckon Thomas might let me go to this Nantes place if he gets his System?'

'I reckon he might,' Milo nodded. 'But are you going to be able to deliver it? That's the question. I'm guessing that whatever your friend is producing isn't going to amount to a crock of shit.'

Raffy met his eyes. 'I can do it,' he said. 'I know I can. But I want to go free afterwards. I want Thomas's word.'

'I'll see what I can do,' Milo said, standing up. 'And you'd better get back to work. No ogling girls when you're meant to be building the System, mind.'

Raffy nodded firmly. 'Wouldn't dream of it,' he said, a little twinkle in his eye. 'Oh, and Milo, one other thing?'

'What?' Milo asked, frowning.

Raffy looked at him cautiously. 'It's Benjamin,' he said.

'What about him?' Milo asked, his eyes narrowing.

'I'd like to spread his ashes. He meant everything to me. He was a good man, a great man. I know Linus and Evie would . . . well I know it would help. It would help wounds heal, if that makes sense?'

Milo sighed heavily, then rolled his eyes. 'It's unlikely,' he said, 'but I'll see what I can do. Just don't get your hopes up.'

'I won't,' said Raffy. 'But I really appreciate the effort. I really do.'

'Good,' said Milo, then he looked at his watch. 'Right, got to go. Things to do, places to see.'

He patted Raffy on the back, turned and left, his polished shoes tack tacking on the floor as he walked out of the apartment.

Raffy watched him go, then turned back to Cassandra and started to type.

Evie heard Milo leave, then she stood up and padded over to Raffy's cubicle. She'd told herself not to, told herself it would achieve nothing, but she couldn't help herself, wouldn't either. She didn't knock; she just opened the door and stood there silently until Raffy turned round, his eyes wide in surprise.

'I'm saying this because of what we used to mean to each other,' she said then, the words that she had rehearsed falling away, forgotten. 'Because you used to be someone I cared about. Whatever that man is saying to you, you can't listen to him. He's like Thomas, Raffy. He's evil. They all are. You can't give them what they want. You just can't.'

She felt her bottom lip start to quiver and stopped talking.

Raffy raised an eyebrow. 'Is that it?' he asked.

Evie nodded.

'Right,' said Raffy. 'So you want me not to help the one person who can help us get out of here, do you?'

'He'll never help us escape,' Evie said incredulously. 'Are you mad?'

'I don't mean he'll help us escape. I mean we might get out of here. When Thomas has what he wants. Evie, there's a world out there full of people I want to meet and places I want to go. In the City, in the Settlement, we thought the rest of the world didn't exist. We thought we were it, fighting for survival. But we're not. The world is amazing and I want to be part of it. Linus can't see that because he's too old, too entrenched, too bitter. But I'm not. You're not. We've got our lives ahead of us. And people here live well. Better than we ever have. They're happy, Evie. We could be too. Imagine that. Happy!'

He shot her a smile that she didn't return. 'I don't want anything to do with Thomas's world,' she said quietly. 'Don't you get that? Don't you see that he's the one who blew up the Settlement, the reason Benjamin's dead? He's keeping us prisoner, Raffy. Why would you want anything to do with him?'

'Because he's all there is,' Raffy said then, his tone suddenly cold and angry. 'Because Linus and Benjamin failed. Thomas won. He was always going to win. And I'm not fighting Linus's battles anymore. I want to live.'

'Then you do what you want,' Evie said, shaking her head in despair, in dread at what Raffy was going to do. 'But know that I will hate you, Raffy. Know that I will delete from my mind every memory, every smile, every touch, every conversation we have ever had. Everything.' She turned and left, allowing the door to close behind her.

'You do that,' she heard Raffy call after her. 'You do that from your glass tower, while I'm out having a good time with Sara from Nantes.' But she'd stopped listening; tears were cascading from her eyes as all her pent up rage and desperation flooded out of her. There was no hope anymore. Thomas was going to win. Benjamin had died in vain. And she was never going to see her beloved Lucas again.

17

Lucas looked around the room, breathing in, wondering if any of her breath remained here, whether there was something of her on this chair, on the keyboard that she used every day.

Evie wasn't here; she was long gone and he knew it. But of all the computers in the City that were connected to the System's now-defunct mainframe, he still chose to use the one that she had worked at years before, changing labels, dreaming of something better. She had despised him back then; had believed the lies that he had told in order to protect himself and Raffy. But he didn't care; that's what he had fallen in love with, Evie's strength, her defiance, her quiet confidence. Everyone else in the City had been seduced by his A label, his position of authority, the armour he had built for himself. But not Evie. She had seen only his cold, hard exterior and had shrunk from it. It was only when he had revealed the truth, revealed his ulterior motive, his pain, that she had looked at him differently. He had always loved Evie, but when he had seen her eyes change, seen her hatred dissolve into something warm, something intoxicating, his life had changed. He'd known right then that he would never be happy until he held her in his arms, until he lay with her on his bed, until he knew that the two of them would be together for eternity. And yet he'd known that it was impossible, that she loved Raffy, that there could never be anything between them, that he was destined to die alone, just as he had always been alone, confiding in no one, revealing himself to no one.

He closed his eyes, remembering the night Evie had come to him in Linus's cave, the night Raffy had betrayed them all, the night she had answered his prayers and told him that it was him that she loved, only him. He heard himself cry out, felt his fist slam down on the desk in front of him, Evie's desk, because it wasn't fair, because she had been wrenched from him again, because he hadn't protected her, hadn't been there when she needed him.

Then he took a deep breath, calmed himself, forced his mind away. Martha had been right; self-indulgence had no place now. He had a City to defend, friends to track down and bring back, and as for Thomas . . .

He felt his chest clench with anger and he breathed in slowly again. He would leave Thomas until last, but he would make sure that he suffered. For everything he had done.

Outside the window Lucas could hear children laughing, playing, their parents chastising them gently as they talked freely. Things that should have been commonplace but which, until recently, would have been unheard of in the City. Where once people feared the judgements of the System, were afraid to speak their minds or reveal too much of themselves, now they were free to talk, to argue, to laugh. Mostly argue, Lucas had to concede; the end of the System had unleashed a million and one plans and ideas for how to organise the City, and passionate debates that sometimes spilled into fights were now commonplace. But Lucas would take disagreement any day over fear. And he'd upped the police guard presence on Saturday nights just to make sure that things didn't get out of control.

He turned back to the screen in front of him, feeling a surge of pride as he moved his fingers to the keyboard. The fact of the matter was that it was worth fighting for. The City was worth fighting for, just as it had been worth sacrificing everything for when he was a boy, taking on the responsibilities of his father, handing his own father in to the Brother to ensure that his integrity and loyalty would never be in doubt. Lucas had lost so much that day, but he had gained so much too, including strength of mind and patience that he would utilise now, that would help him stay focused.

He typed quickly, finding the connection that Linus had hidden so cleverly, that had taken him over a week to find, desperately searching his memory for everything his father had taught him about the System, about Linus, about how to cover your tracks. They had been comrades, his father and Linus; when the Brother had suspected him, he had sacrificed himself and handed the baton to Lucas. And now . . . now it was up to him. The connection was embedded in code, almost impossible to find, but Lucas had followed the path of the original connection, the secret messaging post that had enabled him to communicate with Linus all those years ago. Now he was connecting to a world so much bigger than he'd ever thought imaginable; a world that had been hidden from him, from everyone. Lucas could see nothing of this world, could only imagine what it might be like. But that didn't matter. What mattered was that he made sure the rest of the world knew of the City's existence, knew the truth about Thomas. What mattered was that he found Evie, wherever she was, brought her back and never, ever lost her again.

18

'You're sure this is a good idea?'

Thomas smiled. 'Milo, we wouldn't be doing this if it wasn't a good idea. And if I remember correctly, it was your idea.'

Milo pulled a face as he watched Linus, Evie and Raffy standing together, minders positioned around them. He blamed himself for even mentioning it to Thomas and had been baffled when Thomas had immediately agreed. But that was the thing with Thomas; you thought you knew him and . . . Well, you never did. Which was why they were on the roof of the building, a spot chosen by Thomas for the funeral Raffy had been so desperate for. Was funeral the right word? Milo didn't know. Scattering of ashes. Linus was apparently going to say a few words. To be honest he didn't really care; couldn't be sure the ashes he'd given Raffy were even Benjamin's. 'Yeah, I guess,' he said. 'It's just, you know, being out in the open like this? These people are supposed to be a secret.'

'On the roof,' Thomas said. 'Where there are no cameras. Where we are many, many stories higher than any other building, where no one can see us unless they decide to fly overhead in a helicopter, which they won't because there is a no-fly zone. Why do you think we are up here?'

'You're right,' Milo said immediately. 'You know me, I'm too cautious sometimes. But with Frankie still missing . . . after everything that happened . . . I guess I'm just a bit paranoid.'

After what had happened . . . After what hadn't happened, more like. He folded his arms, tried not to think about it. But he couldn't do it. It was meant to have been simple. Just like all the others. Chip removed, new identity, damage limitation exercise, all done and dusted within twenty-four hours. It was what happened to people who crossed the line, who threatened the status quo. Even Frankie. Even his girlfriend. Thomas had talked him through the plan in detail – how she would be de-chipped, left to wander the streets of Paris for a while, to watch the new Frankie on screen, to realise that she wasn't as important as she'd thought, to learn a little humility. It was only meant to have lasted a day or two. But things hadn't gone according to plan. Not at all. Frankie was meant to be licking her wounds, feeling aggrieved, but also realising the error of her ways. And instead she'd gone AWOL. And now the new Frankie had been 'killed off' because Thomas said it was too risky having her around, because people would start to notice it wasn't the real Frankie. It all made sense when Thomas explained it; it was only when Milo was left on his own, trying to work it out, that nothing seemed to fit together anymore. Still. He'd find her. He'd find her eventually. And then everything would make sense again. Everything would be fine.

Thomas nodded. 'Paranoia is good, Milo. But I think I can safely say that there is no way off this roof except through the hatch, and there are guards positioned all around it. Our friends need some fresh air, need to remember what it feels like. I want them to miss it. I also want them to be grateful to me. Gratitude can be a very powerful thing, Milo. But most of all I want Linus to realise that he can't stop me getting the System, that Raffy can build it if he won't, that Raffy is on our side. I want them to see that there is no hope. Because when they see that, Linus will build the System.'

'I thought Raffy could build it anyway,' Milo frowned as he watched Raffy look up at the sky. He was an alright kid really. Bit weird, bit intense, but what did you expect? He'd had a pretty intense life in a pretty intense place.

'Possibly. But he's unproven. I want Linus's work. He's the reason all of this is here. Linus is the one, Milo. It was all his idea.'

Milo considered this. He had never really spent much time with Linus; tried to avoid it whenever he could. The guy was seriously strange, with eyes that seemed to look right inside you. And the way he spoke made Milo feel stupid, like there was another layer he was missing, like Linus was playing with him, laughing at him behind his back. If it were up to him, they'd be scattering Linus's ashes as well as Benjamin's. And one day maybe it would be up to him. If he played his cards right. Thomas couldn't live forever, after all.

'So,' he said. 'Shall we start?'

Thomas nodded and walked towards the group; Milo followed a few steps behind.

'So nice to see you all,' he said. 'Although I am saddened by the circumstances. Naturally you want to say goodbye to Benjamin. And naturally you will be reassured to know that we are in a very safe environment here. There is no way down from this roof except the way we came. So please don't ruin this solemn occasion with any escape plans.' He looked at

Linus meaningfully; Linus smiled back, his expression opaque. Milo rolled his eyes in irritation.

'Okay,' he said, stepping forward. 'Linus, you can say a few words, then you can all scatter the ashes. We have five minutes up here and then we're going back to the apartment. So, Linus, would you like to begin?'

Linus nodded, moved forwards, brushing past Evie as he reached to take the ashes from Raffy. He held them silently for a few seconds, gazing at them as though trying to work out what to say. Then he looked up.

'Benjamin was a good man and a good friend,' he said eventually. 'He was wise, he was brave, he was clever. And he knew what it meant to have failed, to have been weak, found the wrong path. He did all those things, and his understanding of failure made him a perfect leader, made him the good person that we loved so much . . .'

Milo cleared his throat then turned away. He had messages to read, messages to return; he didn't intend to stand here listening to Linus, of all people, eulogising some freak from the UK who'd fried himself within minutes of arriving here. Particularly when he still hadn't managed to track down Frankie, in spite of Paris having the best camera system in the world. How those imbeciles had let her go was, quite frankly, beyond Milo. Then again, they weren't his men; Thomas had insisted on sending his own men to do the job, so Milo couldn't even sack them for screwing up. But even so, she should have turned up by now. On some camera, somewhere.

Instead, the last film they had of her was walking away from that little prick Jim who had already been questioned several times with considerable force and who had insisted that she'd said she was going to Madrid to track down her father. He said he had no idea how she got a new chip; how the chip she'd been given was subsequently found on a lorry heading south. And Milo didn't believe him, not for a minute, but he had no proof. Nothing. All he could hope was that she'd contact Jim again, and that meant letting him go, making him think that he wasn't under suspicion. And in the meantime, the messages Frankie had received about the UK couldn't be traced either; they appeared to bounce around the globe then disappear into the ether, just like she had apparently done.

Milo sighed in irritation. He missed her. He wanted her back, apologising for being such an idiot, telling him how she'd learnt her lesson. Not disappearing into thin air.

If he ever found out who had sent her those bloody messages in the first place, he would personally wring their neck.

Evie was looking at Linus but she didn't hear a word he said. All she could hear was what he'd whispered to her a minute or so before. 'You have to run, Evie. You have to jump. Level with the flag pole. When I say the word "pray". Jump off the roof, Evie. Do it for Lucas.'

It was as though he'd looked into the darkest pit in her mind, read the thoughts festering there and agreed with them. It was over. There was nothing to do but follow Benjamin's path, make sure that Thomas didn't win. She would never see Lucas again. She would never . . .

She gulped, felt herself choking; she wanted to scream out, wanted to launch herself at Raffy, throw him off the roof because this was his fault, because time and again he had betrayed her, betrayed them all, made a fool of her because she had loved him once, because she had thought he was someone else.

And because she couldn't do it. Wouldn't do it. She had to live; she had to fight. She had to believe. She wouldn't leave Lucas in this world on his own, waiting for her.

'There are things that Benjamin understood. Things that he instilled in everyone who joined his Settlement. That the more we learn, the more we understand, and understanding is the key to peace, to fulfilment. Benjamin created a civilisation in which people co-operated freely, happily; in which the common good was everyone's aim. He was a man of hope, a man who had created this paradise out of hell; who had seen the darker side of life, who knew how easy it was to allow temptation and greed to consume us. But Benjamin also knew his limitations, knew the limitations of man. He was no idealist; he pinned his flag to no ideology. In fact he feared ideology; feared the rabid belief in any one system because he knew that it led only one way: to factions, to hatred, to resentment, to war. That is why he took his own life. He did not want to be part of what we are now part of. He wanted neither to open himself up to temptation, nor to be a pawn or hostage that would prompt others to act against their better judgement. He had lived a free and happy life and he died freely, too.

'Benjamin was not a man of God; like me, he believed in the redemption of humankind, but by their own hand, using strength of will, belief and a desire for good. And yet, I believe a moment of reflection is important, thinking of Benjamin, what he meant to us, how significant he was and what a difference he made.'

Evie was sweating. She knew what was coming. She had to jump. For Benjamin. Had to jump off the roof. Had to be brave. She had to do this. So that Thomas wouldn't win. So that Raffy had no reason to do Thomas's bidding. She had to do it.

Her heart was pounding, she could barely hear, barely think; it was pounding, in her chest, in her head, her blood pumping through her like an out-of-control train. She saw Linus's head turn, briefly, towards the spot he had shown her. The spot where the roof barriers dipped down just slightly. She had to run, step up on top of them and jump.

She couldn't.

She couldn't.

She thought of Lucas, thought of what he would do. Lucas, who had sacrificed himself again and again for what he believed in. Sacrificed himself out of loyalty. Sacrificed himself because he could; because he had no choice but to do what was right. Even if it caused him suffering. Even if . . .

'And so, as we release Benjamin into the wind, let us all close our eyes, and pr . . .'

Evie didn't hear him finish. She ran, desperately, before she could stop herself, before she became paralysed with fear. She ran to the barrier, climbed on top of it. She could hear shouting, could hear Raffy's voice screaming through the wind, could hear footsteps running towards her. She could feel the wind on her face, the moist, cool air. 'I love you, Lucas,' she cried. And then she let herself go. She didn't jump. She just stopped balancing, let herself fall. Into oblivion. Into a better place. A different place. Into a place where she could hold her head up high because she, too, had sacrificed.

Milo stared open-mouthed as the girl fell; rushed forwards, but it was too late. This was no escape plan. This was . . . Well, this was just weird. Were they all psychotic? Did they have some kind of self-destruct code that made them want to kill themselves?

'Evie! Evie! What have you done? Evie!' Raffy's voice was all Milo could hear; he raced to the barriers to hold the boy, to stop him doing something stupid.

'Raffy, easy there. She's gone. She's gone, Raffy.'

'You killed her.' He was like an attack dog now, his eyes wild, throwing himself at Milo. Milo looked over at the security guards, who immediately dragged Raffy off him. 'I didn't kill anyone, Raffy, and you know it. Take him downstairs,' he ordered the guards. 'Both of them.'

He looked over at Linus, who had not moved, his face as expressionless as always. And suddenly Milo knew that he knew something. He'd seen Linus talking to the girl. Had he put her up to it?

Milo walked towards him. 'So you're a murderer now, are you?' he asked. 'You told her to do that. You killed her. And for what? To make a point? There's no point. This is the most fucking pointless thing you've ever done.'

Linus's face turned thoughtful. 'Thomas is running out of hostages, Milo,' he said, quietly. 'Power is a funny thing, you know. One minute you have it, the next . . .'

Milo stared at him then, without warning, hit him square in the jaw. He didn't like Linus. Didn't like the way he looked at him, didn't like the way Thomas revered him. And he didn't like people who killed other people to make a point.

The guards dragged Linus off, more aggressively than was necessary; Milo enjoyed watching them twist Linus's arm behind his back, forcing him through the trap door so that he half fell down the steps.

Then, slowly, Thomas walked towards him. Thomas, who, like Linus, hadn't moved when the girl had jumped, had simply watched silently, his expression unreadable.

'Clear her up,' he said. 'And move them onto hunger rations. I want my System and I want it soon. Do you understand?'

'Of course.' Milo frowned. 'Look, I told you I was paranoid, and now . . .'

'Now you will clear up,' Thomas cut in frostily. 'Do it now.'

And before Milo could answer, Thomas turned and walked silently away, leaving Milo staring at the heavens.

He hated when things didn't go according to plan.

He bloody hated it.

Evie felt herself wrapped in white. Like a sheet. The clouds, she thought to herself. So this is what it's like: I am being wrapped in clouds. She closed her eyes, waited for the nothingness that she knew would come. She felt no pain; the clouds had caught her, broken her fall. Perhaps down below there was a body, her body, but it was not her. Not anymore. She was safe. She was comfortable. She was—

'Quick. Stand up.'

She opened her eyes uncertainly to find two men staring at her. She wasn't in the clouds. She was wrapped in a sheet that had caught her. She looked back up; could see the roof, like a speck, metres above. She looked back down again. She had jumped from the only bit of the roof that was indented, walls either side directing her fall. She had been caught by these men on purpose. Linus had known. Linus had planned it . . .

She felt disoriented, felt dizzy; she steadied herself against the wall and tried to work out what she was supposed to do now, where she was supposed to run.

Suddenly she felt a hand grab her arm.

'Quickly,' he hissed, as a car with blacked-out windows stopped in front of them. 'Get in, quickly.'

She did as she was told; as the door closed behind her, the two men disappeared and the car sped away. She was alone in the back seat, unable to see who was driving her, no idea where she was going. All she knew was that Linus had done this, and that he had a plan. He always had a plan.

And she was alive.

That, for now, was something.

19

Evie sat in the back of the car staring at the world outside, her eyes wide, her whole body trembling, not with cold but with trepidation, with the realisation of what had just happened, of who would be chasing her, of what this meant.

The landscape whizzing by was so unfamiliar, so grey. And she felt a million miles away from home, a million miles away from anything she knew.

But she had escaped.

It was a small victory over Thomas, but a significant one.

They were not powerless.

The car stopped and the driver turned around. 'You get out here,' he said. He was thick-set, large, intimidating, but his eyes were kind. 'You run that way. There's a disused warehouse. A garage next to it. You're to wait in there.'

Evie stared at him blankly. The man looked uncomfortable. 'I have to go,' he shrugged. 'I have to get out of here. There's a path right here. See it? Right where your door opens. Run down it; it veers to the right, just follow it round, okay? You'll find the warehouse. You'll find the garage. You'll be fine. Someone will come for you. But me, I have to go.'

Evie nodded. 'Thank you,' she said, then she got out of the car and started to run. She heard the car speeding off. She had no idea where she was or where she was going, but she didn't have time to worry. The path appeared to stop abruptly, but as she got closer she realised that it did indeed curve round to the right so she followed it onto a scrap of wasteland. There was another path on the other side; behind it she could see the warehouse.

Evie followed the driver's instructions blindly; she had no other choice. She stumbled several times on brambles as she ran, but kept herself low, joined the path, ran past the warehouse and, sure enough, behind it there were three garages. Two of them were locked; the last was open. She was panting, but it felt good to be moving; for months now she had been virtually immobile, a prisoner, watching the world on screens as others lived their lives in front of her, as she sat, unable to join them, unable to do anything except hope and pray that one day it would end – that she would escape or die. Now she realised how much she had been hungering for activity, for sunlight, for the smell of outside air. The scratches on her legs were welcome; they were real, they reminded her that she could feel. And it made her want to cry, made her want to shout with anger and rage at what Thomas had done, made her want to pull out her own hair so that she could gasp with the pain. But now was not the time; she knew that. She was out; that was enough. Now she had to do as the driver had told her. Did he work for Linus? How was that possible? She didn't know, but now wasn't the time to ask questions

Instead, she opened the garage door, ran inside and closed the door behind her. It was empty; it was damp. There was no one here, and no instructions to follow. Evie paced around; she was thirsty but there was nothing inside this cold, concrete building except some metal cans, a net of some sort and three wheels propped up against the wall.

Eventually she pulled out one of the wheels and sat on it; it was warmer than the floor, more comfortable, too.

She drew her knees into her chest. She was cold, and not a little bit scared.

But it was still the most alive she'd been in months.

Gritting her teeth, she closed her eyes and waited.

20

Frankie pulled her leather jacket around herself more tightly and looked at Glen archly as they stumbled over thistles. 'This is insane. We're in the middle of nowhere.'

She could see from Glen's expression that he shared the same doubts as her, that he too was wondering if this whole enterprise was some kind of trap, some wild goose chase that would lead them right into the arms of Infotec. But she also knew that Glen wasn't stupid; otherwise he'd never have stayed hidden for so long, would never have challenged Infotec the way he did, drawn followers to him, acted as a continual thorn in Infotec's side. The doubts floating through her head were, mainly, her own mind trying to talk her out of what she was doing. Not for the first time she wondered if she hadn't been a little rash insisting on staying, on fighting Infotec, on revealing the truth. She could be halfway to Australia by now, a new identity waiting for her. It was warm in Australia. They had beaches. What had she been thinking?

She took a deep breath and focused on Milo, focused on the bastard who had tried to kill her, as she stalked after Glen. No, she told herself. Australia could wait. Right now, she wanted revenge.

They were on the outskirts of Paris, shrubland that used to be something but wasn't now. There were old industrial buildings that had been abandoned years ago; the train connections and roads had been irreparably damaged during the British Horrors when violence had, briefly, spread across the Channel. The French government's response had been to close off all travel routes, to stop those bent on devastation from entering France at all. And pretty soon after that the violence had stopped. Everything had stopped. The denouement, as her parents used to tell her, their eyebrows raised, a look of fear in their eyes, fear tinged with relief that France hadn't been caught up in it, that such a thing would never happen now. Because of Infotec. Because of openness of information.

It was soon after the Horrors that Paris had started to have its own renaissance as all the Brits who had fled the UK stayed, moved their businesses there, Infotec's head office moved there, and before too long native Parisians were muttering in bars about the '*invasion Anglais*'. But the truth was that it wasn't the English survivors who made a difference to Paris; it was Infotec alone. Infotec, with its voracious growth, thousands of jobs. It was Infotec that established a new financial centre in Paris; Infotec that, bit by bit, made it so difficult to undertake a single transaction in French that soon schoolchildren were speaking only English, the global language, the only language that Infotec chose to do business in.

And the company was only ever welcomed because it brought prosperity, brought safety, security. Infotec could see everything, hear everything; now there was nowhere left to hide. And what made it worse was that Frankie had believed in it. She'd swallowed all the bullshit. And so had her father.

She looked at Glen, chewing her lip, like she always did when she was under pressure. 'You really think it didn't happen? I mean, you really think there are people alive in the UK?' she asked as she half walked, half ran after him. She didn't know where they were going; Glen had been incredibly secretive ever since he'd heard from the stranger direct. He'd just announced that they were leaving, that there was somewhere they had to go. Which was fine by her. She didn't care who the stranger spoke to, didn't care if Glen made arrangements without including her.

No skin off her nose at all.

'Infotec are hiding something and we're going to find out what,' he replied. 'Come on. It's going to start getting light soon. We have to hurry.'

'Yeah, but where are we hurrying to?' Frankie asked with a sigh. 'Where exactly are we going?'

'To retrieve something,' Glen said, then he stopped as a message flashed in front of his eyes.

'Okay, she's there,' he said. 'She's in the garage.'

'Who?' Frankie asked, her face creasing with incomprehension. 'Who's there?'

But Glen didn't answer; he just started to walk again, more quickly this time. Frankie ran to catch up with him; she didn't want to be behind anymore. Who was in the garage? What the hell was going on?

They marched across the scrubland, then turned down the path. In front of them were three garages. Glen walked to the last one and reached out to take the handle.

'You wait around the corner. Just in case we've been intercepted. If it's a trap, you run. Don't try and rescue me, just get the hell out, do you hear?'

Frankie considered this, then shook her head and folded her arms. 'I'll go in,' she whispered firmly. 'You wait around the corner. You're more important than me. People depend on you.'

Glen shook his head, but Frankie wasn't taking no for an answer. Pushing him out of the way, she opened the door and stepped inside. Then she frowned, and moved further in. And that's when she saw her. The girl.

'Okay, I don't think it's a trap,' she called out quietly, then walked towards the back of the garage where a small, bedraggled girl was fast asleep on an old tyre. She looked about fifteen; her hair was long, her skin deathly pale, almost other-worldly. Frankie saw Glen hovering at the door and motioned for him to come in. 'Is this who we came here to find?' she asked.

Glen looked at the girl uncertainly, then they both jumped as her eyes opened and she threw herself at them angrily, pushing Frankie to the ground before tearing out of the garage.

Frankie and Glen stared at each other incredulously for a second then Frankie pulled herself up from the ground. 'What the . . .' she muttered, then immediately turned to run after the girl. Glen, as always, was two steps ahead of her, already chasing the girl down. Friend or foe, she'd seen them now, and that meant danger. That meant that the girl wasn't going anywhere.

21

Milo stared at the guard standing in front of him. 'What did you just say?'

His palms were covered in a light layer of sweat and he tugged at his shirt collar, wiped his forehead. The guard had to be mistaken. Had to have made a mistake.

'I said, sir, that no body was found. We were there within minutes of the incident and there was no body, no sign of anything untoward, sir.'

Milo felt a wave of nausea wash over him. Too many people were just disappearing. It wasn't right. 'You went to the wrong place, then,' he said.

'No, sir. We checked. Couple of the lads went up, looked over at the right spot. Could see us below. We were in the right place, sir.'

'Then the wind blew the body further away,' Milo said impatiently. 'She got stuck in a tree. Something.'

'No, sir. There are no trees, sir. We checked a ten-metre radius. No body, sir. No blood, no nothing.'

Milo took a deep breath and started to pace around his desk as he thought rapidly. There had to be a body. He saw her jump. Everyone did. She went right off the roof; there was no way she could have clung on and climbed back up, or down, or some other feat that was only possible in multimedia fiction. She jumped. Ergo, there had to be a body. And he was going to find it. Just like he was going to find Frankie.

'If you are mistaken about this,' he said, a warning note in his voice. 'If you are wrong, then . . .' He didn't finish the sentence; he didn't need to – a veiled threat hung in the air that didn't need spelling out.

'Yes, sir, I understand, sir, that's why I checked myself, several times. That's why we combed the area, sir. There's no body, sir. Categorically, sir.'

Milo nodded wearily. He loved his job. Loved it. Loved the prestige, the power, the money, the perks. He was a someone. He was known by everyone on the globe. He was a superstar. But recently . . . Recently things had got seriously fucked up. Ever since Thomas had brought those weird people back from the UK. From some satellite City that had somehow escaped the nuclear fallout of the Horrors, conducting some weird experiment for Thomas. Milo didn't know the details; he didn't want to. He just knew that ever since they'd got here, things had started to go wrong. And he was sick of it. The sooner that crazy loon's new System was up and running the better.

'Fine,' he said. 'Leave it with me.'

'Leave it with you, sir?'

'Yes. Leave it with me.'

'You mean don't report it further, sir? Don't file any reports, sir?'

'I mean,' Milo said, his voice slow but firm, 'leave it with me. Just walk out of this office and forget about it until I ask you to do otherwise. Do you understand?'

'Yes, sir. Absolutely, sir. Consider it left, sir.'

The guard nodded and disappeared. He would stay quiet, Milo thought with relief. Buy him some time before he had to tell Thomas, before he had to face Thomas's rage, his paranoid, crazed rage that would reverberate around the building and make life miserable for days. Hopefully he wouldn't ever have to tell Thomas. He'd get to the bottom of the situation before Thomas needed to know.

Putting his feet up on his desk, Milo closed his eyes, then he opened them again. Frankie must have had help. Perhaps Evie had, too. If he could find one, perhaps he could find the other. Perhaps this nightmare would come to an end.

'Get me image recovery,' he barked into his chip. 'I want facial recognition throughout Paris, photograph coming through now.'

22

'Evie? Is that your name?'

Evie stared in shock at the girl standing over her. Tall, beautiful, a baggy sweatshirt covering her slender frame, a leather jacket in her hands, dark hair like a boy's. She looked different, but Evie knew who it was immediately, and she felt herself beginning to shake, because Frankie was dead. Which meant that either Evie was seeing things, or that there was a ghost standing in front of her.

'You don't need to be afraid. We're friends. We're here to help.' The man was talking now; Evie regarded him suspiciously. She had run on instinct; had assumed the worst when she'd heard voices, seen two people approaching her. Now, on the ground, the two of them standing over her, she was looking around desperately for something to hit them with.

Frankie crossed her arms across her chest and looked

over at her friend. He shrugged. 'Do you recognise Frankie? She's on the run like you. Infotec tried to kill her. You can trust us.'

Evie stayed silent; she had learned long ago that talking was the easiest way to get into trouble.

'My name is Glen,' the man said. 'Friends of mine helped you escape. Caught you when you jumped off that roof. Drove you here. Are you okay? Are you thirsty?'

He handed her his bottle of water and Evie took it tentatively. He had a nice face.

'Glen,' she said, her voice barely audible. She cleared her throat, drank some water. 'Thank you,' she said, a little louder this time.

'You're very welcome.' He looked at her curiously, his eyes darting away every time she looked back at him. 'Okay,' he said. 'We can't stay out here. Back into the garage until we work out what we're doing next.'

'You don't know what we're doing next?' Frankie asked quizzically, her right eyebrow shooting up. Evie reddened; it was strange seeing her in the flesh, the girl she had watched for hours on the screen, the girl whose intimate secrets she had been party to, whose decisions she had judged, whose every thought had been plastered across the screen for all to see.

Glen ignored Frankie's question; he opened the door to the garage and ushered them inside.

'So, watch my funeral?' Frankie asked her.

Evie shook her head, refusing to admit that she'd watched the whole thing.

Frankie looked slightly taken aback. 'Oh. Right. Well, it wasn't me anyway.'

Evie met her eyes but still said nothing.

Frankie folded her arms. 'So you're from the UK?'

Evie nodded tentatively.

'I thought the UK had been blown to smithereens,' Frankie said. 'I thought it was too radioactive to get close. Guess things aren't always how they seem.'

'No,' Evie said, biting her lip. 'I guess not.'

'You really don't know who I am? I mean, you never watched me?'

Frankie was looking at her curiously, like she couldn't believe anyone wouldn't be riveted watching her day after day. Maybe they had tried to kill her, but it certainly hadn't taught her any humility. Evie's face hardened. 'I'm not that interested in parties and clothes,' she said. 'Where I come from there are more important things to worry about. Like people being murdered. Like Infotec ruining people's lives.'

Frankie stared at her open-mouthed, then her eyebrows lifted in her trademark expression. 'There are important things to worry about here as well,' she said, tartly. 'But that doesn't mean we can't look presentable while we worry about them. Or enjoy ourselves from time to time, something that apparently you know nothing about.'

She looked Evie up and down and wrinkled her nose in distaste; Evie felt her temperature rise and looked the other way. What was Linus thinking sending this airhead to find her? Had he made a huge mistake?

'So,' Glen said, closing the garage door behind them. 'Raffy is a friend of yours?'

Evie frowned. 'How do you know about Raffy?' she asked.

'He's been in touch with us,' Glen said, crouching down on the ground. 'He orchestrated your escape. You're pretty brave, by the way, jumping off the roof like that, trusting us to catch you.'

'It wasn't Raffy; it was Linus,' Evie said immediately. 'And he didn't tell me I'd be caught. He just told me to jump.'

'Off a roof? And you did it?' Frankie asked incredulously.

Evie stared at her. 'Yes,' she said. 'I did it. When you believe in something, when you trust someone . . . He asked me so I did it. Do you have a problem with that?'

Frankie shrugged and looked away.

Glen frowned uncertainly. 'Okay. Well, I'm glad we were there. But listen, Raffy wants us to get you back to the UK. That's why we're here.'

'We're going to the UK?' Frankie turned back immediately. 'Are you serious?'

'It's not Raffy,' Evie said, looking straight at Glen and ignoring Frankie. 'It's Linus. You've got the wrong person. Raffy is the reason we were captured in the first place. Raffy wouldn't help me escape. He wouldn't help me do anything. But of course I want to get back to the UK. Can we really get there?'

Glen pulled a face. 'Hold out your hand.' Evie did as she was told, then cried out as Glen took out a knife and cut her, putting something cold and hard under her skin.

'Sorry about that,' he said. 'But you need one of these.'

'A chip?' Evie whispered. She knew about chips from watching the screens day in, day out.

'Got it in one,' Glen nodded. 'Okay, so now your friend can reach you. Raffy. Linus. Whatever he's called.'

Evie waited, not sure what to do, not sure how the message would reach her. And then there it was, in front of her eyes, words flashing in pinks and blues. 'Are you okay? Are you hurt? I'm so sorry. You couldn't know about Glen, otherwise you'd have jumped differently, Thomas would have known. I'm so sorry, Evie. But you're okay? Tell me you're okay.'

Evie looked around awkwardly, but soon realised that no one else could see the messages. 'I'm fine,' she said out loud, then blushed. 'How do I reply? What do I do?' she asked Glen.

'Open your hands. A keyboard will appear that only you can see,' Glen told her gently, showing her what to do. Evie copied him. It was incredible. It appeared, right in front of her, like it was real. Frankie was smirking at her, but she didn't care. Not anymore. She was going back to the UK. She was going to see Lucas.

'I'm fine,' she said. 'Why did you tell them you were Raffy?'

There was a long pause.

'This is Raffy. Linus is being scrutinised too closely to communicate with anyone except me. Evie, I'm sorry . . .'

But Evie had already closed her eyes, turned away; when the words refused to disappear, she tried shaking her head from side to side.

Glen frowned. 'What's the matter?' he asked.

'Nothing,' Evie said. 'I just . . .'

'Evie, you have to trust me. I'm working with Linus. You have to believe me.'

Evie shook her head again, less violently this time. 'I can't trust you,' she typed.

She looked up at Glen. 'Raffy,' she said. 'It's Raffy.

Not Linus.' Her voice was faltering; this was another of Raffy's tricks. She knew it was. He was playing with her, teasing her. She wasn't going to get to the UK. She had to get out of here.

'That's right,' Glen said. 'Well, I'm glad we cleared that up. So, has he told you the plan?'

'But you don't understand,' Evie said, beginning to shake now. 'You don't understand. If it's Raffy then that changes everything. If it's Raffy . . .' She stood up, ran towards the door, but Glen got there before she could open it.

'Let me go,' she screamed. 'Let me go! I want to go home. I want to get out of this place. You have to let me leave.'

She was banging her hands against the door, kicking her legs, but Glen was too strong for her. 'Evie, you have to listen to me,' he said, his voice low, right next to her ear. 'You're going to the UK. We all are. Your friend Raffy told me that you've got mixed feelings for him, but right now he's on your side. This was all his idea. Frankie's going to film your City. Show the world the truth. Show Thomas up.'

Evie shook her head, but immediately a message appeared in front of her eyes. 'Evie, you have to believe me. You have to trust me. I know this is all my fault. I know that. I've only ever let you down. But right now

I'm doing my best to make it up to you. You're going to the UK. With Frankie. When people see her there, see that she's alive, see that Thomas lied about everything, they'll see what he's like. It'll be over then, Evie. We'll be free. Thomas and the System, they'll be over. I'm so sorry Evie. About everything. But believe me now. Please?'

A huge lump appeared in her throat that felt like it was going to choke her.

'No,' she said, her voice breaking. 'I don't believe it. I don't . . .'

'You should,' Glen said, still holding her. 'We're in this together now. We need to stay focused.'

'No,' Evie said, trying to break free again. Then she stopped, looked at Glen. 'What did Raffy tell you? What did he ask you to do?'

'To catch you when you fell off the roof,' Glen said quietly. 'To have a car waiting. He had it all mapped out. Sounded crazy to me, terrifying in fact, but he'd worked it all out, got the blueprint of the building, the air patterns. He asked me to get you somewhere safe, to come and get you myself and to take you to the UK.'

'How?' Frankie asked, walking over, kicking some mud off her boots. 'How the hell are we supposed to get to the UK? Fly? On which plane exactly? And who's going to stop us being shot down? It's a no-fly zone, remember.'

Glen pulled a face. 'We're not going by plane.'

'Okay,' Frankie said dubiously. 'So how then? Boat? Again, how do you intend to get us past the armed coastguard?'

'I don't know, but Raffy says he has a plan and right now we have to trust him. So far he hasn't let us down. So can I let you go, Evie? Are you going to try and run again?'

Evie shook her head. 'I'm not running,' she said, only half sure she was telling the truth.

'Evie, are you there?' A message flashed through from Raffy. 'Do you believe me? I don't need forgiveness, just to know that you can trust me enough to let me help you. Glen and Frankie are on your side. You can trust them.'

Evie read the words slowly, trying to process what she was being told, trying to reconcile it with everything she knew. 'And what about you, Raffy? Whose side are you on?' she typed into the air.

'Your side.' The reply came back straight away. 'Only ever your side, Evie.'

Evie stared at the words, watched them as they glowed in front of her before gradually evaporating into nothingness.

Like her and Raffy. They had glowed once. They had been everything to each other. But now it was all just empty space.

'Evie?' She realised Glen was talking to her.

'Evie, we have to get going. We've got a long walk ahead of us. Are you okay to leave now?'

Evie stood up. Was she okay to leave? She wasn't sure she was okay to do anything. Everything was terrifying and unbelievable, from the dead Frankie staring at her like she was an idiot, to the words flashing in front of her eyes, to the news that Raffy was behind all of this. She hated Raffy; that was something she knew, something she could hold on to. When he had betrayed them and brought Thomas to Linus's cave, it was as though his transformation from the boy she'd loved back in the City to the man who had proved to be weak, flawed and dangerous was complete. He was a different Raffy, a Raffy she could not look at, would not acknowledge.

But now ... Now Raffy was working with Linus and helping her to escape; he was urging her to get to Lucas. She had seen him laughing with Milo; now was she expected to believe that he had been faking it? Or was he faking this? Was it a trap? A plot?

'You okay, Evie? Tell me you're okay. Glen's a good person. He'll look after you.'

More words flashing in front of her, messages from

Raffy. And it reminded her of when she'd been little, living in the City, and had been sad and afraid; reminded her of the way she'd come to the tree hollow where she and Raffy always met, and would find notes from him, telling her that everything would be okay, telling her that she lit up his life, that she was more precious than the sun, that one day things would be different, that they'd be together, that everyone else would be proved to be wrong and they would be right and . . . and . . .

She closed her eyes. That had been a long time ago. She took a deep breath. 'Sure, let's go.'

'Good,' Glen said, carefully opening the door of the garage and starting to walk.

'So the UK really wasn't blown up?'

They'd been walking in the moonlight for over an hour, mostly in silence, Evie refusing all offers of help to climb walls, cross bridges or scrabble down steep hills. Every time they heard so much as a bird flap their wings they dropped down onto the ground, pressed their faces into the mud and waited; the tension and fear in the air was thick as they followed Raffy's instructions, moving towards whatever lay ahead. Frankie, she couldn't help noticing, was remarkably agile and graceful, her long legs striding purposefully alongside Glen, her expression revealing no fear or trepidation. On film,

Frankie had seemed an inoffensive airhead; in the real world, she was far worse. Cocky, arrogant, she thought she knew everything. But she knew nothing. The worst thing that had happened to her in her whole life was probably breaking a nail.

Glen, on the other hand, seemed okay, as far as Evie could tell. As they'd left the garage he had briefly introduced himself, explaining how he'd been in hiding for years, about how crossing Thomas meant his life was in constant danger, about how he'd made his peace with that and now just wanted the world to know the truth, whatever that was. It felt strange listening to him, realising that he had gone to ground at the same time Lucas's father and Linus had been fighting against the Brother, against the System, against Thomas. They were brothers in arms, kind of, but neither had known the other existed, and now . . .

She realised Glen was waiting for an answer to his question and shook herself. 'No,' she said. 'I mean yes, the Horrors happened but people survived. There's the City, and the Settlement and other places where people have built communities, where people . . .' She felt a lump appear in her throat as she thought about her friends from the Settlement that Thomas had destroyed. Were they still hiding in the mountains? Did they have enough food, enough water? Were they trying to rebuild the Settlement even though they hadn't heard from Benjamin? 'We thought we were the only survivors. In the world, I mean. We were told the rest of the world . . . that it was destroyed.'

'Seriously?' Glen asked, shaking his head. 'Jeez, Thomas really thought it all through, didn't he. And it was all because of this System? Why? What's so special about it?'

'Yeah,' Frankie said, catching up so that she was the other side of Evie. 'What exactly does it do?'

Evie hung back slightly; she didn't want to be quite so close to Frankie. 'The System sees everything.' She shrugged. 'And Linus built it. He wanted it to be a good thing, a System that saw what everyone needed, that made sure everything was fair, that people were happy. But that wasn't what Thomas wanted . . .'

She paused. She didn't have the energy to tell them everything, not right now. It had taken her so long to piece it all together; to understand just what lengths Thomas had gone to, all because he believed that, given the right environment, the right circumstances, Linus would produce the System he had boasted about as a young intern in Thomas's department. Thomas had engineered a series of terrorist attacks that sparked a civil war; had allowed the UK to virtually destroy itself. He had allowed the world to believe that it was a dangerous mound of toxic nuclear waste and enabled the Great Leader to establish a City with Linus. He'd allowed the Great Leader to operate on and brain damage hundreds of people to test his theory on evil. He had ruined so many lives, torn so many families apart, spread so many lies, and all so that Linus could build the System. And now he thought Raffy was rebuilding it for him. Or maybe Raffy really was building it; maybe he was lying to her, Glen and Frankie, just like he'd lied before. Evie didn't know and she didn't have the energy to care. Not really. She just wanted to get home. She just wanted to see Lucas.

She stopped walking, mentally drew herself up, imagining what Lucas would think if he heard her thoughts, imagining his disappointment in her. Of course she cared. She cared deeply. 'He has to be stopped,' she said, softly. 'Thomas has to be stopped because if he isn't . . .'

'If he isn't, then it's very bad news for all of us,' Glen said, grimly.

'So come on,' Frankie said impatiently. 'Tell us how we're going to get there. Because I'm not swimming, if that's the plan.'

Evie glanced at Glen, then at Frankie. 'Raffy hasn't told you about the train tunnel?' she asked. He'd told her about it an hour ago, told her how he'd spent hours studying history pages, learning about the Horrors, or at least what had been written about them, studying maps of Paris, the history of Paris, anything that would help him. He'd been sending her messages every minute; she hadn't replied to most of them.

'Train tunnel?' Frankie asked. 'What are you talking about?'

Glen stopped walking and slapped his forehead. 'Genius!' he said, a smile breaking out on his face. 'Bloody genius! The Eurotunnel. Of course!'

'Eurotunnel?' Frankie stared at him.

'Under the Channel. People used to take the train from Paris to London all the time. I'd forgotten all about it – it was closed before I was born. But I bet it's all still there. So that's where your friend's leading us?'

Evie nodded cautiously. 'Yes, the Eurotunnel,' she said, realising as she spoke that this was real now, that they were actually going back home, to the City, that she was going to see Lucas again. She was shaking, with cold, with fear, with excitement. 'So come on,' she urged the others, upping her pace. 'Come on, we have to be quick.'

Frankie, though, didn't appear to share her enthusiasm; instead, she stopped walking. 'You're kidding me. A tunnel? Under the sea? No way. No sodding way.'

Evie's eyes narrowed. 'Don't come then,' she muttered, shoving her hands in her pockets and walking off. Glen reached out to stop her then turned back to Frankie.

'I thought you said you weren't going to swim?' he said gently. 'Come on, let's keep walking.'

'No,' Frankie said, shaking her head defiantly. 'I don't do tunnels. I don't do underground. There is no way on earth I am going into some old tunnel that goes under the sea. It's the stupidest plan I've ever heard. It's probably fallen in by now anyway. Look, I'm going back. I'll take my chances in Paris.'

'In Paris? You won't last five minutes,' Glen said then, his voice suddenly very serious. 'Frankie, Thomas is looking for you and he will find you. Unless you want to live like I have, underground, always hiding, he'll find you and when he does, he'll kill you.'

Evie could see Frankie's face twist uncomfortably and she tried not to derive pleasure from the fact that the party girl was crumbling under pressure. 'You said you could get me a new identity somewhere. Australia or something. Why can't I do that?'

'Because it's too late for that now,' Glen said. 'If we go back now, Infotec wins, and it will all have been for nothing. If what Raffy and Evie are telling us is true, if we can get proof and get it out there . . . It changes everything. Finally, we'll have something to fight Infotec with.'

He walked over to Frankie and put his hands on her shoulders. 'So, are you coming?'

Frankie looked at him reluctantly, then her eyes moved towards Evie. 'How old are you anyway?' she asked, her tone condescending. 'You're a baby. Is your friend Raffy a baby, too? Are we doing all of this because of some kids?'

'We're nineteen,' Evie said, her eyes narrowing. 'Same age as you,' she added, enjoying for a moment the knowledge that came from following someone's every move.

Frankie looked genuinely surprised. 'Really?' she said. 'Like, seriously?'

Evie glared at her.

'Seriously,' she said, her voice low.

'Huh,' Frankie said. 'Maybe it's because you're so thin.' She exhaled slowly then stared into the middle distance; Evie guessed Frankie was messaging someone. Raffy. She watched as Frankie frowned, then rolled her eyes. Then, slowly, the corners of Frankie's mouth edged upwards.

'What did he say?' Evie asked before she could stop herself. She didn't care. Raffy could message Frankie all he liked. But she didn't like the way Frankie was smiling, like there was some joke that Evie was excluded from.

Frankie raised an eyebrow. 'That would be telling,' she said. 'But let's get moving shall we? I'm cold.'

Evie rolled her eyes and started to walk again, Frankie and Glen at her side, two strangers who knew nothing about the world she'd come from, nothing about Linus, about the Settlement, about Raffy, about Lucas. And yet Frankie dared to smile like she and Raffy had their own little secrets, like she somehow knew more than Evie. When really, until recently she was just one of Thomas's spokespeople, running around worrying about her clothes and make-up, like there was nothing else that mattered in the whole wide world.

'Nearly there,' flashed in front of her eyes. 'I am going to make everything okay. You have to believe me, Evie. You have to believe that I didn't mean any of this . . . I only ever wanted us to be happy . . . And I screwed everything up . . .'
Evie read the message thoughtfully. 'Yeah, you did screw it up,' she messaged back silently, and carried on walking.

Raffy read the message and wondered if he was imagining an element of thawing in Evie's anger, in her utter hatred of him. Then he shook himself. Of course she wasn't thawing.

'You're really nineteen? Kind of young to be ordering us all about aren't you?'

The message from Frankie flashed up suddenly, making him laugh. She was way feistier than he'd thought she'd be, far cleverer, funnier than he'd given her credit for when he'd watched her on Cassandra as she made her way from one social event to another.

'I have a God complex,' he messaged back. 'What you going to do about it?'

As soon as he sent the message he regretted it; she might not get the joke, might take offence, might change her mind and he couldn't afford for that to happen. But within a second another message came back.

'I've already dated a man with a God complex. Not so much. Maybe you should try a new angle?'

Raffy stared at the message. Was she . . . flirting? No. She couldn't be. And anyway, he was doing this for Evie. To get Evie back.

But even so, he found himself smiling.

23

The room had no windows, no screens, no sofas. There was a camera in the corner, its red light flashing intermittently to show that it was recording; on the floor a poor cleaning job had failed to remove the blood-spatter stains from the room's previous occupant. Probably on purpose, Raffy thought to himself.

Linus was smiling at Thomas, knowing how much it would irritate him, knowing how much Thomas still wanted him to appreciate his vision, to be impressed, to congratulate him. Like a child, Raffy thought to himself. Thomas was like a frustrated toddler.

He took a deep breath, forced himself to focus. He couldn't afford to make any mistakes. Not now. He was pretty sure he was here as a witness, nothing more. Thomas wanted him to see how angry he was, wanted Raffy to understand what it meant to cross him. He glanced over at Linus, but Linus was refusing to meet his eyes and for that he was grateful.

'You like the room?' Thomas asked Linus.

Linus nodded. 'It's more honest,' he said. 'If I'm going to be in a prison, I'd rather that it looks like one.'

'Well then you'll really enjoy it here,' Thomas said smoothly, walking over to where Linus and Raffy were sitting on hard chairs, their ankles shackled, their hands tied behind their backs.

Linus refused to let the smile leave his face. 'Benjamin's dead. Evie's dead.'

Raffy swallowed the discomfort bubbling up inside him. Evie wasn't dead, but it didn't stop the words hurting. Because she wasn't safe either. Not yet.

'And now you want to torture us?' Linus continued. 'Was that part of your plan, Thomas? Or is it all falling apart? You must be devastated.'

Thomas reached out and hit Linus across the face. Linus looked him in the eye. 'Feel better now? Make you feel like the big man, hitting a guy tied to a chair? Impressive, Thomas. Really impressive.'

Raffy could see the rage boiling up within Thomas, knew that it wouldn't be long now before he lost control completely. Was that what Linus wanted? To what end? Things were going okay. They should just try and mollify him, surely? Then again, Linus and Thomas had history. Maybe Linus was enjoying this. Maybe this was the whole point.

So long as Thomas only took his anger out on Linus. So long as this didn't go horribly wrong.

'What is it exactly that you want from everyone anyway? Is it fear? Or do you have some twisted notion that people actually like you? That they respect you?' Linus asked, not letting it go.

Raffy saw Thomas's eyes change and Linus laughed. 'That's it, isn't it. Respect. That's what this is all about? You think that by controlling the world that somehow people respect you?'

He shook his head in amazement and Thomas hit him again. Linus was still smiling, even though blood was trickling down his face, around the crevices of his mouth. 'Now that really felt good, didn't it?' he said quietly. 'You should do that again. You won't enjoy it as much as the last couple of times, but it'll still give you great satisfaction, hitting me. The guy with the silver bullet, the guy who refuses to hand it over, the guy who promised so much and has delivered so little. I've been such a disappointment to you, Thomas, I see that now. You had such high hopes; you were so sure I saw the world like you did, that I could be manipulated just like everyone else. And look at me now, an old fool, sitting in a chair, refusing to give you the one thing you've wanted your whole life, making you look weak and stupid even here in the world you've built, a world whose primary aim is to make people respect you. I'd want to hit me if I were in your shoes. Hell, I'd want to do more than that. I'd want to kill me, right here, right now. Show me who's boss. Show me who's in charge here.'

'Shut up! Shut up, will you,' Thomas shrieked, hitting Linus across the face again and again. 'You will stop talking now.'

Raffy wished he would. He was sweating. With fear, he supposed. He wanted to get out of here. He had to focus on Evie. Had to focus on the future. Had to keep telling himself that there was one.

'Or what?' Linus asked gently. 'You'll hit me again? Threaten me? It's a bit late, Thomas. We're kind of already there, aren't we? But you're right. I should stop talking now. I've done enough. Evie's gone, and that's vexing isn't it? Two deaths. It isn't a great record. And you're losing leverage. You're beginning to panic, I expect. And me talking like this is just making it worse, right?'

Thomas stared at him; Raffy could see a vein in his neck throbbing. He looked straight ahead, tried not to shake; Thomas was about to seriously lose it.

Then, suddenly, Thomas's expression changed, became calmer, his eyes glinting almost with triumph.

He leant down so that his face was just inches from Linus's. 'You want me to kill you so that the System will never be built,' he said, his voice thin; it was evidently taking a great deal of effort to control it. 'That's your plan, isn't it? But I won't do it. You will build me the System, Linus. And if you don't, Raffy will. He's smarter than you, Linus. Less idealistic. Fewer scruples.'

He turned to Raffy, who offered him a nervous smile.

'Raffy can't build my System,' Linus said immediately. 'He's trying to copy it, remember it. He doesn't understand its lifeblood. I created the System, and only I can do it again. Only I never will. You know that, don't you?' He swivelled round to look at Raffy.

'You're a disappointment to me, Raffy,' he said, his voice low. 'But you've still got time to think again. Remember what Thomas did to you. He's the reason Evie is dead. Don't give him what he wants. For once in your life do the right thing.' His voice was impassioned, his eyes imploring, but Raffy just glowered at him. It was time. He'd heard his cue.

'I saw you whispering something to Evie,' he growled angrily. 'You made her jump. It was you, all you. Just to prove your point, just to make sure I didn't build your precious System. Well it's not going to work. You're a murderer, Linus. You think you're so good, but you're no better than Thomas. You use people, just like he does. You used Evie. You used Lucas. But you're not using me.'

Linus looked down wearily.

Thomas studied the two of them for a few seconds. 'Hmmm,' he said eventually, walking towards Raffy. 'Is Linus right? Are you incapable of doing what I want you to? Are you?'

Raffy shook his head. 'I can do anything Linus can do,' he lied.

Thomas took a deep breath then exhaled slowly. 'I want to believe you, Raffy, but I fear Linus is right. It's his System. He created it. And I want the genuine article, not a copy, not a knock-off. Then again, Linus, you don't have the work ethic I'm looking for. You've lost your humanity, lost your soul. And, quite frankly, I don't trust you. So here's what we're going to do. You have one week. And after that, if you don't deliver what I want, I will kill every single person in the UK. And make you watch. Watch them writhe in pain. Your brother, Lucas. Your friends Martha and Angel. Stern. Everyone you know and love. They will be told that you are the reason they are dying. And then of course I'll kill you both.'

'You can't do that,' Raffy seethed.

Thomas laughed. 'Oh but I can,' he said lightly. Then

he turned to Linus. 'Since you like it down here, you can stay. I'll have everything you need brought down. Raffy, you will be shown back to the apartment in a few minutes. Good day, gentlemen.'

He swept out of the room; Raffy turned to Linus immediately, glancing as he did so at the walls, wondering where the cameras were hidden, what types they were.

'This is all your fault,' he said, his eyes flashing. 'I hope you rot here.'

'There seem to be no better alternatives open to me,' Linus said, no trace of emotion in his voice.

'Yes, there are,' Raffy said passionately. 'You can build the System, Linus. Can't you see he's won anyway? Build the System. Please, Linus. Please . . .'

Linus pulled a face. 'I thought you can do it on your own with one hand tied behind your back?'

'Maybe I can,' Raffy said, stiffly.

'You know they'll test the System on the shadowframe first. Make sure it works before they let you leave. So don't make any mistakes, if that's what you want.'

Raffy caught his eye for a second, then shrugged. 'I don't make mistakes.'

'I'm glad to hear it,' Linus said, as two men walked into the room, carrying a hood, the same hood that had been shoved over his head roughly an hour before, when he'd been dragged from his desk. Raffy let them untie him and held his head forward for the hood to be pulled down over his face, but not before he'd exchanged one final glance with Linus, a glance that told him everything he needed to know.

He needed to get in touch with Glen, he realised, and he needed to do it quickly.

24

'So what, we're supposed to dig now? This is completely insane.' Frankie was looking at the hard, cold ground and shaking her head in irritation. And Evie didn't like to admit it, but she did have a point. They were standing exactly where Raffy had told them to go, on open, barren land, the wind whistling around them, a few derelict buildings dotted around. They'd walked all day; now it was evening but the dark sky was clear, and a full moon as well as an overhead light lit the area. But whilst they might be above the mystical tunnel, there was no sign of any way into it. None at all. 'This isn't a plan,' Frankie sighed, 'it's a joke. Your friend Raffy is having a laugh.' She shot a look in Evie's direction; Evie ignored her. Her drama queen antics might have got her a zillion Watchers, but this was the real world now and Evie just wasn't interested. She was, however, getting increasingly frustrated with Raffy, who hadn't answered a single message in the past hour, who had brought them here and was now probably laughing at them from inside his stupid cubicle. Would Infotec Inforcers be here in a minute to round them up? Was this all some kind of game to him?

Glen kicked the ground with his heel and looked thoughtful. 'The tunnel is going to be a long way down,' he said. 'If it's been sealed up completely, then . . .' He paced around a bit as though wanting to buy some time. 'It doesn't look great,' he said eventually.

Evie took a deep breath. There was no way on earth she was giving up now. 'If Raffy says we dig, we dig,' she said, looking around for something to dig with. There was nothing. And actually Raffy hadn't said anything about digging. But what else were they going to do? She certainly wasn't going to walk away now. Not when she was so close. Not when she knew that underneath her was a tunnel that could take her to the City, to Lucas. She dropped to her knees and started to scrape at the ground with her fingers. It gave nothing; even as she ripped her fingers to shreds she knew it was pointless, knew that it would achieve nothing. But that didn't matter, because admitting defeat was worse. And so she carried on until eventually Glen joined her, kicking at the ground with his feet. Frankie squatted down and looked at them as though they were mad, which Evie conceded they were, but she didn't care; at least they were doing something.

And then, finally, just as she cut her finger on something hard and metal, words flashed in front of her face. 'Sorry. Been . . . otherwise engaged. So you're there. Great. Go past the building on your left, the warehouse. There's a smaller building behind it with a blue door. You have to break down the door somehow. Behind it are steps . . .'

Evie read the message and stood up, glancing over at Glen, who had evidently received the same message. They looked at each other sheepishly. 'Steps,' Glen said.

'So no more digging?' Frankie asked pointedly, jumping up and walking towards them.

'Let's just find the door, shall we?' Evie retorted. She was sick of Frankie with her arched eyebrows and her way of making out she was so sophisticated and knowing. She knew nothing; she hadn't even realised Infotec was using her.

Evie started to move towards the warehouse, picking up speed as she saw Frankie start to move too. She didn't know why it mattered that she get to the door first; she just knew that it did. And so, when she realised that Frankie was also walking at pace, Evie broke out into a little jog, and before she knew it, she and Frankie were racing past the warehouse, their eyes scanning the horizon for a door, a blue door . . .

They arrived in front of it at the same time. It was easy to spot because whilst around it everything was falling apart, decaying, greying with age, the door was covered in a highly artificial bright blue lacquer; had it not been facing slightly away from them, they'd have seen it the moment they arrived. It was tall and solid with several locks and a handle.

'Found it,' Frankie said triumphantly. 'Come on, Glen.'

'Yes, found it,' Evie said, pulling at the handle, her voice barely disguising the irritation she felt. With Frankie. With Raffy, for making her look stupid.

Glen, apparently doing his best not to notice the hostility between the girls, surveyed the door. Evie and Frankie stepped aside. He kicked it, pulled the handle, rattled it against its locks. Then he frowned. 'Anyone seen a battering ram lying around?' he muttered under his breath.

Evie scanned the horizon. Then, as Glen and Frankie started to kick in tandem, she remembered the metal that had cut her fingers. It was half buried in the ground; a bent piece of metal. Perhaps it was part of something bigger, Evie thought to herself as she ran back and scraped around it, trying to dig it out.

Perhaps it was a tool; she didn't know, didn't care. She just knew that she had to get it out of the ground. Her fingers were bleeding but she ignored the pain; there was nothing to be done about it anyway. She set the end of it free, then stood up and managed to get her toes underneath it, wedging her foot until she had some leverage, then pushing it up. Finally she held it in her hands. It was rusty and heavy, but it was also the right shape to push into the side of a door to break it open. Maybe. Possibly.

She jogged back to where Glen and Frankie were staring mutinously at the door, and moved towards it, pushing the metal between the frame and the door and pulling back. Glen stared at her, then clapped her on the back.

'Brilliant! Where'd you find that?'

'Over there,' Evie said lightly. 'I saw it when I was digging.' She pushed again, tugged at the other end.

'Here, let me help,' Glen said, stepping closer. He helped her wedge one end in further, then they both pressed the other end; Evie heard Glen gasp with exertion. And then, there was a creak. They looked at each other; Glen's eyes were shining. 'Again,' he said, pressing the metal back into the crack. They pushed, pushed again; Evie's cheeks turned pink as she used every ounce of strength in her body. And then another creak, a groan, and the door gave way, revealing rusty locks, a bolt that had collapsed years before.

Beyond the door were steps down, down into darkness, down into the tunnel. Frankie peered in then stepped back. 'Your friend Raffy seriously expects us to go down there?' she said, her voice catching slightly.

'Yes,' Evie said. 'Yes, he does.'

She looked at Glen for corroboration, but instead saw his face fixed into a slight frown, his eyes staring into the middle distance. Another message from Raffy. But none for her. Why? She looked at Glen anxiously. 'What is it? What's wrong?'

Glen looked thoughtful for a moment, then he smiled. 'Nothing's wrong,' he said. 'But I'm not coming with you into the tunnel.'

'Don't be ridiculous. No fricking way. We're not going down there on our own,' Frankie said immediately, staring at him in alarm.

'Yes, you are,' Glen said with a little shrug. 'I have other things to do. And I also need to close this door behind you, make sure there's no trace of us being here.'

Frankie shook her head. 'So what if we get to the bottom of the steps and there's nothing there? We come back up and you've closed the door. So what, we die down there? Like I said, no fricking way.'

Glen smiled patiently. 'The lock's on your side, Frankie, so you'll be able to get out again if you need to. And Raffy says you'll find the tunnel down there. He's been right so far, I think you can trust him.'

'But where are you going?' Evie asked, doing her best to maintain a regular voice, not to let on that her heart was rattling in her chest like one of the trains that used to use this tunnel.

'Doesn't matter. Just an . . . errand,' Glen said.

'Why don't we all do it?' Frankie persisted. 'And then all go through the tunnel?'

'No time,' Glen said firmly. 'You need to get going now. And so do I. Frankie, just think of the end goal. Infotec revealed for what they are. You and I free again. Vindicated. We have to do this. You want to do this. Don't you?'

Frankie met his eye and arched a brow before shrugging. 'Yeah, I guess.'

'Good,' Glen said. 'So look, Raffy says there should be a torch behind the door, on the right.'

He walked through the door, rummaged around and pulled one out. He gave it to Evie.

'Why her?' Frankie asked immediately.

'She's not afraid of tunnels. I figured she'd take the

lead,' Glen said, a little grin playing on his lips. 'Okay, you ready?'

He held out his hand; Frankie clasped it and held it for a few moments. Then he took Evie's hand. She squeezed it back.

'You two take care. And I'll see you soon, okay?'

'Okay.' They both nodded. Then, cautiously, they turned and walked through the door, neither looking at the other as they started to descend the stairs, neither admitting the chilling fear that set in as they heard the door above them creak shut.

Glen looked at the closed door and scratched the back of his head. He was having to put a lot of trust in someone he didn't know, and it didn't come easily to him. But as he stood and surveyed the horizon, the star-lit waste ground on the outskirts of Paris, he knew that he had no choice. He had lived a half-life for too long; it was time for change, time to fight back, properly, not by causing Infotec minor irritation but by blowing the whole thing apart. Or not. And if it was 'not', if Raffy's plan came to nothing, well then at least Glen would know he had tried. He was unlikely to live very long to regret anything anyway.

He took one last look at the door, did what he could to cover their tracks, then ran, not back the way they had come, but north-east, towards Lille. He had to get to a train station, and Paris was too risky. But there were things he had to co-ordinate first.

He ran for an hour, until he got to a bus station; a bus was leaving for Lille in forty minutes. Relieved, he got on, waving his hand over the security bar. This identity chip should last him until he got to Lille, but he would need a different one to get on a train. Frankie would be being hunted, her movements traced historically, and it was only a matter of time before they pieced it all together.

He opened up his web centre and input some code, forcing his way through the system so that he could message someone without being traced. It took him ten minutes; he was cold and tired and his brain wasn't working as quickly as it usually did. But finally he was there.

'I need to get to Sweden,' he wrote. 'I'm planning to get the train from Lille to Copenhagen and then take a boat. I need chips, three at least. And a warm coat would be nice.'

Jim messaged back immediately, just as Glen had known he would. Glen had never made direct contact with the young man before, but he had heard only good things about him and he needed someone he could rely on.

'Sweden?'

'Sweden.'

There was a pause before Jim's next message.

'I'll bring them myself.'

Glen smiled. 'Thank you.'

'I'll be on the train platform in Lille at 6 a.m. Don't leave without me.'

Glen hesitated before replying. He wanted a coat, not company. Perhaps he had chosen Jim too hastily; he was obviously excited, might make a mistake. And he might be under surveillance after Frankie's disappearance. But everyone else was under surveillance too; Paris was in lockdown. All he needed was tickets and a coat. Jim could handle that. Of course he could.

'Try to lay your hands on some thick socks,' he typed eventually, then closed his eyes and allowed himself to snatch a little sleep.

Jim left the library in a hurry. Knowing that he was being watched, he walked in a nonsensical direction, doubling back on himself, walking in circles and finally reaching Haussman Parade. From there, he ducked down into the shopping centre on the corner of Paradise Road and Faubourg Lane, and travelled up in the lift to the top floor, where he bought a ticket for an atrocity of a film, bought himself a large coffee and walked inside.

He never came to places like this; the only cinemas he frequented were the small, independent types that showed old French films, the ones that Infotec hated. But this cinema had one very specific advantage; it had a bathroom with two doors, one leading back into the cinema and one leading out to a staircase.

Sitting at the back of the cinema, he waited until the beginning of the film before slipping his chip out of the fleshy mound beneath his thumb and leaving it carefully on the seat, next to the coke and his coat. Then he ducked down and made his way stealthily towards the men's room; once inside, he put in a new chip, changed his clothes and pulled on a woolly hat, scrunching up his old clothes to dispose of later. Then he ran out of the other door, down the stairs, out of the shopping centre, up towards Fayette Drive, until he got to a camping shop. He replaced his chip again then quickly purchased two heavily padded coats, some thick socks and woolly hats, using preloaded credit, then walked into a party shop, where he made some more purchases. Finally, having ditched the bag of old clothes, he came up onto street level and made his way to the eastern side of North Station, where he had arranged to meet Pierre. Sure enough, Pierre was there in a camera blind spot, cap pulled down over his head, a coffee in his hand. Jim walked towards him, lifting his hand as though checking for messages. Two seconds later, he collided with the coffee, shouted out. Pierre dropped his coffee, grabbed him, shook him, then let him go. Jim walked around to the northern side of the station before checking what was in his hand. Three chips.

He pulled on one of the hats and walked into the station, his eyes glancing furtively around him. The film he'd chosen at the cinema was a long one; his chip was next to the coffee and would stay warm for at least an hour, so it would be automatically scanned for updating purposes. If all was well, no one would question his position for another hour and a half. And by then he'd have met Glen; they'd be on their way to Stockholm. Jim had no idea what Glen was planning to do in Sweden; he couldn't take on the might of Infotec, not even close. But whatever it was, he was going. Glen hadn't asked him and would probably resist, but Jim was sick of Paris, and sick of working the sidelines. He was going to do something meaningful, or he was going to die trying. Either way, he wasn't taking no for an answer.

25

Frankie held onto the rail as she made her way down the stairs and tried to pretend she wasn't grateful that Evie was ahead of her. There was no way Evie should be carrying the torch; the girl was tiny, fragile – she might drop it, and then what? She watched the outline, just visible, of Evie's slender frame as she almost ran down the stairs, apparently not concerned by the darkness, by the fact that they were going to be attempting to cross to a nuclear zone in an undersea tunnel that was probably partly destroyed during the Horrors, was probably full of water, or cracks, at least, which would break open once they started to walk through it . . .

Except it wasn't a nuclear zone, was it? And the Horrors, well, the Horrors hadn't been what she'd been taught they were. Her eyes narrowed as she watched Evie curiously. Had she and this Raffy person really grown up in the UK? In some strange city, cut off from the rest of the world? It seemed so far-fetched, so unlikely. And yet Evie didn't seem the type to lie. She seemed the type to judge, to give nothing away and to generally be incredibly sanctimonious and irritating, but not to make things up. Jesus she was irritating though. She'd been so keen to get into this damned tunnel, virtually skipping down the stairs like there was no danger at all. Frankie was used to being the confident one, the brave one, the rebel, the leader. And now she was following some scrap of a girl who knew nothing about anything, who thought she had the moral upper hand simply because she had grown up on the other side of the Channel, who knew no fear and who was faster than a bloody rat scampering down into the darkness.

'Can you just . . . slow down a bit?' she called out. 'You're going too fast and you've got the torch.'

Evie didn't even turn around; she just shook her head. 'We have to be fast. The tunnel is twenty-three miles long and we're not even at the beginning of it yet,' she said flatly.

Frankie stared at her angrily. 'I can't see what I'm doing,' she called after her. 'Like I said, you've got the torch. If you want to run, at least give the torch to me so I don't break my neck.'

Evie stopped and turned, her expression withering as she looked at Frankie. 'Fine,' she said. 'Take it.'

She handed Frankie the torch, then turned on her heel and started down the stairs again, her feet barely seeming to touch the ground. Frankie followed her, but found that now, holding onto the rail with one hand and the torch with her other hand, her progress was even slower; far from lighting the way and making it easier, the torch was heavy and cumbersome and getting in her way.

'Fine,' she called out. 'You can keep the torch.'

Evie stopped and turned again, a look of impatience on her face. She held out her hand and Frankie handed her the torch, irritation flooding through her. 'You know, I don't have to be doing this,' she said. 'I mean I'm doing this as a favour. It's not my home. Raffy's not *my* boyfriend.'

She arched her eyebrow and watched Evie's face darken.

'Raffy is not my boyfriend either,' she said, hotly, 'and if you don't want to come, don't.'

Frankie sighed. 'Yes, well, I don't exactly have a choice now, do I? I mean we're in the middle of nowhere, Glen's gone, so I'm hardly going to go back up through that blue door and wait for Infotec to come and find me, am I?'

'So then let's get going,' Evie said, no trace of sympathy in her eyes, no indication of gratitude. She was like a robot, Frankie decided. Like a cold, hard, tiny robot. If everyone else in this precious City of hers was like Evie, no wonder Thomas wanted to cut them off from the rest of the world.

'Fine,' Frankie said. 'Just bloody fine. Let's run, shall we? Let's just run under the sea, probably to our deaths. Because hey, what else is there to do? I mean, really, I'm so pleased I'm here with you. So pleased to be appreciated.'

Evie stared at her levelly. 'I didn't ask you to come,' she said. 'Raffy did. I get that you don't want to be here; you just want to be back promoting Infotec and worrying about what dress to wear next. Trouble is, as far as I know, you're supposed to be dead. And dead people can't have millions of Watchers. So stop acting like I've forced you to come with me. I haven't. I just want to get to the City. And I want to get there before your best friends, Infotec, figure out what we're doing. So I'm sorry if I'm rushing. But I don't have the luxury of time. Okay?'

She looked so fierce, her eyes flashing, her jaw set firm, that Frankie was almost full of admiration. But only almost. 'I did not promote Infotec,' she said, icily. 'I was a serious blogger who just happened to be very popular. I'm sorry if you have a problem with that. I guess you don't know what it's like to have loads of people interested in everything you say.'

'No,' Evie said, 'I don't. But that's probably because I don't talk all the time about the minutiae of my life. "Oh, I've broken a nail!" . . . "Oh, my shoes are so pretty!" . . . "Oh, I'm so in love!" Shame about your boyfriend. Wasn't he the one who tried to kill you?'

Frankie stared at Evie in shock, then she reared up and took a step forward. 'Take that back,' she said, her voice low.

'Take what back? You were in such thrall to Infotec you didn't even realise they were using you.'

'Take that back, you sanctimonious bitch,' Frankie seethed. 'You think you're beyond reproach because you grew up in the UK? Well bully for bloody you. If Milo hoodwinked me, then what the hell did Infotec do to you? You say you had no idea the rest of the world even existed. I mean, how pathetic is that? And you dare criticise me. I've met people like you before. Jealous, bitter people who hate me because they can't be like me. Well you know what? I don't care. And I'm not spending another minute with you. I am going back. I don't have to do this. You fight Infotec. If you're so bloody clever, you don't need me to help you.'

She turned and started to climb back up the stairs, taking two at a time.

'And where exactly are you going to go?' Evie demanded. 'Where are you going to hide? You think they won't find you? You think this is only my fight? You're wrong.'

'I'll take my chances,' Frankie called back. 'I think I'd

rather Infotec find me than be stuck in a tunnel with you.'

She continued to climb, doing her best to ignore the pain in her calves. She was fit, usually, but after walking for so long she was tired, hungry, thirsty and physically exhausted. She ached everywhere; her legs in particular were killing her, but she wasn't stopping now. Not until she was as far away from Evie as possible. Not until she . . .

She screamed; her leg, went from underneath her, causing her to stumble then fall, down the stairs; she grasped at the wall, at the rail, but she couldn't steady herself, couldn't stop herself from tumbling further down. To her death, she found herself thinking, desperately. To nothingness, pointlessness, to . . .

She stopped abruptly; looking up, she saw Evie looking down at her. Evie had somehow pinned her shoulders against the wall and her feet against the opposite one, breaking Frankie's fall and stopping her in her tracks. She heard a clatter and looked up in alarm. 'The torch?' she asked.

'The torch,' Evie said.

Frankie tried to move but she couldn't; her leg was trapped underneath her, throbbing with pain.

'What happened?' Evie asked.

Frankie sighed heavily, 'I've hurt my leg. But please don't worry. Just keep on running, I'll be fine.'

'Did it feel like something snapped?' Evie asked.

Frankie shook her head, then realised Evie couldn't see her in the darkness. 'Not snapped,' she said. 'I think I've just pulled a muscle.'

'Okay,' Evie said. 'I'm going to stand up. Are you feeling steady? Hold on to the wall if you need to.'

Frankie did as she was told; Evie lightly stood up and bent over her. 'I'm going to move your leg,' she said, her voice different somehow, gentle, almost tender. 'Okay?'

'Okay,' Frankie said morosely, then yelped in pain as Evie manoeuvred her into a sitting position.

'Can you move this leg?' she asked, patting Frankie's right leg. 'If so, can you move it forward?'

Frankie duly swung it round.

'Okay, and now the other one.' Frankie winced as Evie gently manoeuvred her left leg forward. It hurt like hell, but there was something about the way Evie was touching it, pressing it, that made her not want to cry out. There was nothing rough in her touch; nothing impatient. Instead, she was methodically moving her hands up and down, asking Frankie what hurt, where the pain was, which movements caused it.

Eventually she stopped. 'I think you've sprained your ankle and possibly torn some ligaments around your knee. It's going to hurt. But if we can support it somehow . . .' She paused. 'Are you going to be okay if I go and get the torch?'

'Yeah. Of course,' Frankie said gruffly, not really wanting her to go at all but wanting to admit that fact even less.

'Okay. I'll be back in a minute.'

Frankie barely heard Evie running down the stairs; it was as though she was entirely weightless. She stared after her into the darkness. She felt really alone. More alone than she'd ever felt. There were no messages from people telling her how amazing she was; there was no one cheering her on, admiring her courage. There was no one at all.

Frankie bit her lip and sniffed, doing her best to push back the tears that were pricking at her eyes. She didn't want to be in a bloody tunnel with a sprained ankle. She wanted to be in her apartment, getting ready for a night out, asking people whether to wear blue or green. And yet, even as she longed for the camaraderie of her Watchers, she knew that she didn't want them. Not really. Because they weren't real. Because they'd been just as happy to follow an imposter. Because she might have felt like she had a million friends, but actually, apart from Jim, she'd been pretty much entirely alone; even her boyfriend hadn't given a shit about her.

'Okay, it's still working,' Evie said, arriving back with the torch, shining it on her face and revealing a little smile. 'And I found a few sticks at the bottom of the steps which we can use to support your knee. It's not going to be the best bandage ever, but . . .'

She took off her cardigan, placed the sticks against Frankie's knee and started to wrap. 'I'm going to need your tee-shirt. For your ankle,' she said as she worked.

'That's fine. I've got two on,' Frankie said, quickly taking off her sweatshirt and slipping one over her head.

'You look like you know what you're doing.'

Evie shrugged. 'Not really. I mean, we all had to learn . . . at the Settlement. There wasn't a hospital like there was in the City. There was a doctor, but we all had to learn the basics.'

Frankie absorbed this. 'What was it like?' she asked. 'I mean, what is it like? In the UK, I mean? Is it like here?'

Evie shook her head. 'The City is. A bit. I mean, there are computers and electricity, although it's rationed. And they get food from other settlements because they can't grow enough themselves. They don't tell people that, but . . . There. How does that feel?'

'Good,' Frankie said as Evie surveyed her knee. 'So come on, how about the Settlement? That's the place you lived when you left the City?' The truth was, Frankie had barely listened when Evie was telling Glen about the UK; she'd been too absorbed worrying about tunnels, about the turn her life had taken. But now, now she really wanted to know.

Evie nodded. 'The Settlement . . .' She went misty-eyed. 'It was amazing. It was this wonderful place, started by someone called Benjamin. He was an incredible man. Strong and brave and . . .' She paused, took a breath. 'Everyone was kind and happy. Everyone had enough to eat and they had teachers so you could read books and learn about history and . . .' She met Frankie's eye and reddened. 'But it isn't there anymore. Thomas destroyed it because Benjamin wouldn't hand us over. Everyone's hiding in caves and Benjamin is . . . dead.'

'Oh,' Frankie said. 'Sorry about that.' She wiggled her ankle and looked at Evie incredulously. 'Wow. That feels much better, thank you. Bloody hell. I just . . . it's hard to take in. What you're telling me, I mean.'

Evie pulled a face. 'Discovering that the world hadn't been all blown up was quite hard to take in too,' she said lightly. 'We thought we were the only survivors of the Horrors. We thought we were the lucky ones.'

Frankie breathed out and pulled herself up. 'Thanks, Evie,' she said. 'I mean really. Thanks.'

'It's nothing.' Evie shrugged. 'Do you want to hold on to me?'

'No,' Frankie said, forcing a smile; there were limits to how much charity she could accept from this strange girl. But as she watched Evie walking carefully in front of her, as she hobbled after her, she knew with a sudden conviction that they were truly in this together now;

she and Evie probably needed each other. And if she was quite honest, Evie probably wasn't a bad person to have on her side.

'So if Raffy's not your boyfriend, why were you both taken by Thomas?'

Evie turned sharply; Frankie's initial questioning had turned into a full-fledged interview and Evie wasn't used to sharing information like this. In the City she'd always been too scared to share, too fearful that she'd be judged, that the System would be alerted; in the City no one shared confidences – they buried them, denied them, terrified about the consequences of admitting anything, whether a feeling or a thought, in case it veered from what everyone else thought, what the Brother thought. In the Settlement the women had been friendly and had always chatted as they worked, but Evie had been too shy to join in, still too nervous that she might say the wrong thing or reveal too much.

'We . . .' She frowned, not sure how to answer the question, how to explain her history with Raffy, the complicated twine that bound them so closely together. 'I was matched with his brother, Lucas,' she said eventually. 'But Raffy was in danger in the City. We were . . . very close. So when he had to escape from the City, I went with him.'

'Leaving Lucas behind?' Frankie asked curiously.

Evie bit her lip; just the thought of Lucas made the hairs on the back of her neck stand on end, made her eyes fill with tears. 'We were together. When Thomas found us,' she managed to say. 'But Linus helped him escape. We were all meant to get away, but . . .' She closed her eyes, the painful memory of Raffy rushing forwards to stop her following Lucas as he took the left turning in Linus's cave, the steep drop that led him to freedom, that should have taken her, too . . . She had hated Raffy in that moment, loathed him so much she would have happily killed him if they hadn't been held at gunpoint by Thomas. But now . . . Now she didn't know what she thought about Raffy. 'It didn't work out like that.'

'So now I get why you're in such a hurry,' Frankie said, a little smile on her lips. 'So this Lucas. Is he hot? And how about Raffy? Is he hot, too? I like his sense of humour.'

Evie found herself smiling at the ridiculousness of their conversation. Normally she'd have barked back a sarcastic comment; lives were at stake and Frankie's questions were stupid, infantile. But they were also comforting, friendly. And Evie wanted a friend. She needed one.

'Lucas is . . . beautiful,' she said after a long pause. 'He's strong and he's had to hide who he is for so long . . .' She glanced over at Frankie, whose eyebrow was raised quizzically. 'He's hot.' Evie giggled.

'And Raffy?'

Evie thought for a moment, remembering Raffy the boy she used to meet secretively at night; Raffy the farmer who had proudly worked so hard at the Settlement; Raffy who had risked everything to help her escape. It was weird having someone ask about him. Weird having Frankie ask about him. Like she . . . liked him, or something.

She pulled a face, trying to remind herself that Frankie wasn't being rude, or patronising. In this world, what people looked like mattered a lot. Half the people she'd watched in the apartment spent most of their time in front of mirrors, or describing other people's appearance in great detail. 'I guess he's hot too,' she said, thinking of his dark, soulful eyes, which always seemed to show Evie the thoughts he hid from everyone else; sometimes she warned him to keep them closed in company because it made him too much of an open book. She realised Frankie was waiting for her to say something and bit her lip as she tried to work out how to describe Raffy. 'He's darker,' she said eventually, trying to mimic the language she'd heard on screen, the relaxed way people talked about each other. 'Tall. Kind of brooding.'

'Mmmm,' Frankie said as she hobbled down the last few steps. 'Interesting. Okay, Evie, holder of the torch. Where to now?'

26

Hovering in the shadows, Glen watched the station concourse. There were three or four police people visible, but he had already spotted a further two undercover Infotec guards, their eyes narrowed, focused, as they checked faces, watched the platforms.

Glen looked at his watch. Ten minutes until the train left. Had Jim been detained? Had they linked him and Frankie?

His eyes darted around the concourse, taking in every piece of information available, clocking what people were wearing, who was being watched on the myriad screens, which trains were leaving from which platforms at what times. He had spent years underground and he had learnt how to disappear, how to blend in to the landscape so that no one noticed him, no one remembered him. But he had also learnt that information was power, that you always had to be two or three steps ahead, that looking carefully at any situation would always eventually provide the route out of it.

He rubbed his eyes. It was morning and he hadn't slept. He was cold, colder than he should be, colder than the weather demanded. He knew why: he was hungry. But there was no time to eat, and he couldn't risk a problem with his chip if he tried to buy something. Maybe Jim would bring some food. He hadn't thought to ask.

He looked around furtively, eyeing up each person on the concourse as possible Infotec Inforcers waiting for the right moment to move towards him. He wasn't on any screens, but he knew they were still looking for him. Knew they would never stop looking.

He took a deep breath; tried to calm himself down. But he didn't feel calm. What if the cameras had seen him? What if they had picked him up on the outskirts of Paris with Frankie and Evie? They'd been so careful, changing chips so many times, changing direction, using every trick Glen knew in order to confuse the cameras, in order to throw Infotec off the scent. But what if Infotec had found them anyway? What if they were, right now, opening the entrance to the tunnel, dragging Frankie and Evie out?

He felt a hand on his shoulder and jumped in the air, his heart racing now, ready to run, ready to charge through the station. But the hand held him down, a voice muttered in his ear. 'It's me. Come on, this way.'

Jim linked his arm through Glen's and led him around the concourse, away from the platforms. His face was disfigured, nothing like the images Glen had seen of him. It was impressive; he had disguised himself well. 'Here's your stuff,' he said, thrusting a bag into Glen's hands. 'I'll wait here.'

Glen looked at him uncertainly. 'Wait? You go now. I can't thank you enough, but you should leave.'

'I'm coming with you,' Jim said then, his voice low but firm. 'It's not safe for me here anyway. Quick. The train leaves soon.'

Glen opened his mouth to protest, then realised there was no time and turned instead, keeping his head low as he ducked into the men's, so as not to have the facial recognition cameras spot him. He went into a cubicle, clocked where the cameras were, angled himself away from them and got to work. The silicon slipped on easily and the wig was unobtrusive, thinning on top, realistic. He put on the shirt, flushed, and came out, allowing himself a quick glance in the mirror as he washed his hands. He looked like someone else.

He put his hands in his pockets and wandered out

onto the concourse, more confident now, but his eyes still flickering, still noticing everything. He frowned as he looked around. There was no sign of Jim. No sign at all.

He turned, scanned the platform announcements. Platform 11 for Stockholm. It left in four minutes.

He walked towards Platform 11, up the escalator, towards the gate. But as he walked he felt his head begin to throb. Jim must have been apprehended. He was in danger. And all because Glen had asked for his help. Yet again, because of him, people were in danger, people's lives were being ruined.

No, not because of him, he told himself firmly, ignoring the sweat on his palms, the anger welling up inside him. Because of Infotec. Because of Thomas.

He got to Platform 11, waved his wrist, and felt mild elation as he got through the checkpoint. He upped his pace as he got close to the train, then stopped as he heard footsteps behind him. Footsteps that were getting quicker. Glen braced himself. He would fight. He would run. He would find another route, but he would get to Sweden. He wouldn't let them win, not now, not with so much at stake.

He turned, ready to throw himself at his pursuer, ready to hurl them aside and race away. Instead, he stopped dead.

'I forgot to buy socks,' Jim said, looking at him strangely. 'You know it's minus twenty degrees in Sweden right now? So, shall we get on the train?'

Milo's door opened and Thomas walked in, unannounced, as was usual. But for once Milo struggled to shoot him his trademark smile. Instead, he turned, a little wearily. 'Thomas. What can I do for you?'

Thomas was jumpy; Milo could tell from the way his eyes wouldn't settle, instead wandering around the room; the way he paced around the room instead of standing still. 'Found the body yet?'

Milo shook his head. He'd wanted to keep that particular piece of information to himself, but when all attempts at finding Evie's body had failed, he'd been forced to tell his boss. 'I just don't get it,' he said. 'I can only think someone saw her fall and, for whatever reason, took the body.'

'Took a dead body? From outside the Infotec building? Who would be so stupid?' Thomas rounded on him, his eyes flashing angrily. 'Who would get past our security? Who would be able to move her without being caught on camera? Do you realize how ridiculous you sound?'

Milo did his best to keep his expression neutral. 'Then perhaps she disappeared into a puff of smoke,' he said.

Thomas's eyes narrowed. 'So you're reverting to sarcasm?'

Milo sighed. 'Look, I'm on it,' he said, diplomatically. 'There must be some explanation and I will find it.'

'Good,' Thomas barked. 'And I need some drones to be made available for next week. To travel to the UK. I want anthrax dropped to cover every inch of the land. Do it carefully; none can drift back across the channel.'

Milo frowned. 'Anthrax?'

Thomas nodded dismissively. 'It's something I've been thinking about for a while – the whole thing is a loose end, a vexation. We've kept everyone away with tales of radioactivity, but eventually someone is going to get over there and we can't afford for our dirty little secret to get out. You know how quickly Anthrax kills people? How quickly it covers a large area? It's ingenious, really. Problem solved within twenty-four hours or so. The bodies will decompose eventually and in the meantime, anyone who decides to go and see for themselves will be dead before they can report anything back home.' He smiled. 'I know. I'm brilliant. But we wait a week. If the System hasn't been delivered, I'm going to make Linus and Raffy watch before they are flown over themselves and dropped by parachute. I want them to live long enough to know what's about to happen to them.'

Milo nodded uneasily. Until recently Thomas had kept what Milo called his 'dirty laundry' a secret. The first time he'd confided in Milo was when he'd brought those people over from the UK. Now he talked about killing people pretty much every day and sometimes Milo just wanted to stick his fingers in his ears because this wasn't what he bought into when he got this job. He wanted women, power, money. Not violence, torture and murder. 'Anthrax. Sure.'

'Good,' Thomas said, evidently pleased with himself. 'And find another girlfriend. Someone you can control. The world misses Frankie. We need to find someone new, and fast.'

Milo pulled a face. 'You know she's not actually dead?' he said tentatively. 'I mean, she's still out there, somewhere.'

'She's as good as dead. Forget about her. You need to find someone else, and soon. Understood?'

'Loud and clear,' Milo said, clearing his throat as Thomas headed for the door. 'I'll get on it right away.'

He waited until Thomas was several feet away before turning back to his screen and typing in his code. He had to find Frankie. He had to find her now.

The Swedish outpost of Infotec was positioned in the north of the country, in an area twenty-five miles north-east of the Abisko National Park, far enough away to ensure that no one ever visited, that no one in fact really knew of its existence except for the hundred or so people, including five security guards, who worked there. All the employees had been recruited from Germany or Paris and were shipped up for a year at a time, a rite of passage for ambitious Infotec employees who were sworn to secrecy before leaving. No one knew exactly where they went and, on their return, no one ever breathed a word, but still stories abounded amongst younger employees of a training ground, a central hub, a place where truths were revealed, where the brilliant were able to excel. No one ever admitted on their return, particularly to themselves, that in actual fact they had spent a year being bored out of their minds in the middle of nowhere, monitoring the Infotec mainframe, ensuring that it was backed up every sixty seconds, and nothing more. It was less a rite of passage, they generally realised after a week or so of being there, and more like a penance or test; survive Sweden and your career would be on track. Try to leave, as some poor fools had done, and you'd never be seen or heard of again.

Jim knew all of this although he'd never been to Sweden before; he had written a blog about it years ago, when he was just a boy; had interviewed one brave woman who had just got back and who described a year of misery, of loneliness, or boredom that was eased only by bullying within the ranks, drinking and abuse often bordering on rape.

He'd been naïve back then, stupidly naïve. He'd wanted to be balanced, believed that there was a free press, free speech, just like they were told there was every day, just like they were told that the sharing of information meant that there could be no more lies, no more dark secrets, no more conflict. He'd believed it all, and he'd believed that he could make the world an even better place by shining a torch on things that others might have missed, to make them better, to make everything better.

So he'd gone to Infotec to get their viewpoint. Milo had met him at the Infotec offices. And just like Frankie, Jim had been warmly received, reassured, flattered. He hadn't been flirted with, of course, but instead he'd been offered money for his studies and a job at the end of it. A very nice job that he'd been sorely tempted by. He'd very nearly accepted. Only Milo made a mistake. Or perhaps had simply been arrogant enough to think that he had Jim just where he wanted him. Either way, the woman, Jim's source, had disappeared. Completely and utterly disappeared off the face of the planet, leaving no message, no trace. And she'd disappeared before Jim had accepted the Infotec money. That had been Milo's mistake. Jim had been suspicious, suspicious enough to call Milo on it, to ask more questions, questions that Milo, it turned out, was not interested in answering. The choice was made clear to him: in or out, join us or take the consequences. Without his source, Jim now had no story, as Milo pointed out with a shrug. And anyway, she'd been troubled, mentally unstable; she was receiving treatment. A second mistake: having claimed no knowledge of the source, Milo then started to fabricate a whole web of lies about her mental health, about treatment that he couldn't elaborate on, in a health centre he couldn't name.

Jim never saw the woman again. And he didn't take the money or the job. And now . . . Now he felt like he was coming full circle. Sweden had changed his life, changed his outlook, changed everything. He'd discovered that the 'truth' was whatever Infotec wanted people to believe, that transparency was a myth, that Infotec had the power to ruin lives if it saw fit. He had been a teenager with brilliant prospects but following his last meeting with Milo he was turned down for every degree course he applied for, and every job. He had never found the woman again; his Swedish story had evaporated and enough rumours started to circulate to make people suspicious of him, to not want to get too close to him, to ensure that his watcher numbers were always around the 'embarrassingly low' level.

And so he had slipped into being a second-rate blogger and part-time Infotec saboteur, doing anything and everything he could to help Glen, Sal and anyone else he met along the way. It meant he spent his days always looking over his shoulder, never trusting anyone, sometimes wondering whether he had made a huge mistake all those years ago but generally knowing that he hadn't, that one day he'd get his own back, that one day he'd get his chance to tell the truth – not just about Sweden but about everything he now knew.

And now, that time had come.

Either that, or he and Glen would be caught, tortured and killed.

One of the two.

He guessed it was probably fifty-fifty which way this was going to go.

'So,' he said, a cup of cooling coffee cradled in his hands, leaning forwards so that only Glen could hear him as the train rocketed through Denmark. 'Why exactly are we going to Sweden and what's the plan when we get there?'

27

The journey to Stockholm took fifteen hours on the direct shuttle train. Every time the trolley wheeled towards them, Jim felt his stomach clench in fear; every time the train slowed or, worse, stopped, he braced himself for guards boarding and taking them away. But as the rainy landscape was replaced by snow and the world became more hushed, he felt himself relax, allowed his eyes to gaze out of the window, allowed his breath to become deeper as his head started to nod, and he found his eyes closing . . .

Suddenly he felt Glen tugging at his shoulder. 'We're here,' he whispered.

Jim woke up with a start. It was dark on the train; the few people seated around them were all asleep or trying to be.

'We are?' he whispered back.

Glen nodded and motioned for him to put his coat on. Then he led him out of the carriage to the connecting passageway. The doors, like all shuttle train doors, were sealed shut; they would open only when the controller released the mechanism. But Glen either didn't know that or didn't care.

He moved towards the door, opened a panel and input a code; immediately the red light in the corner turned green and the door slowly slid open. 'Ready to jump?' Glen asked, a little smile playing on his lips.

Jim nodded apprehensively.

Glen winked. 'The snow will break your fall. And you're wearing a nice padded jacket. You'll be fine.'

Before Jim could question his logic, Glen opened the door and held out his hand. Jim took it, and immediately felt himself being hurled out of the train; he heard a thud a few seconds later and realised it was Glen, a few metres away.

Jim, who hadn't had time to put his hood up, felt something trickling down the back of his head; he reached round to feel a gash where he'd hit something hard. He turned to look but it was too dark.

He heard something, felt a light being shone on him. 'You hit a rock? Bad luck,' Glen said, sounding genuinely sorry. 'Let me have a look.' Too shell-shocked to do much else, Jim let Glen peer at the back of his head. 'It's a graze,' he said. 'Here.'

He pressed some snow against it; Jim winced in pain but managed to stay silent.

'We're in Stockholm?'

'Near enough,' Glen said. 'We're better off making our own way from here.'

Jim digested this. 'And the door?' he asked. 'How?'

Glen smiled secretively. 'I kind of banked on them not changing the override code since I designed them,' he said, his eyes twinkling. 'Guess they never thought they needed to.'

'Right,' Jim said, pulling himself up. 'So what else did you design when you were at Infotec?' he asked, trudging after Glen, who had already started to move.

Glen turned round, a little smile playing on his lips. He looked much younger all of a sudden, like he'd suddenly come to life. His face, which had been virtually grey when Jim had seen him for the first time earlier, seemed to glow in the moonlight. Maybe he wasn't the only one who saw this mission as a chance to do something real, Jim realised. Maybe he wasn't the only one who'd been frustrated lately.

'Not much,' he said. 'Just most of the place we're going to. Come on, we've still got a long way to go.'

The snow was knee deep; Jim's trainers were no match for it and so he resigned himself to cold, wet feet and started to follow Jim, his legs doing an odd sort of march that was, he found, the only way to get any kind of pace. Ahead of him, Glen seemed almost oblivious to the environment; he was walking purposefully, quickly, as though the snow didn't even exist.

'Come on,' he called back; Jim did his best to hurry but instead found himself tumbling into a wet blanket of cold. He scrabbled to his feet and started again, cursing his shoes, his trousers, the feeling that he was out of his depth, that he wasn't helping at all.

And then, suddenly, the ground changed; the snow ended and a path appeared. 'And now,' Glen's eyes scanned the horizon, 'just about now . . .' He looked up and down; Jim's eyes followed his gaze, but all he could see was the dark sky shimmering with stars, the white snow surrounding the icy white path they stood on. 'Can you hear that?'

Jim listened; first he heard nothing, and then, then he started to hear it, a rushing sound, some barking, something coming towards them. But what? Who? The sound got louder; Glen grabbed his arm and turned him around so that he could see the sled careering towards them, pulled by four wolves, an old man sitting on it, his face covered by a big, white beard. Father Christmas, Jim found himself thinking. It was Father Christmas coming to their rescue.

The man pulled on the reins and the wolves stopped. 'Glen.' He stood up, shook Glen by the hand. 'It's been a long time. I wasn't even sure it was you. Could be you. I'm glad it was. Glad you're alive.'

'For now,' Glen said grimly, but there was warmth in his eyes. 'Christopher, I want you to meet Jim, a friend of mine.'

Jim held out his hand and felt Christopher's clasp it.

'We'd better get going,' he said then. 'There are only another five hours of darkness and we have a long way to go.'

Glen motioned for Jim to get into the sled, then sat beside him. 'You'll think you're going to fall out,' he warned him. 'But try not to.' He tapped Christopher on the shoulder. 'Is the pass still clear? They haven't closed it?'

Christopher shook his head. 'You'd be surprised how little has changed,' he said with a little shrug. 'They pay us little attention up here. So long as we leave them alone.'

'You're lucky,' Glen said, then gripped the rope in front of him. Jim did likewise and was pleased he had because at that very moment the sled moved off and only by holding on for dear life did he prevent himself from spinning right out of the back.

It was a good ten minutes before Jim trusted himself to speak. 'Who . . . is this guy?' he managed to shout eventually, his voice almost disappearing in the wind rushing past.

Glen turned to face him. 'A friend,' he said.

Jim raised an eyebrow. 'I get that,' he shouted. 'But who is he? How is he a friend? How did he know to come and get us just now? Where did he come from?'

He saw a little twinkle in Glen's eyes and realised how much the man he'd revered was enjoying this. He had only ever known Glen as a shadowy figure, too important to meet, the guy running the show, the guy who knew everyone, knew everything. He could arrange for people to disappear; he always seemed to know what Infotec were planning next. But Jim had never thought of him as a person, as someone who might get frustrated, who maybe wanted to get out more, who missed living in the open air. The man next to him was no longer a man of mystique; he was a man, a man who was looking at him now, his eyes suddenly deadly serious.

'Christopher was one of the builders of the site,' Glen shouted over the noise of the sled. 'He led the crew; he knew the terrain, knew what was possible and what wasn't. But Infotec reneged on its promise to him. It paid him half of what he was owed. To my shame, I believed head office when it told me there were discrepancies, that Christopher had lied. I refused to listen to him. But when

I realised the truth about Infotec, realised what was going to happen to me, I tracked him down and apologised. And paid him what he was due. He said to let him know if I ever needed him. And now . . . Now, we need him.'

He told the story matter of factly, with little drama, but Jim could see that Glen's misplaced trust in Infotec agitated him still; he realised that his determination to bring Infotec down was personal as well as ideological. It had used him; it made him a lesser man.

'And the path you talked about?' he asked Glen.

'It was the path the builders used to pull equipment in. More dependable than the roads. Hidden from view every time it snows, but it's been kept operational just in case.'

Jim considered this. 'You were here how long ago?' he asked.

'Ten years.'

'And whose idea was it to keep the path operational? Why? What for?'

Glen smiled again, looking suddenly boyish, pleased with himself. 'Because you never know,' he shouted, a little glint in his eye. 'Because when I left this place, Christopher and I promised ourselves that one day . . .'

'One day?' Jim asked when he realised Glen had stopped talking. But he didn't get an answer; Glen was staring at his hand.

'They're searching for you,' he said to Jim grimly. 'They know you were at the station. It's not going to take them long to put two and two together.'

Jim's heart skipped a beat. 'So?'

'So we'd better get there quickly and not screw up,' Glen said, his face suddenly grim as he turned to Christopher and the dogs.

It was her. Milo squinted at the grainy image. Dark, cropped hair – that had to be a wig. And she looked pale. But it was definitely her.

He'd come to a dead end at first; had seen her running down the street, meeting her friend Jim, walking with him, then leaving him outside a café and walking off. And it had made no sense, none at all. He couldn't trace any messages between them, couldn't work out how she had even arranged to meet him, unless perhaps she'd arranged it before, earlier that day, not knowing what was going to happen. But after, after she'd left him, she seemed to disappear.

The chip she'd had in was found in some other girl's bag; Milo had smiled at that, at her cleverness; few people knew that Infotec kept tabs on each and every person through their chip, that chips stored every message, every journey; that they communicated everyone's co-ordinates 24/7. People didn't need to know; they only cared that it opened up the latest technology to them, enabled them to type messages in the air, update their status and communicate with their Watchers on a constant basis. But how had Frankie known to be so clever? Where had she got the other chips? And how had she disappeared off the radar in the most-watched city in the world?

He'd been stumped. And then he'd extended his search. Twenty miles outside Paris. And that's when he'd found her. With her new cropped hair. With two other people.

And that's when he'd known that things had moved to a whole new level. Because they weren't just people that she was with. One was dead, for starters. And the other one was the most wanted man on the planet.

He watched the grainy film, watched them making their way towards a disused industrial site. A place that could mean only one thing.

He closed his eyes. None of this made any sense at all. This was Frankie. Frankie the party girl. Frankie his girlfriend. She was spirited, yes; she liked to think that she had important things to say. But she wasn't this person. What could have induced her to hook up with terrorists? With people who wanted to bring everything that Infotec had worked so hard for crashing down? Who wanted to destroy the peace and security that made the world a great place to live?

He sat back against his chair, his mind whirring. Why had she run?

How had she run? There were two Inforcers with her, and she was strong for a girl but not so strong she could see off two athletic men.

What had happened after he'd lost sight of her in her apartment, after the replacement Frankie had taken her chip to teach her a lesson?

Milo leant forward, but before he could do anything a message flashed up. 'Drones ready to depart in six days' time 0800 hours. Please message back to confirm.'

Milo read it several times, then looked at the images of Frankie, at the industrial site. He knew exactly what it was. Knew exactly what Frankie and her new friends were planning to do, where they were planning to go.

In some ways it made everything cleaner. In some ways it was better like this.

He closed his eyes. Thomas was right; Frankie was replaceable. Everyone was replaceable. People were nothing nowadays; they were vessels of technology, mini-robots who could be manipulated, led, told what to do. Hadn't he done exactly that with Frankie? Told her how to dress, how to act; told her how to be seen, how to work her Watchers? She was his creation, nothing more. He could do the same with anyone else, any time he chose.

He looked back at the screen. Except she didn't. She didn't do what he told her to. She wouldn't let him control her. Not completely. That's what had always made her so attractive to him; her independence, the spark in her eye.

And that's what had led to her downfall.

It was kind of ironic.

He took a deep breath. He had to do this; had to stop thinking. There was nothing to think about. Nothing at all.

'Confirm,' he wrote back, waited a couple of seconds, then pressed send. Then, heavily, he walked away from his desk.

They travelled the rest of the way in silence. As they hurtled through the snow, Glen remembered the first time he'd come to this beautiful land, the first time he'd seen this huge, exposed landscape and wondered what he was doing here, wondered why they had chosen such a remote place for such a complex build. It had been Thomas's idea, of course; everything was Thomas's idea. First he cleared the land, closing the national park, putting up signs warning of contamination, moving those who lived nearby to apartments in Stockholm, just as he had moved whole swathes of people from other remote areas of the world. For safety, he told them; for security. And if there were protests, Glen saw little of them. But then the work had commenced and it had become clear that the builders brought over from Paris were out of their depth here, where snow fell daily, where temperatures dipped to minus twenty-two, where morning sometimes failed to arrive. And so a group of local men were brought back to work, to build this place that would house the mainframe, the centre of everything that Thomas had created. Here, in the cold snow, the mainframe would whirr, watch, control; here no one would know.

And Glen had been happy that they had this secret place; had thought how great it was to have something so important so tucked away. Here, in the peace and silence of northern Sweden, he would help to keep the world safe.

He took a deep breath; they were nearly there. The wind was beginning to howl around them; a storm was coming. He knew that inside the Infotec building, Protocol 23 would be being followed: windows checked, doors checked, the water butts checked, drains cleared. If it was a bad storm, the windows may not open for days.

Well, all except one.

The wolves began to slow; Glen turned to look at Jim. He was staring straight ahead, clinging on for dear life. Did he know what danger lay ahead? Perhaps he did, perhaps he didn't. It made no odds either way, Glen told himself. He had learned himself that knowledge isn't always power; that knowledge can instil paralysing fear. Sometimes it was better to go boldly into the unknown. He had lived with fear for too long; now, he wanted to stop fearing what lay around the corner.

He leant forward and grabbed Christopher's shoulder. 'Thank you,' he said. 'You're a good man.'

'I'll be waiting for you,' Christopher said. 'I'll wait a day, no more. The snow will be too high.'

'We'll be there.' Glen patted Jim on the back and motioned for him to get out of the sled; he caught him as his legs wobbled. 'We have to walk now,' he said. 'About an hour. You up to it? You can stay with Christopher if you'd prefer?'

Jim looked at him angrily. 'I'm coming,' he said, his jaw setting firmly. 'Of course I'm bloody coming.'

Glen grinned. 'Glad to hear it,' he said, accepting a plastic bottle from Christopher and filling it with snow. 'Put this under your coat so it melts,' he said to Jim, taking another and doing the same. 'Easy to get dehydrated, and eating snow just gets you colder.'

He gave Christopher one final nod then watched as the wolves turned and the sled sped away.

'So,' he said to Jim. 'Are you ready to change the world?'

28

'So tell me more about Lucas.'

Evie looked at Frankie uncertainly.

'Come on,' Frankie said, rolling her eyes. 'We're stuck miles below the sea in this disgusting tunnel full of rats and God knows what else. I've told you about Milo. You tell me about this person you're so crazy about. So far I know that he's beautiful and good and noble. It's not much to work on. What does he do with his spare time? What kind of things do you two do together?'

Evie cleared her throat. Lucas. She didn't even know where to begin, didn't know how to explain, how to describe him, who he was, how she felt about him. Frankie seemed to find it so easy to talk; she'd been talking for the past hour, telling Evie all about how she'd met Milo, how she thought she'd been streetwise, how she'd been totally suckered in by his charm. And that wasn't all she'd told her; Evie knew pretty much everything about Frankie's childhood, her ambitions to be a successful blogger, the constant tug between getting high Watcher numbers and writing about stuff she believed in . . . Evie had felt her ears burning at times, so unused to listening to such intimate details of someone else's life. And now Frankie was expecting her to reciprocate. And she had no idea how to even begin. The truth was that they had shared such precious little time together. 'Lucas,' she said, desperately trying to conjure up the light tone with which Frankie had revealed her innermost secrets and failing miserably. There was nothing light about Lucas, about her feelings for him. She couldn't encapsulate her childhood in an anecdote with an arched eyebrow and wry laugh. She had buried her stories deep inside herself; occasionally she would take them out to carefully look at them, consider them, feel the pain of remembering, before forcing them back to where they belonged: hidden, suppressed. 'He's . . .'

And then she stopped. In front of her the tunnel appeared to stop dead; she shone her torch up and down but it was entirely blocked. She turned to Frankie. 'This doesn't look good.'

'You're telling me,' Frankie said, her voice low. They both moved forwards and felt the wall in front of them. 'Mud,' Frankie said. 'It's damp. Do you think that means the tunnel has collapsed?'

Evie didn't say anything; a lump had appeared in her throat, because they were so close, because Lucas was so close, because she was not giving up now, not walking away, no way.

She moved slowly along the wall, painstakingly feeling every inch that she could reach, from one side of the tunnel to the next. The wall wasn't really a wall; it felt, like Frankie had suggested, like the roof of the tunnel had collapsed; the wall was curved, uneven. And utterly dense. She examined it for about fifteen minutes, looking for openings, for gaps, for areas of weakness but there were none.

Frankie was sitting on a rock, watching her. 'Evie, we're screwed,' she said with a sigh.

Evie felt her chest clench with anger. 'We can dig our way through it,' she muttered.

Frankie looked at her incredulously. 'You're joking, aren't you?' she asked, standing up and walking towards her.

Evie shook her head.

'You want to dig through mud that has probably collapsed in from the sea? Mud that is quite possibly the only thing stopping water from flooding into the tunnel and drowning us both? Sorry Evie but there's no way. We're turning back.'

'No,' Evie said sharply. 'We're not. I'm not anyway.

We're an hour from the UK. About that anyway. We're going to keep going.'

'How?' Frankie retorted. She patted the wall, kicked it. 'How, exactly?'

'I don't know,' Evie said mutinously. 'But there has to be a way. We have to find a way.'

'Good luck with that,' Frankie said, her eyebrow shooting up, to Evie's irritation.

'You turn back,' Evie said, glaring at her. 'You turn back and you hide from Infotec, run from them for the rest of your life. You're welcome to it if that's what you want. But I'm going to the City.'

'You mean you're going to die trying to dig your way through wet mud,' Frankie said drily.

'I mean I'm not giving up,' Evie said through gritted teeth, starting to claw at the mud frantically.

Frankie stood watching her; Evie suspected she was laughing inwardly but she didn't care. She didn't care about Frankie and her worries about whether writing about parties was affecting her integrity as a blogger. Frankie didn't know what it meant to feel a hopeless cavern of pain open up inside her. She had never really known loss. Even when Milo had tried to kill her she'd been helped. She knew nothing of fear, nothing of heartbreak, nothing of love. And nothing of Lucas.

'Okay, well I'm going back,' Frankie said eventually.

'I admire you, Evie. I admire your determination and your strength, and I'm really grateful for this bandage you made me. But there is no way either one of us is getting through that. We need help. Or an alternative route. I'm going back to Paris. If I can't find Glen I'll go to Sal; maybe he'll have an idea.'

Evie ignored her; she didn't know who Sal was and she didn't care either. She just knew she wasn't going to give up. Not now. Not when she was so close. Lucas had never given up. Never.

She dug her hands into the mud, took out a handful and threw it on the ground. Then she dug her hands in again. It was slimey and slippery; the more she removed, the more she realised how futile the exercise was because more mud would just slip downwards into the hole she had created. But she didn't care; she was going to get through the wall or she was going to die trying. There was no going back. There was no alternative.

'Last chance, Evie. Please come with me. You've got to know when you've been beaten. And we've been beaten.'

'No we haven't,' Evie growled.

'Suit yourself.' Frankie shrugged and began to walk away, hobbling slightly. Evie watched her for a few seconds, then turned back. Desperately she dug into the mud with her arms, yelling with the exertion of pulling it out; within twenty minutes she was caked in the stuff, her face, her clothes all covered; it was in her nose, in her throat, threatening to choke her when she didn't spit it out quickly enough. And then, suddenly, she felt something. Or rather, she felt nothing. A gap. Behind the mud. She felt air.

Frantically, she dug; her arms were aching but she barely noticed as she clawed her way through, made a hole big enough to climb through before yet more mud sank into it, shouting into the space, hearing an echo, feeling her head spin as she realised that it was big, that the wall wasn't impenetrable after all. She pulled herself up, through the hole, into the space. And then her mouth fell open because it was vast, like an ocean, the bottom filled with water; it looked like the tunnel continued on the other side but it was maybe twenty metres away. She tried to grip the wall behind her, but there was just wet, slippery mud. Instead, she turned around and slowly lowered herself down into the water. It would be shallow; it was only a metre or so above the bottom level of the tunnel. She could wade through it. She would have to wade through it. Holding onto the ledge, she felt her right foot enter the icy water; then, taking a deep breath, she let go and let herself fall. The water was so cold it made her gasp, but seconds later she was doing more than gasping. The water was deep. She couldn't feel the bottom. She was sinking, her legs kicking frantically, her arms moving wildly as she desperately tried to get to the surface, to get oxygen in her lungs. She opened her mouth to cry out but instead filled her lungs with water; she could no longer see the surface as her arms and legs thrashed pointlessly, as she realised with excruciating pain that she was drowning.

She closed her eyes, wondering frantically if Lucas would ever know that she had tried, if he would ever find her body. And then, suddenly, she felt a tug; she was moving quickly through the water. And then she felt air on her face, she gasped as more water filled her lungs. Then pressure on her chest, an arm throttling her, forcing the water upwards, out of her mouth. She couldn't see, could barely hear.

'Lie on your back,' she heard a watery voice say. 'Stop bloody moving will you? Lie on your back and let me pull you.'

Evie did as she was told, felt herself gliding across the water. And then they stopped. Evie was pushed up onto a moist surface, put on her side. She heaved, threw up, gasped, then lay still. They were on a kind of muddy platform; below her was a large pool of water; she could see the thick wall of mud that she had pushed herself through. She turned her head; the tunnel continued from where they were lying; a few feet away she could see the ground was dryer, the roof higher.

'Well I guess I was right about you wanting to die trying,' the voice said, a few minutes later. Evie opened her eyes to see Frankie leaning over her.

'You came back,' she managed to say.

'Yes, I came back,' Frankie said, shaking her head. 'Jesus, Evie, what were you thinking? Can't you swim?'

Evie shook her head.

'But you thought you'd just jump into this cesspit anyway? I watched you; I thought you'd seen me. But you just hurled yourself into the water. And then you started thrashing. Gave me a bloody heart attack. And it's freezing too.'

Evie pulled herself up; she could see Frankie now, beside her, shivering; her own flesh was white, covered in goosebumps.

'Cleaned off the mud, I guess,' Frankie continued, pulling her knees into her chest. 'But we're going to get hypothermia if we don't get moving soon. You okay to walk? Looks like the tunnel got compressed or something. It looks okay from here.'

Evie nodded, pulled herself up. 'Thank you,' she said. 'You saved my life.'

'Yeah, whatever,' Frankie sighed, her teeth chattering as she spoke. 'So we'll take it easy, okay? Shit I'm cold.'

Evie nodded. Her head was spinning, her body felt like it wasn't hers and her throat and chest felt as though they had been stamped on. But she pulled herself up. 'Ready,' she said. 'Come on, let's go.'

Frankie stared after the mad scrap of a girl who was running into the distance, a dot of crazy energy, and found herself hotfooting it after her. And as she ran, she found herself trying to fathom how someone so tiny, someone who must be as hungry and thirsty as she was, could find the energy to run so fast, could find the determination not to give up. And it dawned upon her that she no longer pitied Evie, was no longer quite so irritated by her. She realised that her overwhelming feeling was one of respect. Because there was no way Frankie would have jumped into that pool of water of her own accord. No way she would have pushed herself through a wall of mud. Particularly with no one watching her, no one cheering her on, no one to tell her how amazing she was afterwards.

Frankie had only come back because she'd realised she'd never get up the steps on her own; had hoped that she would find Evie broken and dejected, ready to turn back. And instead she'd watched her jumping into the water; had realised immediately that she couldn't even swim. And it was only the realisation that Evie was going to drown that had propelled Frankie to dive in, to drag Evie to the surface, to somehow get them both to the other side. She'd never have done it on her own, not for anything.

And as soon as they were over the water, even though Evie had just almost died, she'd been up immediately, looking for the way back to the tunnel, her body juddering with the cold, her lips blue but her eyes steadfast. And it made Frankie want to know what was on the other side of that tunnel, made her want to see it for herself if it was the last thing she did. Because she had never felt like that about a place, about a person, about anything. And it made her feel like it had been her, not Evie, who had been living in the shadows. It made her feel like she was finally living.

And as she ran, she felt a kind of euphoria rush through her, because it was actually going to happen. They were going to go to the UK. They were going to do something incredible, something that would have repercussions for years to come. She was finally going to make a difference. A real one.

She was finally going to make herself proud.

'Wait,' she called after Evie. 'Wait up.'

'No,' yelled Evie, her voice more high-pitched than usual. 'Look, there's light. Ahead!'

Frankie forced herself forward, ignoring the pain in her ankle. And then her face broke into an excited smile. Because Evie was right. They were just fragments, but there was sunlight. Sunlight ahead. They were in the UK. They were so close. They had done it.

'You're amazing,' she shouted. 'You know that, don't you?'

Evie stopped and turned, her expression one of surprise, then she grinned, her mouth stretching from one side of her face to the other. 'Take my hand,' she called to Frankie. 'Let's get out of here together.'

29

The Infotec mainframe was housed in a large, squat building in the middle of what looked to Jim like army barracks, a huge sprawling mass of small, low buildings. Not that he had first-hand experience of army barracks; there was no need for an army now that the world was peaceful, now that criminals and terrorists were unable to cause problems, unable to spark unrest, unable to unbalance the status quo. But he had seen images; everyone had. They learned about war in school; they read Wilfred Owen, saw pictures of bodies brought back from Afghanistan, listened to the first-hand experiences of those who had lived through the Horrors, those who had managed to escape in time. Everyone knew these things; everyone knew what a violent, angry world people used to live in, a world full of hate, jealousy, anger and revenge.

Jim didn't know exactly when it was that he started to

question it all. He couldn't ever remember being entirely convinced; he could picture himself, aged eleven, putting his hand up, asking questions that his teacher brushed aside, questions about whether anger sometimes had a place, about whether terrorists were always on the wrong side. The mantra was that the world was now a safe, good place, and no one would tell him any different. Even though there were countries where Infotec offices were attacked over and over, where governments used surveillance not to maintain peace but to track down and murder current and former dissidents, their price for allowing Infotec into their countries. In other countries, resistance to adopting English as the national language ran high, and across the world bloggers wrote of their disgust at their freedoms being curtailed, before their words were wiped clean by the Infotec filter.

And now, now he was in the midst of the Infotec power base. Now he was looking at the control centre, the mainframe, the place where all the information was held, ordered, stored.

At least, he was close to being in the midst. Actually, he was just outside it, in a bunker, surrounded by snow. But every time he peeked out, he felt the same sense of awe, of hatred, of fear.

'Right,' Glen said, sitting down in the bunker and furiously typing into the air. 'We go in at 2000 hours.

That's in twenty minutes. That's when the rubbish trucks leave through the north gate. That's our chance.'

'And the north gate is . . .'

'Directly in front of us,' Glen said.

Jim nodded slowly. 'Okay,' he said. 'Just one other thing.'

'Yes?' Glen looked at him impatiently.

'What exactly are we going to do once we're inside? I mean, what is this mission all about exactly?'

Glen looked at him for a few seconds, then his face crinkled into a smile. 'I haven't told you yet?' he asked.

Jim shook his head. 'Not so much,' he said wryly. 'And that's fine, I mean, you know, need to know basis and all that. But bearing in mind we're going into the centre of Infotec's power base in twenty minutes, it would be kind of helpful to know why.'

Glen laughed softly. 'I'm sorry,' he said. 'You're right. Okay. So this place houses the mainframe, the centre point of all the information that passes through the Infotec System. Which is basically everything: every message, every image, every movement of every chip. It's all here, stored for three years, longer if your chip is of interest to them. Or rather, if you are.'

'Yeeees,' Jim said uncertainly. 'I know all that.'

'Okay,' Glen said. 'But you may not know that there's also a shadow mainframe. It copies everything on the real mainframe, is exactly the same, and acts as a back-up in case anything goes wrong with the mainframe. Not that anything ever goes wrong, but it's there if any maintenance work has to be done or any changes are made.'

Jim frowned. 'So?' he said.

'So our job is to flick a switch,' Glen said with a little shrug. 'From one to the other. Simple as that.'

'Just flick a switch?' Jim asked.

Glen nodded. 'Exactly. It just happens to be a switch that is guarded night and day, behind several electronically locked doors in the bowels of the building,' he said lightly.

Jim contemplated this. 'Right,' he said eventually. 'So we sneak in, past the security, through the locked doors, and we flick a switch. And that's it?'

'Not quite,' Glen said.

'Not quite?' Jim stared at him uncertainly. 'What else do we have to do?'

'We have to flick it back again when we're asked to. Then we have to wait for a signal, and then we have to do a bit of . . . deconstruction work.'

'We have to stay there?' Jim felt his blood run cold. 'How? Everyone in the building will be after our blood.'

'Only if they know we're there,' Glen said, wrapping his arms around himself.

Jim did likewise, trying to digest what Glen had just

said; he had more questions, so many more questions, but already Glen was staring into the middle distance, messaging someone. Who? Jim wondered. This Raffy guy? Christopher perhaps? Someone else entirely? Jim had always known that Glen had secrets, had contacts; he had survived, after all, in the middle of Paris with Infotec Informers all around. He had helped countless Infotec targets to leave the country with new identities; had established a worldwide network of unbelievers, of rebels, of dissenters. But until now he had always been a shadowy figure; until now he had rarely been seen by anyone, his power all in information. And it was a suitable weapon, Jim figured, seeing that he was up against Infotec, whose entire power base was forged from the same thing. To see him now, though, crouched down in the snow, planning such an audacious act . . . Jim found himself staring at Glen partly in awe. But he was also staring at him in fear. Because what Glen wanted them to do, what he was planning . . . It was suicide, plain and simple. And he didn't even look worried about it.

Jim, on the other hand, was worried. Very worried. Scared, even. Terrified. His heart was pumping, his palms were hot and his thoughts were full of excuses, reasons he had to leave, explanations he could offer up to Glen for why he'd love to stay but actually couldn't because of a previous engagement that had completely slipped his mind. He was a blogger. He was a cynic. He didn't like to be told what to do; he didn't like Infotec's bully-boy tactics and he didn't believe everything they told him, particularly since their version of history made them the ultimate good guys. He enjoyed existing slightly outside the centre, looking in, finding fault; if he was honest, he enjoyed the thought of being on Infotec's watch list because it made him feel important, made him feel like there was a point to him.

But he wasn't a hero. He wasn't a soldier, or a terrorist, or anything like that. He didn't want to die. Didn't want to be tortured, to feel pain. He really, really didn't.

He looked around nervously. He was sweating in spite of the cold; could feel beads of the stuff dripping down his chest. He wasn't cut out for this. He was going to get dehydrated. Dehydrated, then tortured, then killed. He'd been stupid for coming. He should have just done what Glen asked him to. He should have walked away. He should have . . .

'Ready?' Glen asked.

Jim looked up at him, finding it hard to focus.

Glen took a step towards him. 'Everything okay? You don't have to come if you don't want to. You can wait here. If I don't make it back I'll ask Christopher to come for you tomorrow. What do you say?'

Jim pulled himself up. His mind was whirring, incoherent, his body was hot yet frozen, his limbs barely able to move. And he could stay here. He should stay here. He was no use to anyone. Not really.

'Jim?' Glen asked. 'Look, I have to go. But thank you. For coming. For helping. And I'll see you afterwards, okay?'

He started to trudge off; Jim watched him a few seconds, then stood up. Afterwards? Sod that. 'Wait,' he shouted, forcing his legs to walk. None of his blogs had changed the world; none of them had changed anything. Nothing he'd ever done had ever meant anything significant to anyone; he didn't even have a girlfriend. Or a boyfriend. He wasn't even sure which one he wanted.

But now, now it probably didn't matter. Because what he was about to do . . . well, it might change things. It might change them a lot. And if it didn't, if he was shot or electrocuted before managing to do a single thing, then he wouldn't be around to have any regrets, so what did it matter?

Glen had turned around, was looking at him quizzically.

'I'm coming,' Jim called out, trying to ignore the nausea washing over him, trying to forget that he really wasn't cut out for this kind of thing. 'Wouldn't miss it. Lead the way, Glen. Lead the way.'

30

'Your cortisol levels are high. Would you like me to play some soothing music?'

Raffy nodded distractedly; his cortisol levels were high because he was more strung out than a tightrope; he could barely sit still, couldn't stop his mind from turning a thousand images over and over in his head, of Evie, of Lucas, of Benjamin killing himself, of Martha, Angel, of the System he and Linus had painstakingly destroyed. A lifetime ago. In a different world.

He'd been so naïve.

He'd been so stupid.

And then, suddenly, it was there, in front of him, the message he'd been waiting fifteen hours for, the message he'd half thought he'd never receive. 'The System is ready.'

Raffy stared at the coded message in front of him for a few seconds before feeling able to reply. 'Ready?' he typed back. 'Are you sure?'

'Finished,' came back straight away. 'You can check it, but I know it works. Tell Thomas he's got what he wanted.'

Raffy nodded and, his body pumping with adrenaline, he typed a message to Thomas, copying in Milo, telling them the news. It was starting. It was happening. And if it worked . . . If it didn't . . .

Thomas replied seconds later. 'I'm on my way. If this is some kind of game, you will regret it.'

'No games. You want it, you've got it,' Raffy replied.

'Thanks, Cassandra,' he said, turning off the music, his mind trying to process what was happening. 'Maybe later, okay?'

'Your cortisol levels . . .' Cassandra started to protest, but Raffy was already furiously sending a message to Glen, all the time looking through his glass door at Thomas, who was striding towards him.

Thomas opened the door and looked at him expectantly. 'So?' he said. 'Shall we?'

'Sure,' Raffy said, his message sent, his legs almost buckling under him when he stood up. 'Why don't you lead the way?'

*

Lucas watched the throngs of people carrying food, putting up tents, their faces full of purpose, a hum of intense activity everywhere, and he felt something radiate through him that was almost close to happiness. Fifty metres away he could see Martha organising teams of people who were supplying soup to the hundreds of refugees now camped within the City walls, throngs of people adding a new vibrancy and energy to the City, which had stagnated for so long. Now there was no stagnation; now there was a sense of urgency, of fear, but also of determination. The City had suffered, just as the new communities within it had suffered, and now they were ready to fight.

What the fight would entail, Lucas didn't know; how they could fight an enemy as powerful as Thomas, he had no idea. But he knew that they had to try. The UK was Thomas's dirty little secret, and he would want it to stay that way. Once he had his precious System up and running he would murder everyone. If he could.

Lucas shivered as he remembered listening to Thomas talk, heard his disregard for human life, for suffering, his total inability to understand what he had done. He saw only what he wanted; the lives he destroyed along the way were meaningless to him. And now he had Evie. Evie, Linus, Benjamin, Raffy . . .

Lucas shook himself. Martha was right; he had to focus on what he still had, what he could still save.

It had been so much easier than he'd thought to convince the City's people to open the gates wide, to send messengers to communities up and down the country and invite them in. Together they were going to send a message to the rest of the world. Together they were going to make sure that the truth was known.

A man walked towards him; Lucas lifted his hand in greeting. 'Stern. How are things?'

Stern grimaced; he and the entire Settlement community had arrived that morning, frightened, hungry, exhausted, having walked for days. 'We shouldn't be out in the open,' he said. 'If the bombs come . . . we need shelter. What he did to the Settlement, he will do here.'

Lucas nodded slowly; he understood Stern's fear. And yet Linus's message had been very clear. 'I know why you are afraid,' he said. 'But the message I have received . . . We are not to hide. Linus is with Benjamin; with Thomas. He knows what Thomas intends to do. And his message was unequivocal. We are to stay together. Above ground. Someone is coming. A friend.'

'A friend who will show the rest of the world that we are here; yes, I know that's what Linus said,' Stern cut in, his deep, laborious voice rather more impatient than

Lucas had heard it before. 'But what if he is wrong? What if the friend doesn't get here? What if the bombs arrive first? You asked us to come here and we did. But we are not safer here as you promised. I can see only that we are sitting ducks. My people trust me and I have to put their safety first.'

'Your people will be safe,' Lucas said.

'So you keep saying,' Stern said insistently. 'And yet you give me no evidence. Lucas, you are a good man, I can see that. Benjamin trusted you and your friends, and so I must trust you, too. But you asked me to bring the Settlement people down here and with Benjamin missing it is beholden on me to ensure their safety. Simply being told that they will be safe is, I am afraid, not sufficient.'

Lucas looked at him carefully, took in the wizened face, the dark, lugubrious eyes. 'Everyone is being given blankets and an emergency bag of provisions,' he said.

'Yes.' Stern nodded. 'Yes, I know. But that won't help us when the bombs come, when everything is destroyed.'

'No,' said Lucas. 'They won't help on their own. But the reason people are being asked to carry these things with them at all times is because we have a back-up plan. A plan that we are keeping utterly secret because we do not want to induce panic or suggest that we fear a bomb attack. Fear can spread quickly, Stern, as you well know.'

'And what is your back-up plan?' Stern asked gruffly.

'You lived in London,' Lucas said. 'Before the Horrors?'

Stern's eyes narrowed. 'I was in prison in London. With Benjamin.'

Lucas nodded. 'Right. But you lived in London before that?'

Stern grunted. 'I lived in London. I grew up there.'

'Right,' Lucas said, relieved that he'd got his facts right. 'Well *there* is *here*. We're in London now. What used to be London.' It felt strange talking of a place he'd never known, a place his father used to tell him about secretively, a place that everyone knew had been full of evil and yet which his father talked of wistfully sometimes, as though he missed it. It was only later that Lucas understood; only much later that he realised that the only real evil lay within Thomas's heart. 'You remember the London Underground?'

Stern froze for a few seconds, then he started to nod. 'The tube,' he said.

Lucas smiled, remembering his father using the same word when he had told Lucas about the series of passages underneath the City, passages that trains used to run up and down, taking people wherever they needed to go.

'Well it's underneath us,' Lucas said, lowering his voice as though someone might hear, lowering his voice because in his mind, retreating to the tube would mean defeat, would mean losing. Even revealing the back-up plan to Stern felt like failure. 'A secret team has opened up three of the stations along one line which runs the length of the City itself. That is where we go if Linus is wrong. That is where we will be safe if the bombs come. We have provisions down there, enough for everyone for a week. We have marshals who will ensure safe transit down into the tunnels. And enough space for everyone. That is our back-up plan, Stern. That is why I know that I can keep everyone safe.'

Stern considered this, then he nodded slowly. 'Good,' he said. 'Then I'd better get back to work.'

He walked off; Linus watched him in admiration – he was an old man now but he still carried himself tall, accepted no help from anyone, in spite of Martha's best efforts. Whilst others from the Settlement queued up for bandages, Stern had spent every minute since he arrived getting food for his people, making sure everyone had what they needed.

'Stern,' Lucas shouted after him. Stern turned, slowly. 'Get yourself some food. I need you to be strong today. Make sure you rest. Your people are going to need you.'

Stern opened his mouth to protest, then turned, lifted a hand in a little wave. And then he was gone, leaving Lucas on his own again, wondering what was coming, wondering what the day would bring.

31

Thomas pulled a face, then stepped back. 'Shall we?'

The two men who had been behind him since Thomas had walked into Raffy's cubicle now took Raffy by the arms and handcuffed him; they then followed Thomas out of the room. There was no hood over his head this time; he saw a long corridor with plush carpet, saw a lift, saw Thomas press the button to go down, saw him press the number '10' once inside.

'It's the maintenance floor,' Thomas said, noticing Raffy's eyes. 'Not as comfortable as yours. But I guess you know that. You remember.'

Raffy nodded as he was pulled out of the lift onto a concrete floor; there was the sound of machinery, a chill that he hadn't felt further up the building. They were on the floor he had been brought to before, the floor where he and Linus had been tied up together.

Thomas stopped in front of a large metal door, then stepped aside; the man holding Raffy's left arm dropped it and stepped forward, taking out a key. The door swung open slowly; Raffy was shoved roughly through the doorway. 'Thank you gentlemen,' Thomas said then; the men stepped backwards and the door closed in front of them.

The room appeared empty; high grey walls stretched upwards and metal shelves sat against the walls, carrying computers, books, machinery, papers and files. Thomas walked around the corner; Raffy followed him. And there, sitting in the corner, was Linus, his usual impenetrable smile on his face.

'Thomas,' he said.

'Linus.' There was no warmth in either voice. 'So you've finished?' Thomas walked towards him. 'I thought that perhaps changing your scenery might encourage more of a work ethic. I'm so pleased I was right.'

'You have never been right about anything, Thomas,' Linus replied benignly.

Thomas stood over Linus; Raffy noticed how much he obviously enjoyed the dominance. 'Show me,' he said, curtly. 'Show me now.'

Linus shrugged lightly and began to show Thomas and Raffy what he'd built. And Raffy, who at one point had truly believed he could build the System himself if necessary, found himself staring in awe at what Linus had created, the subtlety, the sophistication, the beauty of a System that truly appeared to breathe, to understand, to feel. It was different from the System he'd built in the City; closer to how Linus had described his original ideas to Raffy – ideas for a System that could pre-empt people's needs, that could monitor happiness levels, look for unrest, for dissatisfaction, for despondency, depression or unhappiness, so that those affected could be helped, so that their lives could be improved, so that they did not lash out and take their anger out on others. Or, Raffy thought heavily, in Thomas's world, they would be tracked down and eliminated, as would anyone found to be questioning his authority, planning any kind of protest or simply breaking any one of his rules.

'It's really here,' Thomas breathed, as Linus walked them through it. 'It's extraordinary, so complex and yet so simple.' Then, suddenly, his eyes narrowed. 'But why? Why, Linus. It wasn't this room. It wasn't any of my threats. You'd have died before building this System for me. So why did you do it?'

Linus took a deep breath then exhaled slowly. 'I'm tired of the bloodshed, Thomas. I'm tired of people dying, tired of all the pain. It made me wonder what

I'm fighting, if my fight is causing so much pain. I'm an old man, Thomas. I don't have any fight left.'

Thomas shook his head. 'No fight? Linus, you'll always have fight in you. Don't you realise that's what's kept you going all these years? You think you hate me for everything I've done, but really you should be grateful. I provided you with the perfect environment.'

'To build my System? Yes, you did that,' Linus said quietly.

'No,' Thomas shook his head again. 'No, I don't mean that. I did that for me, not you. I mean the City, your rebellion. It's what you thrive on, Linus. You've always been a loner, but until I started the Horrors, you didn't have a cause. Think about when you've been happiest. Was it before the Horrors, when you were walking in and out of jobs all the time? Was it in the City, when you were building your System? Or was it in that camp of yours, starting the rebellion, planning the fight back against the evil Brother, the corrupt System? That's when you came alive, Linus, admit it.'

Linus frowned. 'And I should be grateful to you for that? For starting a war, for creating a City that was corrupt from the beginning, that lied to its people and made them afraid?'

Thomas smiled. 'So indignant, Linus. So aggrieved. Yes, you should be grateful to me. Don't you know your

Durkheim? He said that people are happiest when they are at war, when they have a common enemy. It gives their lives meaning. It brings people together. Without me you'd have been a drifter. You'd never have lived up to your potential. And you'd certainly never have had any friends.'

'And that's how you sleep at night? You think that killing all those people somehow saved me so it's okay?' Linus asked, his voice very cold suddenly.

Thomas shrugged. 'I sleep at night because I've done everything I ever wanted to and more,' he said, taking a few steps away from Linus, folding his arms in front of himself. 'Because I have control over everything and everyone. Because I ask for something and I get it.' He walked back to where Linus was sitting, leant in closely. 'Even your precious System, Linus,' he said, his voice dropping. 'Even your precious System.'

'Just be careful what you wish for, Thomas,' Linus said then.

Thomas regarded Linus, a look of pity on his face. 'Oh, Linus. You are so desperate to still be the person who knows what's going on. Don't you get it, though? You were never that person. Back in your little camp, in your cave, you knew nothing about anything. You thought the rest of the world had been destroyed. You believed everything I wanted you to believe. And now you have lost all your bargaining power. You've totally given in, given up. Linus, I used to respect you. Now, I just pity you. You are pathetic. You have served your purpose.'

He stood up. 'I am going to take your System and test it. If there are any problems with it, any problems at all, I will kill Raffy here and then I will kill you. Slowly. Painfully. I don't need you anymore; what's here is enough for my people to develop anything I want them to. So this is your last chance to tell me about any little glitches you've put in there to surprise me.'

Linus shook his head, shot a quick smile at Raffy, who didn't return it.

'Good,' said Thomas. 'Very good. In that case, Linus, come with me. We'll test it together.'

32

Evie had never felt so exhausted, had never felt her muscles and bones groan with so much pain, but she refused to give them a moment's rest. In front of her was a door, a door that led to everything she had ever wanted, and she was going to open it if it killed her.

'Is it locked?' Frankie called up. Evie was perched at the top of a fixed ladder; the door, like the door back in Paris, had been the emergency entrance for maintenance, for access in and out. But this door wasn't opening, however much Evie kicked at it.

'No, it's wide open,' she shouted back, aware that the sarcasm in her voice wasn't entirely necessary but unable to manage any other tone. Now wasn't the time for questions; it was the time to get through this bloody door. They'd come so far and they weren't going to be defeated now. Evie wasn't going to be defeated now.

She kicked again; the metal door stayed resolutely closed.

Frankie scrambled up behind her, then next to her; Evie resisted her angrily. 'I can do this,' she said, but Frankie wasn't listening; she continued up the ladder then started to feel around the wall. Evie rolled her eyes and, holding onto the ladder, started to kick again, pain shooting up to her thigh as she did so. She kicked, over and over and over, each kick as futile as the last, and she could feel the tears running down her face but she ignored them because she was going to get out of this tunnel, she had to get out of this tunnel. And then Frankie squealed. 'Got it!'

'Got what?' Evie shouted, still kicking, left leg, then right leg, then left leg again.

'Stop that bloody kicking,' Frankie shouted. 'I've got the key.'

Evie stopped dead. 'The . . . key?'

'The key,' Frankie nodded, talking slowly, as though to a child. 'People always leave a spare key lying around just in case. There's a ledge up there that goes right around the perimeter of this little tube we're in. And I found the key.'

She shot a triumphant look to Evie and scrambled back down the ladder. Evie tried to take the key from her but Frankie refused, edging Evie out of the way and fitting it into the lock. It took her a few minutes to turn it, but eventually Evie heard the metal move; moments later, Frankie turned the handle and the door opened. In front of it was another tunnel, filled with mud, lots of mud, piles of it as high as the two of them put together. But there was also light. Not far away there was sunlight, a way out. A way home.

Evie stared at it, almost not daring to believe. Then, without warning, she grabbed Frankie, threw her arms around her and squeezed her so tightly Frankie gasped for air, then she released her and took her hand. 'We're here,' she said, her voice barely audible. 'Frankie, we're really here.' And with that, she started to run, not looking back to check that Frankie was following, just running towards the light, towards the City, towards Lucas.

Milo watched the planes leaving. There would be questions, of course there would, but the questions didn't matter now. Milo would obfuscate, would make something up. Thomas had his System; that would be enough for now.

'So!' His door opened and Thomas appeared; behind him, held by two Inforcers, were Linus and Raffy, hoods covering their faces. 'I have it,' he said, his eyes gleaming. 'It's finished.'

Milo stood up, clapped Thomas on the back. 'You've

done it,' he said. 'You've got everything you ever wanted.'

Thomas nodded slowly. 'Yes, Milo. I think perhaps I have.'

'So are you going to show me?' Milo asked, keen to change his screen to something else. 'It's being tested on the shadowframe, right? Show me. Talk me through it. If it's everything you say it is I can't wait to see.'

Thomas's eyes lit up as he ushered the guards in and installed Linus and Raffy on two chairs, their hands tied behind their backs. 'It's more than everything I've said it is. Very well, Milo. I'll show you. Prepare to be amazed.'

33

Frankie's lungs felt like they were about to explode; her whole chest ached, her legs were shaking and she winced every time she landed on her right foot. And yet she kept running, because ahead of her was Evie, and the urgency in the way she was moving, the elation in her face when they had finally seen light, made Frankie as determined as her new friend was to get to this place called the City, to see with her own eyes what Evie had told her about. Evie didn't say very much; Frankie had learnt that pretty early on. But she said a lot with her eyes; the way they clouded over when she met with disappointment, the way they turned to steel during disagreements, the way they danced when she spoke about Lucas. Frankie had never met someone so private who, nevertheless, communicated so much.

At first it had made her wary, mistrustful; after all, sharing was good, sharing meant that you had nothing to hide. But gradually she had begun to see that Evie was just cautious, that by keeping things to herself they stayed more precious. It reminded Frankie of the little jewellery box her father had given her when she was eight; it was full of secret compartments, each containing their own bead or bauble which, joined together, could be made into a necklace. It had been a year before she strung them together; within a few weeks they had been worn, forgotten, lost. But in the box they had been treasures. In the box they had been her secrets that she was determined to protect.

It had been a long time since she'd had any secrets. It had been a very long time since anything had been that precious to her.

And so she ran, gritting her teeth against the pain shooting up and down her limbs, squeezing her chest. Because Evie still had treasures to protect. And Frankie was going to help her find them again. Because nothing else mattered anymore. Because this strange, silent girl had taught her how to feel alive again, and Frankie would never forget it.

She saw the speck in the distance, Evie, stop, and she upped her pace to catch up, panting furiously when she finally reached her.

'There,' Evie said, breathlessly, pointing ahead. 'That's the wall. That's the City.'

Her eyes were sparkling in spite of the bags under her eyes, her matted hair. Frankie knew that she, too, must look unbelievably awful, covered in mud mixed with sweat, her wig plastered around her face. She grinned. 'So come on then, what are we waiting for?'

'I don't know,' Evie said uncertainly. 'Nothing, I just . . . This is it. We're here. And you're going to film it all, right? That's what you said. You're going to show the world that the City exists?'

Frankie put her hand on Evie's shoulder; she could see the nerves on her friend's face. 'We're going to show them,' she said. 'Everything's going to change, Evie. Because of you. Because of Raffy.'

Evie nodded. 'I know,' she said, her voice catching slightly. 'It's just . . . I can't quite believe it. Does he know? Raffy, I mean. Does he know we're here?'

'I don't know,' Frankie said. 'I haven't heard from him.'

Evie considered this. 'He's a good person. Raffy, I mean. He deserves to find happiness,' she said.

'Then I hope he finds it,' Frankie said, doing her best to keep her voice light. 'Now listen, have you thought about doing something with your hair? You're going to be seeing Lucas soon. And I'm going to be filming it for the whole world and . . . well . . . it's an interesting look you've got going on, that's all I'm saying.'

Evie smiled. 'Lucas won't care,' she said. 'Anyway, you can tell your watchers that I'm just working tunnel chic.'

Frankie stared at her in surprise. 'Working tunnel chic?' she asked, an eyebrow raised. 'And where did a backwards City girl learn a phrase like that?'

'I might have watched you a bit,' Evie shrugged lightly. 'Before I met you, I mean. I watched you all the time. You kept me sane. And actually I quite liked that pink dress you wore to the film premiere two weeks ago. It was pretty.'

Frankie's eyes widened in disbelief. 'You watched me? You liked the dress? I thought fashion is a waste of time and, worse, a diversion away from the real pain and suffering that exists in the world? I thought that I was an Infotec Stooge who's as much to blame for the cultural prison we're in as Thomas or Milo?'

Evie shot her a sheepish grin. 'Maybe I was a bit harsh,' she admitted. 'And, maybe a bit jealous.' She bit her lip awkwardly.

'I think I can probably forgive you,' Frankie said, holding her gaze for a few seconds before winking. 'Race you to the City?' she suggested then, running off ahead quickly. 'Winner gets a shower. You do have showers in the City, don't you?'

'Of course we have showers,' Evie yelled, running after her. 'Although I'm not sure that cheating Parisians get to use them. Anyway, you don't even know the way.'

'So show me!' Frankie yelled back. 'Show me your City, Evie. And show the world while you're at it.'

34

As Evie got nearer the wall, she found herself slowing down. The gates were open; she could see people inside. Not swamps, but people, people she didn't recognise, people she did. And then she saw a face and she stopped dead because it made no sense, because it was suddenly so real, that she was here, that things had changed, that she didn't know the City anymore, that she didn't know if Lucas was even alive.

'Martha?' The woman who had comforted her so many times ran towards her, embraced her, held her tightly. 'Lucas,' Evie gasped. 'Where's Lucas?'

'Hi,' she heard a voice say. 'I'm Frankie.'

'Frankie. My name is Martha.' They were talking but Evie couldn't hear them; she pulled away from Martha's embrace, stared around at the people milling about, drinking soup, talking, moving things around.

'Lucas,' she said, then started to run again. 'Lucas!'

She could hear Martha calling her back, could hear Frankie calling after her too, but she couldn't stop, wouldn't stop. 'Lucas,' she screamed. 'Lucas!'

She ran through the crowds, stopping dead when she saw Maggie, an old friend from the Settlement, then shaking herself and running again, towards the centre, towards the place she hoped he'd be. 'Lucas!'

35

Thomas stared at the screen. It was beautiful. Beyond beautiful. It was everything he'd ever dreamt of. He could see everyone, see where they were, what they were doing. But more than that, he could see what they were thinking. Or rather he could see how they were feeling. He could see anger and frustration, joy, tension, boredom, misery.

'You did it,' he breathed. 'Linus, you actually did it. I didn't think you would. I thought when I turned this on the screen would just go black, that you'd think somehow you could outwit me. But you didn't. You built it. The original idea. It's so much better than the one you built for the City. It's incredible.'

'It's the dream,' Linus shrugged, his eyes twinkling. 'So you like it? Mind removing our hoods so we can see it too?'

Thomas nodded to the Inforcers to remove them. 'Like it? It's incredible,' he gasped. The status updates of everyone flashed before his eyes in colours that told him whether they were truthful or not. 'Loving this new job', a lie in red that clearly showed the fear and anxiety the updater was feeling. 'OMG this party is awesome' in purple, the colour of loneliness. Another lie. Thomas rolled his eyes; people were pathetic, always trying to make out that their lives were better than they were, that they had more friends than they did, that they were better, richer, cleverer, more disciplined than they really were. People were pathetic, really. Pathetic, self-deluding peacocks.

But that didn't matter. What mattered was that he knew everything now. Everything. It was extraordinary. It was beyond his wildest dreams.

Milo cleared his throat. 'Listen, sorry to interrupt but I've just had a message from Sweden. Apparently there's some communication breakdown,' he said.

'Deal with it,' Thomas growled. 'I don't care about Sweden. Not now. Don't you realise what this is? What it means?'

Milo raised an eyebrow. 'It's great,' he said.

Thomas looked at him pityingly. 'The problem with you, Milo,' he said, 'is that you've never had any vision. You've never understood the whole picture, never been able to see the potential in things.'

'No?' Milo caught his eye; Thomas thought he saw something in it, hostility perhaps. Then, quickly, he turned back to the screen in front of him, saw for himself the colour of Milo's thoughts. Black for anger, hatred. He would have to go. He would organise it later that day. Perhaps a tragic car accident. Possibly on the way to Sweden.

'Thomas, I think you need to see this.' Milo was talking again; Thomas barely glanced at him.

'Milo, I am not interested. Whatever it is, I am not interested.' He was staring at the screen in front of him, staring at the colours, the thousands of colours washing through it as he navigated through whole towns, cities, countries. Everywhere were emotions, thoughts. Everywhere he looked. And he found himself frowning because the colours were so dark, so flat. Unhappiness, loneliness, worry, hunger, fear, anxiety, pain. And it made no sense. People were happy. People loved the world he had created for them. They told him all the time, told him in their updates, their blogs. Why was there so much sadness? Why weren't the colours bright, light? What was wrong with everyone?

'Not interested in the entire operating system shutting down?'

Thomas frowned. Milo's words had turned white. 'What are you talking about?'

He couldn't look away from the screen, couldn't turn his head away from the blacks, the reds, the purples, the browns. It was as though everyone was shouting at him, crying, sobbing. It was too much; he wanted them to stop, needed them to stop, but they wouldn't.

'Enjoying your System, Thomas?' Linus said, his voice low. 'Enjoying seeing how people really feel?'

Thomas rounded on him. 'You did this,' he said angrily. 'You have engineered it to suggest people are sad when they are happy. You think I can't see through you?'

'You think you have any idea how people miss freedom?' Linus said softly. 'How much they fear you? I thought that's what you wanted.'

'Thomas, you really have to see this,' Milo was saying.

'Turn this off,' Thomas said to Linus, his voice icy. 'Turn it off now.'

'Turn it off? Oh, that's impossible, Thomas. The genie's out of the bottle. Can't put it back in again.'

'Turn it off,' Thomas shouted. 'Turn it off. Now . . .'

And then he stopped. Because in front of him, the screen changed. And in front of him was Frankie. She looked different, thinner, covered in mud, her hair matted, her clothes like something out of a war zone. But that wasn't what made the hairs on the back of his neck stand on end. It was where she was. He recognised it instantly.

'This is the place Infotec didn't want you to see. These are the people Infotec wanted you to think had died long ago in a nuclear attack that never happened. This is the experiment orchestrated by Thomas, our leader, to imprison us, to convince us to turn to him for protection, when the only thing we needed protection against was him. He started the Horrors, controlled them. He told us that the UK had imploded; told the survivors here that they were alone in the world. But now they are fighting back. Infotec didn't want you to see me. They tried to kill me for asking questions about the UK. But I'm not dead. I chose to fight. And I ask you to do the same. Take out your chips. Take down your cameras. Say "no" to Infotec. Say "enough".'

Thomas felt the blood drain from his face. 'Turn it off,' he growled. 'Turn the channel off. Now!'

But Milo was shaking his head. 'I can't,' he said, his voice breaking. 'She's on every channel.'

'What are you talking about?' Thomas shouted. 'Shut her down!'

'I'm afraid you can't shut her down,' Linus said. 'She's beaming right out of the mainframe in Sweden.'

'Then switch to the shadowframe,' Thomas said, rounding on Milo. 'Do it!'

'I've tried.' Milo stared at the screen as though transfixed. 'Nothing's happening. I can't get in touch with Sweden. That's what I've been trying to tell you.'

'You can't get in touch because the communications centre has been switched off,' Linus said, a little smile playing on his lips. 'See, we've got some friends in Sweden who switched from mainframe to shadowframe a few days ago, just long enough for Raffy here to hack into it, put in some code to make it disintegrate once the System went live. Then he gave Frankie the code so that when she started to film, it would be beamed around the world, the only thing anyone could watch. Right now, you're hoping that the mainframe is fine, that you can get someone to flick a switch back again. Problem is, our friends unplugged it. They're destroying it right now. They're quite enjoying it apparently.'

Thomas shook his head. 'No,' he said, blood pumping around his body now. 'No!' He jumped up. 'Milo, get guards out on the street. And you, Linus, you are going to regret this.' He pulled out the gun he always carried with him, put it to Linus's head. 'You think you're so clever,' he seethed. 'You have always been so sure of your superiority, but you will not get away with this. You will not!'

'I think I already have.' Linus smiled; Thomas immediately pulled the trigger. But instead of the explosion he was expecting, there was nothing; he pulled it again, then shook the gun. 'Inforcers! Shoot him. Kill this man. It's an order. Do it now!' He was shrieking, his cheeks hot, his whole body sweating. 'Kill him!'

But Milo pulled out a gun of his own and trained it on Thomas. 'Put your weapons down,' he ordered the Inforcers; Thomas, wide eyed, nodded for them to do as he said. 'Don't do this, Milo,' he said, uncertainly. 'Whatever you think you're doing here, you'll regret it.'

'Maybe I will,' Milo nodded. 'But I won't do your dirty work anymore, Thomas. You were going to kill her,' he said. 'You were really going to kill Frankie just because she wrote that blog. You lied to me, Thomas, and I believed you. I let you pull me into your dirty world because I believed in you, believed what you told me. But this was never about making the world a better place. This was about you controlling everyone. Including me. Including Frankie. But you couldn't control her, could you?'

Thomas stared at him incredulously. 'This is about a girl? About Frankie? Jesus, Milo, she was nothing. Nothing! And she's going to die anyway now that she's in the UK. They all are. Put the gun down. Let's talk like adults, Milo. Put the gun down.'

But Milo was shaking his head 'It's not going to happen, Thomas. Not this time.' He took Thomas's gun, loaded it and gave it to Linus, and suggested that he keep it trained on the Inforcers, then he marched

Thomas into the room next door, empty but for a chair, pushed him aside and locked the door.

'You'd prepare for the consequences, Milo,' Thomas shouted as Milo walked away. 'I have called for more Inforcers. This isn't going to end well for you. It isn't going to end well for you at all.'

Jim watched the screen and felt the corners of his mouth turn upwards. 'She did it,' he breathed. 'She actually did it.'

'She sure did,' Glen replied, his eyes dancing in spite of the sweat dripping down his face. 'And so did we.'

Jim nodded slowly, his brain trying to comprehend what had happened, what they'd achieved. His arm was killing him; Glen had passed out a few times over the past twenty-four hours and Jim wasn't sure how long his makeshift bandages would hold out. They'd been shot at several times; Glen's leg was bleeding heavily. But his knowledge of the security codes had got them in and after that they had watched in wonder as Glen had shut everything down, locked doors, created so much confusion that no one seemed to know what to do. But they had done it. They had flicked the switch, destroyed the mainframe, and held off Infotec's henchmen. They had opened up communication over the UK. And now . . . now they had closed down the communication centre, filling the airwaves with just one channel; just one image. Frankie was being beamed around the world. His friend. His friend, who had turned to him for help. And he'd helped. He was really part of this.

He looked back at Glen, and he saw tears in the big man's eyes. Tears of happiness? Of sadness? Jim didn't know. But he, like Glen, was transfixed by the images in front of them. Of people, of a city, with houses, and roads, of a whole civilisation that Thomas had denied, that Infotec had hidden, its dirty little secret. And then Frankie was going into a building, up stairs, following Evie and a tall, blond man whose arm was wrapped around her as though he would never let her go. And then he ran to a computer and moments later it was filled with a fuzzy recording of Thomas's, describing how he had started the Horrors, how he had created the whole thing so that the man next to him would build the System.

And then Jim was crying too. Because of the lies. Because of the shame. Because it was over. And as he lost consciousness, he knew that it had all been worth it.

He knew that he had finally done something truly worthwhile.

Frankie shrugged apologetically at the nice-looking woman and ran after Evie, trying not to mow people down as she ducked around them, trying to keep up, trying not to stare. She turned the camera on herself. 'Yes, people. This really is Frankie. Not dead, in spite of Infotec's best efforts. In spite of Milo's best efforts. Some boyfriend he turned out to be. So anyway, I'm sorry about my appearance. Tunnel chic, according to a good friend of mine. I've been crawling through a tunnel, you see. A tunnel that people used to travel through all the time. The Eurotunnel. Between France and the UK. Remember the UK? Remember it was destroyed, that everyone was killed, that it was a radioactive wasteland that no one could even visit? Well, I'm here folks. And as you can see, Infotec lied to us about everything.'

She turned the camera around, scanned the horizon from the distant open gate to the path Evie was running down. She started to run again, and as she ran, makeshift tents made way for proper houses and gardens, roads, larger buildings, shops. People were staring at her but she just filmed them, talking as she did so. 'These people have been living here since the Horrors. They were told that the rest of the world had been destroyed. They were left to build their own city from the ruins, to fend for themselves. All because Infotec were conducting a little experiment. That's why they tried to have me killed, by the way. Because I dared to ask difficult questions. Nice, huh? Okay, so we're nearing the centre of the

City. Oh, and those of you who know your history, this City is built where London used to be. Not much left of it now of course. And that shouting you can hear? That's my friend Evie.'

She zoomed in to where Evie was standing, several hundred metres away, her voice hoarse now but still shouting the same thing. 'Lucas. Lucas, I'm here. Lucas, where are you?'

And then suddenly she saw a figure. A tall, blond man was coming out of a building, his mouth open. Frankie rushed forwards, her camera moving up and down as she ran. It was him; she knew it, knew it because of the way he was looking at her, looking at Evie with such elation, such devotion, such seriousness, such . . . love. And Frankie didn't know if she'd ever seen love like this before, but he was moving towards Evie now and Evie had seen him and she was running, and now he was running, and as they reached each other Frankie felt her stomach leap and turn and tears were cascading from her eyes as they held each other's hands, touched each other's faces, stared at each other as though neither thought this possible, as though neither dared to blink in case it turned out to be some kind of mistake.

'Evie was taken prisoner,' Frankie said into the camera, her voice catching. 'She was brought to Paris by Thomas. She came through the tunnel with me to get here. She is the bravest person I've ever met. She grew up in this place, and it is my honour to show you her home.'

Raffy felt something welling up inside him like a tidal wave, a choking, consuming pain that made him bend over, clutching his stomach.

Because they were there, in front of him. Because he knew it was over. Because he knew he'd never had a chance. Never.

Evie didn't love him. Evie loved Lucas. Evie would always love Lucas. And Lucas loved her. Not in a jealous, dominating way, not needing to possess her, not obsessing over everything she did, everything she said, towering over her, blocking her sun, cutting her off from the world she loved. No, he loved her as she deserved to be loved. And it made Raffy want to die.

Linus leant over. 'You okay?' he asked gently, as though reading his mind. 'We did it. You did it. Benjamin would be so proud of you right now.' Raffy turned angrily, opened his mouth, then closed it again. Would Benjamin be proud? Maybe. Or maybe he'd look at Raffy with those piercing eyes, see inside his brain and shake his head wearily.

Evie was gone. Completely. Forever.

'You think there's hope for someone like me?' he

asked, his voice strangled by the large lump in his throat.

'If there's hope for a loner like me,' Linus grinned. Then he leant over. 'Raffy, you made this happen. All of it. So maybe allow yourself a bit of happiness, huh? Maybe let the past go. Just turn it off. Move on.'

Raffy watched as Linus went to turn off the images in front of them both. He was right, as always. Although knowing it was time to let go and actually being able to do it were two very different things. Raffy gazed back at the screen, trying to picture a life without Evie in it, without thoughts of her consuming him from morning until night, and then he felt his chest clench because he could see something in the distance, something that made his heart stand still. 'No,' he said urgently. 'No, Linus. What's that?'

Frankie sniffed, her eyes still on Evie and Lucas; she was all choked up, from happiness, sadness, a bit of envy. And then she frowned, looked up; she could hear something. A plane. She looked over at Evie, who was looking up too. Lucas was shaking his head uncertainly.

'Is this you, Raffy?' Frankie asked, but there was no reply. She looked back up at the sky; she could see more clearly what was up there now, and she started to shake.

They were drones; Frankie recognised them from history programmes. Drones usually dropped bombs.

The bastards.

She looked at Evie and Lucas, so happy, so utterly transfixed, oblivious to everything around them. And suddenly she realised she wasn't ready to let Milo win. Not yet. Not ever.

'Run!' she screamed. 'We need to get under cover. They're going to blow us up.'

Lucas's head swung round to Frankie; then he looked up at the sky. 'This way,' he shouted, then called over two men; moments later, a siren started to sound. 'Underground,' he called out to Frankie, his eyes serious, his arm protectively around Evie. 'This way.'

'Wait,' Frankie shook her head. 'You run. I'm filming. The world has to see this. Before it's too late, the world has to see . . .'

36

Milo heard a door bang as more Inforcers stormed towards the room he was in; he was still transfixed by the screen in front of him, by Frankie's face. She was running, talking into the camera as she moved, then pointing the lens up at the sky, where the drones were nearly over the City. And she didn't even look scared; she looked defiant, angry.

She looked utterly beautiful. More beautiful, even, than she'd looked when she'd first marched into his office, so cocky and insouciant and utterly, utterly mesmerising. He had made her into something she wasn't; he had tried to control her. But now, looking at her, he realised he'd failed. And he was glad to have failed. Because she had shown him what Thomas really was. She had made him realise that he had loyalties that went beyond Infotec.

'Is it bombs they're dropping?' Linus asked tightly. Milo met his eyes; he looked older suddenly, his usual defiance missing somehow. 'Is that what's in the drones?'

Raffy was staring at the screen in disbelief, muttering 'no' over and over. Milo shook his head as he turned back to the screen, watching people running, screaming, flocking into tunnels that he knew would offer them no protection. At least wouldn't have done.

'He ordered a long-lasting anthrax,' Milo said quietly. 'He wanted everyone dead, and anyone subsequently investigating to die, too. He wanted the problem to go away.'

Linus nodded slowly; then he frowned. 'He wanted?' he asked.

Milo let out a long breath. 'Unfortunately for Thomas there was a bit of a mix-up,' he said, raising one eyebrow, thinking of Frankie as he did it.

'A mix-up?' Linus asked, leaning forwards.

'Turns out someone ordered the anthrax to be replaced by fertiliser,' Milo said, raising his shoulders and pulling a face. Then he looked at Linus carefully. 'I'm not a good person, Linus, but she didn't deserve to die. Frankie was in the UK. His plans . . . he doesn't care about people. He calls them technology vessels. But Frankie . . . She isn't a vessel. She was never a vessel.'

He looked away, sucked in his lips. 'It was Thomas's

idea to . . . teach her a lesson. Replace her. He told me it would do her good. Said the replacement would just buy us some time, allow Frankie to come to her senses. Then they'd be switched again. But he was never planning to switch them back. He killed the replacement. Would have killed Frankie if she'd let him. And then, with his drones, it looked like he was really going to do it, I couldn't let him do it.

Linus nodded thoughtfully. 'I see.'

'He was planning to kill both of you, too. And everyone in the UK. All those people he'd categorically promised me didn't exist. I believed him. Just like everyone else did. I suspect he's working out how to have me killed right now.'

'He's a psychopath,' Linus said, looking at him intently now. 'He's a very dangerous man.'

They both turned to watch the screen as the drones flew on, as people dropped to the floor, clutching children to them, bracing themselves, screaming in fear, then, slowly, looking around, pulling themselves up, staring at the sky in incomprehension, watching the drones disappear, then jumping up, embracing one another, shouting out in relief.

And then the door was flung open and six Inforcers trooped in. 'At last!' they heard Thomas call out as they unlocked his door and brought him out into the corridor. 'I want these two prisoners to be executed for high treason. They are a danger to our security. And Milo is to be taken into custody until further notice.'

The Inforcers took out their guns. Then they pulled Thomas's arms behind his back.

'What are you doing?' he shouted. 'Take your hands off me. Kill these men or I will have you taken away. Do you understand?'

But the guards were looking at the screen, at Milo. 'I don't think so,' they said. 'We've been watching that Frankie.' And then they stopped, looked at one another, and, in one seamless movement, ripped off the 'I' badges that adorned their uniforms and dropped them on the floor in disgust. Holding the screaming Thomas by his arms, they walked slowly back down the corridor.

Linus looked at Milo and Raffy thoughtfully. 'Thomas once told me he had made me happy,' he said. 'And I told him he was wrong. But now . . . Now, in a roundabout sort of way, I think he finally has.'

37

'*Encore?*'

Raffy realised that the waiter was looking at him expectantly and he shook his head. 'No. I mean, *non. Merci.*'

He put his hand over his cup to emphasise the point but the waiter had already disappeared, off serving someone else, someone who wasn't staring wide-eyed like a slightly crazy person. He did try to act cool; tried every day. But he couldn't. Not when there was so much to see. Not when he could walk down the street, hail a cab, go anywhere, do anything. Not when just sitting here in a sidewalk café he could see the world go by, see thousands of people, talking, laughing, crying, shouting. Living. They were all living. And so was he.

It had taken a while. For a couple of days he'd refused to leave the apartment in spite of Linus's best efforts, in spite of some of his former captors offering to go out with him, show him Paris, protect him from whatever he was afraid of. They treated him like some demigod, like some kind of saviour; there had been a stream of journalists wanting to talk to him, wanting to find out how he triumphed where no one else could, how he showed Thomas up for what he really was, how he changed history.

But Raffy wouldn't see any of them. It was all bullshit; he hadn't done anything but send a few messages, hack into a computer system. It was Evie who had jumped off a building thinking she was going to die. Frankie who had trekked through a tunnel under the sea. Glen who had risked his life to turn a switch. Linus who had been beaten. Benjamin who . . .

What would Benjamin have made of this place, Raffy found himself wondering. It was a café like any other, just a normal, unremarkable café. That's what the former Inforcers had told him, the same ones who had finally, gently, ejected him from the Infotec building and found him an apartment in the 6th arrondissement instead. It was the café nearest to his new home; twenty paces away, in fact. But there was nothing unremarkable about it to Raffy. Nothing normal at all. There were people in it at all times, from first thing in the morning to last thing at night. And he could sit, unnoticed, all day if he wanted. People smiled at him sometimes, but other than that they left him alone. No one knew who he was; the news reports had mentioned his name, but there were no pictures released, he'd made sure of that. He was just a person in a big city.

He was free.

And each day, he thought about Evie less. Each day, he realised a bit more that he was actually happy for her, happy that she had someone, that she was safe; realised that he couldn't let his antagonism towards Lucas define him anymore. It was time to start again. Time to find a life of his own.

'Your friend coming today?' The waiter was back, putting a glass of water on his table. Raffy shook his head.

'*Non*,' he said, enjoying the sound on his tongue. Languages. The whole idea had kind of freaked him out at first: people all speaking different words, all around the world. But that was one of the first little acts of rebellion when Thomas was revealed as a tyrant, a liar, a war criminal. People started to speak their own language again. A lot of people had grown up only speaking English, but you wouldn't have known it, the way they were confidently talking French like they'd never done differently. Signs were everywhere offering French tutoring and shop posters were all proclaiming their wares in la langue française. According to the news, the same was happening all over the world.

'*Il est ou?*'

Raffy frowned. 'Linus?'

The waiter nodded.

'*En Angleterre*. He's gone to England,' he said. 'In a bloody huge great Mercedes,' he added silently, allowing himself a little chuckle. That had been the only thing Linus had been interested in when he was freed, hailed as a hero, offered anything he wanted.

The waiter's eyes lit up. 'I want to go there,' he said. 'I mean, can you imagine? A country where people have been living in tribes and stuff? It's like so amazing. I am so totally going to go there this summer. You think by then they might have some hotels set up and stuff?'

Raffy wasn't sure what to say. 'Probably.'

'Yeah,' the waiter said dreamily. 'It just shows, you never know, do you? I mean, you just never really know what's going to happen. Or what's happened. From now on I am so never going near a computer again, you know what I mean? I'm going to travel the world. See it for myself. It's the only way, right?'

'Right,' Raffy said quietly. 'I think you're right.'

'Although for now, I need some cash. So I better go and serve some other people,' the waiter said, giving him a mock salute before wandering off.

Raffy picked up the newspaper in front of him, a new paper that had recently started to roll off the presses as chips were discarded and information had to be disseminated in new, or old, ways. And he was astonished at how many problems were already being worried about. Markets. Crime. Immigration. Bank failures, all apparently about to tip the world into anarchy because trust had broken down, because chips were no more, because the old order was being abandoned and the new one hadn't been created yet.

'Anyone sitting here?'

He looked up, then froze. There was a girl standing over him. Tall, blonde bob, trademark leather jacket. And more beautiful in the flesh than he'd ever thought possible. 'Frankie?' He cleared his throat. 'So you ditched the wig?'

She grinned, her mouth filling her whole face as she plonked herself down next to him. 'Would you believe my real hair is now a disguise? Turns out no one's interested in old-Frankie anymore, they want the girl with the short dark hair. Like this, I'm left alone. So listen, I was waiting to hear from you. I mean, you always managed to track me down before. But I didn't hear a thing. Not even a "well done" or a "congratulations", something like that.'

'Well done. Congratulations,' Raffy managed to say. He hadn't contacted her because . . . Well, he hadn't been able to. Hadn't known what to say.

'Thank you!' Frankie affected an expression of huge gratitude. 'And congratulations to you, too. Job well done. So what happened? You some kind of lone ranger? The job's done so you disappear? I had to flirt my ass off with some of these new police people they've got now to find out where you were. But what am I saying? I haven't even introduced myself properly. You realise we've never actually met? My name is Frankie. Very nice to meet you.' She held her hand out expectantly.

'Raffy,' Raffy managed to say, shaking her hand. His mind had gone blank. 'Um, I'm Raffy. Nice to meet you, too.'

She smiled again. 'I need some coffee,' she said. 'But first, I need you to tell me something.'

'You do?' Raffy asked.

'I do.' Frankie nodded, stretching her long legs in front of her. 'Your radio silence, this whole low-key under the radar act. Are you still in love with Evie? Are you here nursing your wounds because she's all lovey dovey with your brother? Because much as I get it – I mean, the whole Evie thing. She's seriously cool, if a bit deranged, but then aren't we all a bit mad really? The point is, I do not need another messed-up guy in my life, you know? I mean, seriously, I do not need any more crap right now.'

She was looking right at him, her eyebrows raised,

just like they used to be when he watched her on screen, only now her eyes were so much more intense, almost black in colour, the light bouncing off them as she talked. And he barely heard a word she said because she talked so fast and her hands gesticulated with every word, hypnotising him, making him forget what he was doing here, what his name was. But she was waiting; he had to say something.

'I don't want any more crap in my life either,' he managed to say eventually.

'Really?' Frankie scrutinised his face. 'You're ready to move on? Because I don't have many friends. Not here in Paris. Apart from Jim, that is, but he's . . . well he's going into politics apparently and good luck to him . . . What I guess I'm saying is that for good or ill, you're pretty much my best friend now. And I kind of need a friend. So if you don't mind kicking around together a bit? You know, while this whole new order thing works itself out?'

'I'd like that,' Raffy said. And as he spoke, he felt lighter. Felt like he'd been carrying something around with him for a very long time and now he wasn't anymore.

'Good,' Frankie said, biting her lip, a tiny indicator that she wasn't quite as confident as she made out, a tiny movement that Raffy noticed, that she noticed him noticing as their eyes locked and Raffy's hand moved forward in a movement he barely controlled; he grasped her hand, squeezing it tight.

'We did it,' he whispered. 'But now what?'

'Now?' Frankie asked, her voice low and soft, a smile, a secretive little smile, on her lips. 'Now, we order more coffee. And then . . .' She winked. 'Then I have no idea.'

Acknowledgements

Huge thanks as ever to my agent Dorie Simmonds whose wise counsel and support knows no bounds. To Kate Howard, my editor, whose enthusiasm has seen me through many a dark patch, and whose brilliant insights and eye for detail I have come to rely on. To my publicists, Leni, Vero and Emilie. To everyone at Hodder who has worked so hard, particularly the designers who created such wonderful covers . . . Thank you, thank you.

Thank you to my sister Maddy, who got me writing all those years ago. Thank you to my husband, Mark, whose mantra 'just get on with it' might be irritating but is always, in the end, what I need. Thank you to my parents with their unwavering support. Thank you to Atticus, Allegra and Diggory for bringing so much joy and mischief into my life, and to Emma Wright for bringing fun (and order) into theirs.

Enjoyed this book?
Want more?

Head over to

CHAPTER 5

for extra author content,
exclusives, competitions – and lots
and lots of book talk!

Our motto is
'Proud to be bookish',

because, well, we are ☺

See you there . . .

 Chapter5Books @Chapter5Books